THE DESIGN OF DUKES

KATHLEEN AYERS

PROLOGUE

Lady Masterson's Garden Party, outside London

L ady Andromeda Barrington stepped discreetly behind a tree, determined to sketch the gorgeous concoction Miss Anne Cummings wore. The frothy gown of pale pink had been designed in such a way to resemble the careful opening of a flower. A fabulous design. Romy wondered who had made the gown. Madame Fontaine? Surely if it had been made by Madame Dupree, Romy would have known.

Pencil clutched in one hand, she pulled out the small notepad she always carried from the pocket cleverly hidden in the folds of her skirts. Pockets were something she insisted on, for they were useful for a variety of things. Just as Romy got the design stitched on Miss Cummings's skirts correct in her sketch, her view was blocked by an enormous pair of shoulders garbed all in black.

Black. At a garden party. Like an oversized vulture.

Still, Romy didn't look away; she stopped her sketch of

Miss Cummings's costume, all her attention taken by the large form in front of her.

Grumpy Granby, as she'd christened the Duke of Granby, was difficult to overlook. The height of Granby, nearly a head taller than all the other gentlemen surrounding him at any event, certainly drew the eye. As did his powerfully built form. Granby's massive shoulders strained against the fabric of his clothes as if he spent his days chopping wood instead of doing ducal things. Large, booted feet encased in expensive leather had been stomping among the lesser mortals of Lady Masterson's party all day while Granby stared everyone down with his patent frosty manner.

Romy had known several dukes; she was the daughter of the Duke of Averell, after all. But never had she encountered a gentleman who seemed to look down on so many of those around him as did the Duke of Granby.

It was shortly after her debut when Granby had first drawn her eye, at the opera of all places. The sheer . . . *enormity* of Granby made him difficult to ignore. He'd stuck out dramatically against the other gentlemen making their way up the steps to their private boxes. Granby himself had easily towered over Mrs. Hammond, the young, glamorous widow clinging to his arm. Oblivious to his lack of interest in her, Mrs. Hammond had been chattering away as Granby dragged her forward.

It had reminded Romy of a bear who hadn't quite decided to shake off the small fox attacking its arm. This observation had not been helped by the fact that Mrs. Hammond's shoulders were swathed in fur.

Granby's chilly gaze had swept the throngs of the *ton* at the opera with disinterest, passing over Romy, who was making her way to her family's box, without pause. Later, during intermission, as her brother Tony had escorted Romy to the refreshment stand, Granby's glance had once again drifted over Romy with indifference even though she was mere inches from him.

Romy was accustomed to being looked at but not with such apathy.

Perhaps his manner had been what spurred her to observe the length of his coat. It had been far too short for a man of Granby's height. The latest fashion dictated a gentleman's coat come to mid-thigh. Had he not nearly stomped on her skirts with his gigantic feet, she might have mentioned such a thing to him as a kindness. He'd nearly torn her gown.

That night, she had added *careless* to the list of attributes she'd assigned him.

Days later, Romy and her mother, the Duchess of Averell, had attended the Cambourne ball. Once again, her gaze had focused on Granby *and* the incorrect length of his coat. Either his tailor was blind, or Granby simply wasn't very observant.

Another aspect of Granby she didn't care for.

At the ball, Granby had stood against a far wall, ignoring the entire herd of twittering young ladies attempting to garner his interest. He viewed them all with the same cold detachment Mrs. Hammond had received at the opera. Couldn't he at the very least put a polite smile on his face? While she couldn't put her finger on why, Granby's disdain bothered her.

As did his bloody coat.

While a gentleman's attire wasn't exactly Romy's forte, she was well-versed in the latest fashions. And the length of his coat was obvious. At least to her. His inattention to this one detail bothered her, for in all other ways, his appearance was impeccable. Cravat always crisp, though Romy didn't agree with the bland color. Boots always polished. Waistcoats also boring, but properly fitted.

But *not* the length of his coat.

It was a glaring, troubling omission.

Romy pressed closer to the bark of the tree, careful not to tear her gown, and peered at Granby. He was nauseatingly wealthy and could certainly afford the best tailor in London. She shook her head, taking in the coat he wore today. As expected, the length fell closer to his hip, and not mid-thigh as it should. Her perusal naturally lent itself to the long length of Granby's legs. It took a moment. He *was* exceedingly tall.

Goodness.

And *impressive*. His trousers strained over the bunched muscles of his thighs, more apparent because the length of his coat was incorrect. Could his tailor not measure properly? It was as if the fabric hadn't been given enough room to account for—

Oh, dear.

A tiny, barely noticeable shiver followed the burst of heat flooding up her cheeks.

Romy *shouldn't* know about such things. The vast majority of young ladies of her station did not. But she had two older brothers. Tony was a notorious rake and the other, Leo, owned a gambling hell and pleasure palace. Romy wasn't entirely ignorant of how her brothers lived. And the Duchess of Averell, her mother, had insisted her daughters not be raised in ignorance, as so many girls were.

Romy also possessed a vivid imagination, useful not just for clothing design.

Her fingers clutched the pencil tighter as she forced herself to look away from the lower section of Granby's body. The Duchess of Averell might be more progressive than most, but she would still object to her daughter ogling a gentleman in such a manner.

"Grumpy Granby," she whispered into the bark of the

tree. "Please move your giant form so I may continue my sketch." Romy focused her attention on the view of Miss Cummings's skirts not blocked by Granby. The design *appeared* to be honeybees.

How clever.

The rest of the embroidery was hidden from her eyes. Granby didn't so much as move an inch, almost as if he knew he was ruining things for her. Her sketches had to be conducted with the utmost discretion, unseen by those she observed, else her hobby would become fodder for the gossips. And she was nearly out of time. Her mother and their friend, Miss Lainscott, would soon wonder where Romy had gotten off to.

Granby turned slightly, giving Romy an unobstructed view of his striking, almost savagely carved profile. Bold slashes of cheek and brow, with not so much as a hint of patrician refinement met her eye. His hair, the exact color of a raven's wing, sparked with blue-black highlights where the sun touched the dark strands, as it did when one thick wave fell over his eye only to be pushed absently away.

The coat is too short. The hair, too long.

Another bit of Granby to puzzle over.

There was a roughness to this duke, as if he'd be more at home in a boxing ring than at Lady Masterson's party. Romy sensed there was something else lurking beneath the rigid, stiff manner, a wildness Granby was desperately trying to contain within the cool detachment he presented.

The allure Granby held for her swirled around her ankles like a small hurricane. She wiggled a foot, trying to shake it off.

A gentleman approached from across the lawn, and Granby tilted his chin in greeting, the scowl so often gracing his lips softening.

"Gran. I wasn't expecting to see you at Lady Masterson's."

"Why not?" The words came from Granby. "I received an invitation."

"Garden parties aren't typically the type of amusement you seek." Granby's friend was carelessly attractive, with hair of burnished gold and twinkling blue eyes. "All this sunlight might give you a hint of color. You should be careful. Someone may mistake you for being human." A grin lit across his face.

The man's name popped into Romy's head. *The Earl of Blythe.*

Blythe had lately become the focus of her younger sister's attention. Theo had spotted the attractive earl in the park several weeks ago and now spoke of him constantly in glowing terms. Highly unusual given Theo rarely cared for anything other than the painting of her miniatures. Romy doubted Blythe had any idea of Theo's interest as, to Romy's knowledge, the two had never been introduced. Theo wasn't out yet. And Blythe was a notorious rake.

Neither of those facts dampened Theo's interest in him one bit.

"My amusement," Granby replied, "is in seeing all the idiots who have bowed to Lady Masterson's wishes and garbed themselves as stags." Granby nodded in the direction of Lord Carstairs who was stumbling about with antlers strapped to his head. "I'm constantly surprised Carstairs hasn't managed to shoot himself while on one of his many hunting trips. Virtually a miracle."

Romy covered her mouth to keep from laughing. Tony was friends with Carstairs and often said the same about his friend.

"But you *are* in costume, Gran, aren't you? Let me guess— a blackbird?" Blythe gestured to Granby's somber attire. "Perhaps a raven." Blythe taunted with a laugh, showing an even row of white teeth. "An overly large one."

No wonder Theo is enamored. Blythe is spectacular.

But Blythe, despite his golden masculine beauty, didn't draw Romy's eye.

"Bugger off, Blythe. Not all of us care to prance about like dandies seeking to ruin any young lady we come across." Granby had a lovely voice. Low and rumbling, laced with delicious undertones of caramel.

The sound was mildly intoxicating, as evidenced by the way her toes curled inside her slippers.

"You make me sound quite immoral." Blythe placed a gloved hand on his chest as if shocked by Granby's appraisal. "I don't take liberties with *every* girl whom I happen upon." He dipped to peer around Granby, piercing Romy with a look. "For instance, the young lady who is eavesdropping on us right now. I've not so much as even made an improper comment to her. Yet."

Bollocks.

Granby turned around, fixing her with a disdainful glare. His eyes were so dark, they resembled bits of obsidian, flat and cold with absolutely no warmth.

"Come out," he growled. "If you please."

This was bound to be unpleasant. She'd only been sketching. The eavesdropping had been entirely accidental. It was doubtful, based on the chilliness with which he regarded her, that Granby would see it that way.

Romy stepped out from the safety of the tree trunk a step, careful to keep herself beneath the shadow of the canopy of leaves above her, hoping to keep her features in shadow.

"Your Grace." She dipped gracefully to Granby. "Lord Blythe."

Blythe raised a brow, the grin splitting his lips stretching further. "I fear you have me at a disadvantage, my lady, for I don't believe we've ever met."

"Nor I," Granby murmured, dark eyes never leaving her face.

"We haven't, my lord." She replied to Blythe, purposefully avoiding looking in Granby's direction, though she felt the press of his gaze touching her skin. "You were pointed out to me during an afternoon at the park." There was no good way to explain how she knew Granby's identity without sounding like a complete idiot. One didn't tell a grumpy duke how fascinated she was by the length of his coat. Or any other part of his person.

"My apologies for disturbing you; it was not my intent." She forced a polite smile to her lips. "I was sketching when His Grace stepped in front of me." She held her tiny notebook up. "If you will excuse me, I must take my leave. Enjoy the party." Turning, she took a step back, intent on escaping to the safety of Lady Masterson's front lawn.

"Stop."

Romy hesitated, not caring for the duke's commanding tone. If she just starting running, would he attempt to stop her?

"Were you sketching Granby's backside?" Blythe laughed out from between his gloved fingers, clearly finding the situation amusing. "I suppose there's a first time for everything."

Heat stung her cheeks at Blythe's scandalous statement. "I was absolutely *not*, my lord."

"Could you find nothing else more worthy of your talent?" Blythe's tone turned flirtatious. "Mine, perhaps?" Blythe turned sideways and wiggled his hips.

Blythe was a shameless rogue. Though Romy had to admit upon inspection, Blythe's backside, like the rest of him, was rather magnificent.

Granby's eyes fluttered shut, head shaking as if Blythe continuously tried his limited patience, before once again fixing Romy with a frosty glare.

He has uncommonly long lashes for a man.

"I was sketching Miss Cummings's costume." Romy waved in the direction of the young lady who was now wandering off, oblivious to the fact that her gown had been the cause of Romy's current situation.

"And eavesdropping." Granby's snarl met her ears.

"Who knows what else you were sketching," Blythe said mischievously. "*I'd* like to take a look."

She immediately hid her notebook within the folds of her skirts. "I'm not certain," Romy snapped back, embarrassed to have been caught looking at Granby while Blythe took notice, "there was anything of merit for me to overhear. If you must know—"

"Oh, I must," Granby drawled.

Worse than being commanded by Granby was being mocked by him. It shouldn't have bothered her—after all, they hadn't even been properly introduced—but it did. Romy had a temper. One that caused her to speak without thinking. According to her family, her temper was one of her biggest failings.

"If you must know"—she imitated in a mockery of Granby— "I was struck dumb at the sight of the duke's coat."

"My coat?" His dark eyes narrowed, blasting her with dislike.

"Yes, Your Grace." She nodded as if truly at odds over what she was about to relay to him. "I noticed the length is incorrect. Two inches longer would be much more in line with what is deemed fashionable."

Granby's massive shoulders stiffened. One gloved hand tugged at his collar, though she hadn't said a word about his cravat. Yet.

"She may have a point, Gran," Blythe added helpfully, looking between his coat and Granby's. "I think I mentioned—"

"I do *not*," Granby said, interrupting Blythe, all his attention firmly on Romy, "take fashion advice from a woman who has the poor sense to come to a party dressed as a *shrub*."

Romy sucked in her breath. Her costume was lovely. She was a dryad. A tree nymph. It was true that very few had seen the vision of her costume today, guessing somewhat correctly that she was a tree of some sort, but she certainly, emphatically, did not look like a shrub. Granby himself was a mountain masquerading as a duke.

"I am a *tree nymph*, Your Grace," Romy stated with determination.

"I beg to differ." His dark eyes ran down her body. "*You* look like a shrub. All you need is a bit of red and I'd mistake you for a holly."

"A holly?"

"Or," he put a finger to his lips, "whatever that small bush is that is beneath the windows of my home. Do you recall the name, Blythe?"

"Hawthorne." Blythe pursed his lips trying to hold back his laughter.

"It is not surprising you don't recognize the difference between a tree and a shrub, Your Grace." Romy's chin jerked angrily in the direction of his coat. "You obviously do not have a discerning eye."

This time, Blythe snorted in amusement.

Granby went completely still, nostrils flaring in apparent outrage, like an angry bull about to charge.

She'd unintentionally hit a nerve. *Good.*

Dressed in all that black, it would be easy for Granby to be mistaken as a bleak mountaintop in some inhospitable place. She could practically see the snowcaps hovering about his shoulders. He was rather intimidating, but unfortunately, her temper had full control of her mouth at the moment. Besides, Granby would hardly assault her with Blythe so close.

"You appear to have more to say, *shrub*. Don't let me stop you."

"Your tailor has measured incorrectly, a situation you should remedy *immediately*, Your Grace. I'm not sure whether he is incompetent or merely lacks talent. At the very least, his eyesight should be checked."

"There's nothing wrong with my tailor," the duke said in a chilly tone.

Blythe, no longer able to control himself, turned his back on both of them, his shoulders shaking with mirth.

"I respectfully disagree, Your Grace."

"There is nothing respectful at all in your tone." The mountain moved in her direction, a dangerous light flickering in his eyes.

Strangely, Romy felt not an ounce of fear, another failing which her brother Leo at times likened to stupidity. But the skin of her arms and chest prickled in a most curious manner at Granby's nearness. She sniffed the air.

Granby smelled woodsy, as if he'd been tromping through the wilderness all day. Like an ogre.

"You should find a better tailor." Romy lifted her chin, daring him to object before taking a step back further beneath the tree. "Your Grace." She dipped politely once more before turning and striding off in the direction of the small crowd surrounding the refreshment stand set up in the center of the lawn. Lemonade and servants would offer her some protection.

A slight rumble sounded in the distance. Thunder. Or Granby. She wasn't sure.

Turning her head up toward the sky, Romy was gratified

to see a darkening of the clouds just as the first drops of rain hit her arms. She doubted Granby would care enough about her condemnation of the length of his coat to pursue her during a rainstorm.

Hopefully, they would not cross paths again.

Eighteen months later, London

R omy rubbed her fingers over the sample of damask. The fabric was beautiful but far more suitable for a sofa or chair than a gown. She made a mental note to speak to Madame Dupree, though she supposed someone like Miss Hobarth, who was chattering away happily beside her, would hardly note the difference.

I can hardly allow Miss Hobarth to go around looking like a sofa cushion.

"I am so pleased to see you, Lady Andromeda. London has been dull without your company. I know how difficult the time away has been." Miss Hobarth gently touched Romy's forearm.

"It has indeed." A mild understatement. The death of Romy's father, the Duke of Averell, had been far worse than any travail Miss Hobarth could imagine, though she meant well. Watching her father's formerly robust form waste away to nothing while her two brothers remained estranged from him had been a frustrating circumstance. The anger still lingered at Tony, now the Duke of Averell, as well as her other brother, Leo. Tony at least seemed to have taken the reins of the family and dukedom firmly while her illegitimate brother fell further into his grief. As did Romy's mother. But Mama was finally starting to recover after a frightening collapse in which Romy had feared for her mother's health.

"Will you be staying in town long?" Miss Hobarth examined a bit of wool dyed a deep green.

"I'm not certain." Maggie, Romy's sister-in-law, had begged the family to visit London as she and Tony could not come to Cherry Hill at present. Leo had taken off for New York on business, leaving Tony to manage his gambling hell, Elysium.

Business. Romy wondered if Georgina, Lady Masterson, would like being referred to as if she were an invoice requiring payment. Leo had gone after Georgina, who had fled England for her native New York, last year. Honestly, it had taken him far longer to follow her than they'd all thought.

Mama, finally starting to wear pewter instead of black, had reluctantly agreed to come to London, mainly so that she could be with her grandson, Freddie, who was beginning to take his first steps.

"I do hope you stay long enough for me to ask your advice. I'm having several new gowns made, and you know better what I need than my own mother." Miss Hobarth snuck a look at Mrs. Hobarth who was across the room. "What a stroke of luck to find you here today."

"Lucky indeed. Madame Dupree was kind enough to inform me of some new silks she'd received, else I wouldn't be here." It was a half-truth. Romy would have been there regardless.

"I'm certain the help you gave my sister was what helped her land Viscount Lowell."

"How is Lady Lowell?" Miss Hobarth's elder sister had

tion. Those conversations naturally led to Romy sketching out entire ensembles which the modiste would approve or make suggestions to before presenting them.

Finally, Romy had been able to express herself through the clothing she created. Madame Dupree had the assistance of another talented modiste. It had been a very satisfactory arrangement. Romy even made a small commission when her designs were chosen.

All of it had come abruptly to an end when the Duke of Averell's health had declined sharply and Romy, along with her sisters and mother, had returned to Cherry Hill. She had continued to send sketches to Madame Dupree from her family's country estate along with suggestions on accessories and trim, but it hadn't been the same. In the end, the Barringtons had spent over a year at Cherry Hill, choosing to grieve for their duke away from the glare of society.

Now that Romy had returned to London, she'd resumed her previous agreement with Madame Dupree and hoped it would evolve into something more.

After assisting Miss Hobarth for the better part of an hour, Romy wandered over to the far corner of the shop where Miss Lucy Waterstone stood frowning over a selection of velvets. She knew Miss Waterstone but not very well and took the opportunity to renew their acquaintance.

Waving away one of Madame's assistants, Romy struck up a conversation with the girl. Miss Waterstone explained she had been invited to a house party scheduled for the following month. Several eligible bachelors would be in attendance, an earl and a marquess among them. Her father wished her to make an impression, she said to Romy, lisping softly as she cast her eyes down.

Miss Waterstone was a shy, lovely young woman, a year or so older than Romy. She was the granddaughter of an earl, but fate had awarded her with a crippling shyness, in addition to her lisp, which accounted for her unmarried state. As well as the fact that Miss Waterstone's father was a tyrant. Few wanted him for an in-law.

"I know just the thing." Romy took her hand and led her around the corner. As she did so, her skirts caught on something.

"Drat."

One of Madame's assistants had carelessly left behind a pair of fabric shears, the sharp edges jutting out dangerously from a table laden with sample fabrics. The shears were wedged into a block meant to secure ribbons, lace and other trimmings while being cut. Thankfully, Romy herself hadn't been sliced due to the thickness of her skirts. But when she tried to move forward, threads snapped along her waist.

"Oh, my lady." Miss Waterstone put up a hand, her eyes widening.

Romy tugged on her skirts, all the while smiling at Miss Waterstone, until the sickening sound of thread and fabric popping apart filled the air. She turned and began trying to work out the edge of the shears without cutting herself, but the slightest movement tore more of her skirts, exposing a large portion of her petticoats.

Miss Waterstone's gloved hand pressed against her lips as she tried to stifle a sound of anguish. As if tearing one's skirts was the absolute worst tragedy which could befall someone.

"I'm sure it isn't as bad as all that," she assured Miss Waterstone. She twisted to the side only to watch the fabric slice again. A small portion of her corset showed through as the entire right side of her dress sagged open at the waist. She should never have used the seamstress in the small village outside of Cherry Hill. The stitches in the hem of her dress weren't as small and careful as they should be, a sure sign the garment was not well-made.

Miss Waterstone looked quite upset, much more so than Romy herself was. "I fear this is my fault, Lady Andromeda."

"Nonsense." Romy gave a small laugh as the material of her dress dragged along the floor. She put her back to the counter so as not to expose the gaping hole in her skirts to Madame Dupree's other patrons. "How could it possibly be?"

Miss Waterstone's fingers tangled together. "Because," she said in a solemn tone. "Things often are."

"I was not paying attention."

Madame Dupree came bustling forward. "*Mon dieu*. What has happened?" the modiste exclaimed, surveying the damage to Romy's dress.

"I am a victim of my own clumsiness," Romy stated sadly, giving Miss Waterstone a look cautioning her not to speak. "I stepped on my own skirts while backing up. This dress, I fear, is not well-made."

Madame's eyes widened.

"Because," Romy stated somewhat loudly for the benefit of the other patrons, some of whom had turned her way, "it was not created here. I fear I purchased this from the local seamstress outside my father's estate. In the country," she clarified. "A mistake."

Madame Dupree's keen eyes took in the shears jutting out from the table. She discreetly plucked them from their spot, her polite smile never wavering as she sought to free them from where they'd been wedged. She cursed under her breath.

"My lady," Madame Dupree said, still smiling. "Are you injured in any way?"

"Of course not," Romy whispered. "But I would prefer not to return home with most of my dress sagging around me. I've no idea how long these poor stitches will hold. Do you have another dress I might borrow? Something ready-made? Or a very large cloak?" She was already trying to figure out how to sneak into the house without running into any of the servants or her mother, who all assumed Romy was out distributing books to the poor.

I was mobbed by the orphans; for the books, Mama, and my dress tore clean away.

"Anything," Romy stated firmly. Her mother hadn't seen her this morning and wouldn't recall what Romy had worn, but she would question a torn dress.

"I do." Madame's brow wrinkled. "It was made for Lady Van de Burgh's elderly aunt who, I'm sorry to say, perished before it could be given to her. You need not return it."

Miss Waterstone looked thoroughly horrified.

"I'm sure it will be fine." Romy took Miss Waterstone's hand. "I'll only be a moment and then I'll return to help you. I think a shade of periwinkle to bring out the beauty of your eyes."

"Oh, but you mustn't waste any more of your time on me," she lisped softly. "I've already caused you enough trouble."

"You caused me no trouble, nor are you a bother. I'll only be a moment," Romy assured her before following Madame Dupree to the back of the shop through a narrow doorway.

"You are so kind not to be upset, especially since you could have been hurt. Monique is on the floor today. She is lazy and knows to put these away." Madame pulled the shears from the pocket of her gown. "I never thought to find such uses for pockets. I am glad I took your suggestion on them."

"I am perfectly fine," Romy said again. "Truly. There has been a crush of ladies in your shop today, and I don't think Monique was intentionally careless. Please don't sack her on my account." Monique supported two younger siblings. Romy would feel terrible were she to be the cause of the young woman's loss of employment.

"I *am* busy. Incredibly so. All the society mamas have flooded my shop because of the gorgeous new designs . . . from *France*." She shot Romy a bland look before they both burst into laughter.

The designs were all Romy's, sent to Madame Dupree while Romy had been at Cherry Hill. She'd paid the courier extra to keep the sender's identity a secret lest her mother become suspicious. Madame had not actually *said* the designs were from France; the modiste merely did not correct her patrons' assumptions.

Romy's merriment filled the back room. It was good to laugh. There hadn't been enough amusement in the last year, and being back in London, especially at Madame Dupree's shop, had lifted Romy's spirits. "I have an entire stack of new sketches. When will you visit Beston's?"

Beston's was one of London's premiere linen drapers, purveyors of the finest fabrics in all of England. Madame Dupree and Mr. Beston were business associates and likely much more, based on the way the modiste blushed when speaking of him.

"I will go next week and replenish our supplies." She moved into another room. "Mr. Beston is expecting a new shipment of exotic fabrics."

"I could go with you," Romy said hopefully.

"My lady, you know you cannot. Especially in my company. If you were to go on your own and order dozens of bolts of fabric? *Mon Dieu*. They would ask why, of course. Then wonder at you visiting my shop three or more times per week, conveniently helping the young ladies. Someone would guess. I do not think you are ready for that to happen. You may never be ready for such a thing. And your brother, the duke? He would be most angry with me."

"You're right, of course." The idea that a duke's daughter was secretly designing clothing for her peers would be a decent-sized scandal. Tony, who had conveniently disregarded his own tattered past, would not approve.

Papa would have.

A brief flash of pain crossed her heart. She missed her father.

Madame Dupree walked over to a large cabinet stuck in the corner, pausing to wave at a gown being pieced together. "I have had my girls working day and night on this." She pointed to a gown of cream silk patterned with a gold geometric design draped over a dressmaker's dummy. "Is it what you envisioned when you chose the silk?"

Romy stood before the gown, admiring the work of Madame's team of seamstresses. The silk alone was stunning, the texture and feel of it like butter between her fingers, but an unusual pattern in gold had been added to the fabric, elevating the gown to something royalty might wear. Romy's design called for alternating underskirts in pale amber which would flash and sparkle when the wearer walked across a ballroom. The neckline would skim the shoulders, the bodice smooth and flat with tight puffed sleeves. An ambitious design. One of her best.

Madame Dupree continued. "Adding the underskirts in various shades of gold was true inspiration. I am jealous I did not think of it myself. You have an eye for such things."

Romy gently brushed her fingertip along the hem, relieved to see the stitches were tiny and placed perfectly. "You taught me well."

"My lady, you have far surpassed my talent. It is I who now learn from you."

What would Romy have done without Madame Dupree? The modiste had given Romy the only means to do what she loved most. She had also become a dear friend.

"I have created clips to adorn the hair of the young lady who wears this," Romy said over her shoulder as she admired the tiny pleats along the neckline. "Suns." It had taken her weeks to get the clips correct. She'd spent hours with bits of

not expecting you and was about to close for the day. Your Grace, what a pleasure it is to welcome you to my shop."

"Your assistant is insolent." Granby snorted in annoyance. "You should have her sacked." The dark eyes lingered on Romy's mouth before dismissing her with a tick of his chin.

Romy swallowed the insult hovering at her lips, though she dearly wished to fling it at him.

Madame Dupree's crimson painted mouth opened with an audible pop, clearly horrified at his assumption that Romy worked for her.

"My assistant?" she choked out, glancing at Romy and then back at Beatrice. "*Non.* Surely you are jesting with me, Lady Beatrice. You are acquainted with Lady Andromeda, are you not?"

Beatrice turned the color of a beet, mottling the perfection of her otherwise porcelain skin. The arrogant tilt of her chin slid down. "Of course." A stiff, false smile graced the rosebud of her mouth. "We are well acquainted. It was a jest, nothing more. Wasn't it, Lady Andromeda?"

Romy enjoyed every moment of Beatrice's discomfort. *Gossiping twit.*

"I don't believe we've been introduced." The rasp of Granby's voice hovered in the air, like winter frost. There was no hint of apology that he'd assumed her a shopgirl and ordered her to be sacked.

Arrogant, rude . . . *vulture.*

Romy's gaze roamed up his form, clothed entirely in black with not even so much as a pattern on his waistcoat. Only the pale cream of his cravat helped break up the dismal monotony.

"We have not." Romy didn't bother to extend her hand.

He doesn't remember me. Somehow that bothered her much more than his condescending behavior.

The right side of Granby's mouth lifted slightly, amused.

Which was impossible because Romy was sure he didn't know how to smile.

"Your dress." Beatrice's gloved hands fluttered about her golden blonde head, clearly unsure of how to continue. "I've never seen you wear—that color before."

"I had a bit of an accident, and my dress was ruined. Madame was kind enough to lend me something to wear home. I find it perfectly comfortable, if not fashionable."

Beatrice's eyes bugged slightly.

Granby's gaze never left Romy, eyes shining like a bolt of ebony silk as he took in the hideous garment.

Romy very deliberately turned her back to him.

"Madame Dupree, if it isn't too much trouble, I'd like to see the progress on my gown," Beatrice said. "You should see it, Lady Andromeda. One of a kind, made especially for me."

"Some other time, perhaps. I need to return home."

Romy pressed a palm to her mid-section, trying to staunch the roll of her insides at the knowledge that her masterpiece, with all those precious tiny suns she'd created, was going to Beatrice.

Beatrice gave Granby a pretty pout, followed by a deter-mined flutter of lashes. "I will only be a moment longer, Your Grace."

His massive shoulders rolled in annoyance, the errant wave of hair falling over his eye once again. "I encourage you to shorten your visit as much as possible."

"Of course, Your Grace. Madame Dupree, if you will." Beatrice bobbed politely in Romy's direction. "I'll call upon you, Lady Andromeda. We have much catching up to do."

"I look forward to it." Romy would not be receiving that day or any day Beatrice decided to call.

Madame Dupree dipped politely to Granby and Romy before escorting Beatrice to the back of the shop.

Once they'd disappeared, Romy turned to face him. "Your

Grace." She bobbed politely before walking quickly to the door, eager to escape his presence. Granby had the most unwelcome effect upon her senses.

"Allow me to escort you to your carriage, Lady Andromeda." The deep gravelly words tickled her skin, lifting the hair on her arms.

"There is no need." Romy didn't halt as she strode by him, catching a whiff of pine mixed with a hint of soap and leather. Woodsy. Just as before. How could she recall how Granby smelled while he didn't even remember her?

"I insist."

His long legs easily kept pace with hers as Romy made her way to the sidewalk outside. Glancing out of the corner of her eye, she studied the austere line of his jaw dusted with dark hair, wondering if the rocky hardness of his features allowed him to smile.

"Is there something you find interesting about my cravat, my lady?" His lips pressed into a line.

"Not in the least," she replied, horrified he'd caught her looking. "I was only observing that though your cravat is finely twisted, I don't care for the color."

"The color?" Humor edged his reply though his lips didn't so much as twitch.

"It reminds me of bathwater that has gone cold."

Granby pushed at the errant wave of his hair again. "Very descriptive. You feel I behaved in an insulting manner by assuming you to be one of Madame Dupree's assistants, so you are returning the favor by disparaging me in return."

Romy didn't care for his observation, mainly because it was true.

He took her arm, the touch sending a tingling sensation up to her shoulder. "How is it that we have never been *properly* introduced, Lady Andromeda?"

"Avoidance, I suppose."

"Why would you wish to avoid me? We've only just met, haven't we?" The chill was still there in his words, but there was something else. A silky, slightly carnal quality that hadn't been present before.

It was rather unnerving.

"I feel certain that should be obvious," she retorted sharply, wishing he would simply stalk off and terrorize some children instead of herself. Surely there were some about.

When finally they reached her carriage, Granby halted, dark gaze fixed on the ducal seal and the livery of the footmen. "Averell." He rolled the name over his tongue as if he found it distasteful.

"Yes. I've two brothers. The elder is the duke." Romy always made it a point to remind everyone of the fact that she possessed not one but two brothers. Bastard or not, Leo was beloved by her and her family just as much as Tony.

Granby's mouth pursed in disdain. He was yet another titled gentleman who adored spending his coin at Elysium all the while despising Leo for being a bastard. If Granby was such a bastion of propriety, it was likely he didn't care for the Duke of Averell either.

Romy decided she found Granby and his rudeness beneath *her*.

The Averell footmen immediately came forward as Romy approached. They were both big, strapping young lads who eyed Granby with a stern look while moving immediately to Romy's side, though the duke towered over them both.

"Hello, Wicks." She nodded to one. "Rondal."

Granby raised a brow at her casual tone in addressing the footmen, probably wondering why she would even bother to learn their names. He was *that* type of duke. The kind she disliked.

She pointedly looked at his hand on her elbow, staring at

his fingers until he released her. Marching smartly to the door of her carriage, she tossed over her shoulder.

"Good day, Your Grace."

DAVID WARBURTON, DUKE OF GRANBY, HAD RECOGNIZED the little termagant the moment he saw her inside the modiste's shop even though she'd been wearing what looked like a flour sack. The last time he'd seen Lady Andromeda Barrington, he hadn't known her name or that she was the sister of the Duke of Averell. She'd been dressed as a tree of some sort, floating about Lady Masterson's garden party with a small notebook, hellbent on insulting dukes and their tailors. He'd returned the favor by stating she resembled a shrub.

The most beautiful one he'd ever seen.

Lady Masterson's garden party had been some time ago, yet David had never forgotten the most *annoying* creature he'd ever met. Andromeda hadn't offered any apology for hurling insults toward a duke. No one of his acquaintance would have spoken to him in such a way, man or woman. Not only was he a duke, but David's size often intimidated those around him, something he generally used to great advantage. He'd wondered, later, why the little shrub had been so unimpressed by him.

Because she's the daughter and sister of a duke, albeit tarnished ones.

After Andromeda had dismissed him and lost herself in the crowd of guests at Lady Masterson's, David had meant to seek out his hostess and ask the identity of the young lady, but a sudden rainstorm had disrupted the party, sending the guests back to London. He'd spent the rest of the season searching for her among the gaily dressed ladies of every event he'd attended, but her slender form had never reappeared.

Now he knew why. Andromeda's father, the Duke of Averell, had died.

As David watched her carriage maneuver itself into the snarl of London traffic, he jerked down the sides of his coat to hide his reaction to Andromeda. The attraction to her was so biting and immediate upon seeing her, it had taken the breath from his body. Desire for her ebbed and flowed through his bones and cock, unwanted and unavoidable.

All things considered, it was for the best she was the Duke of Averell's sister, a man David neither liked nor respected. The family's charming list of eccentricities, as society politely referred to their tarnish, included a bastard, Elysium, and a dowager duchess who'd once been a lady's companion.

A bastard son should be sent to the military as soon as possible with the hope he should be honorably killed in battle. A female should be put into service or shipped off to Australia.

His father's teachings still resonated loudly within him, dictating his actions and molding him into a duke who would make his father proud. The Barringtons, by their very nature, invited attention, something the current Duke of Granby avoided at all costs. He'd learned well from his father's mistakes, vowing never to repeat them.

As the carriage rolled away, David caught Lady Andromeda's delicate profile in the window. She was stunning, as all the Barringtons were rumored to be.

Desire once more curled around his thighs.

"Your Grace."

David turned to see Lady Beatrice Howard gliding out of the modiste's shop, sun-kissed curls sparkling in the late afternoon sun. Another beautiful woman, but one possessing an impeccable lineage and a family tree with no spare branches. She rarely expressed an opinion on anything other than the weather. Beatrice would never insult him. She would be an obedient wife and bring little unwanted attention to the Duke of Granby.

In short, Beatrice, unlike Andromeda, was perfect.

2

Romy picked at the lamb on her plate as Cousin Winnie prattled on and on about Lady Ralston's ball the previous winter. Cousin Winnie, Lady Richardson to those outside her family, could recall with startling clarity the color of each lady's dress in attendance, how many gentlemen had danced with her daughter Rosalind, and who had been caught on the terrace in a compromising situation.

Romy tried desperately to remember exactly how Cousin Winnie and Rosalind were related to the Barringtons. On her father's side, she was certain, but the actual connection had never been made clear.

"Goodness, Winnie. Your memory certainly rivals my own." Romy's mother picked at a piece of lamb with her fork, smiling at their guest.

A foot nudged Romy's. "What a coincidence business called Tony away just as Cousin Winnie's carriage arrived," Romy's younger sister Phaedra whispered. "I find it all rather suspect."

"And poor Freddie," Theo said to Romy's left. "Imagine—

our nephew suddenly had a new tooth come in just as Cousin Winnie stepped into the foyer. And Maggie had to tend to him personally. I'd not thought our sister-in-law so devious."

"Olivia," Phaedra said in a hushed voice to their mother's ward who sat just across the table. "You look quite ill. Pale as a sheet, in fact. Perhaps I should escort you to your room and read to you until you feel better."

Olivia calmly chewed a sliver of carrot, barely raising a brow at Phaedra's audacious suggestion. "I don't think your mother would approve. And I resent being told I resemble a bedsheet."

"Approve of what?" Amanda Barrington, the Dowager Duchess of Averell looked down the table at them, a slight frown marring her pretty features.

"Why, attending Lady Molsin's house party." Cousin Winnie clapped her hands sharply. "Knowing you girls haven't been out much"—she gave Romy's mother a pained expression—"and justifiably so, I have asked Lady Molsin if she has room for two more guests in addition to myself and Rosalind. Isn't that so, dear?"

Rosalind, seated next to her mother, gave the table a weak smile.

"How wonderful," Romy said before Cousin Winnie began to regale Romy's mother with the lavish details of a dinner party she'd once attended at Lady Molsin's, right down to the pattern on the china the meal had been served upon.

"Rosalind." Romy waved her fork in Rosalind's direction and mouthed, "I shall never forgive you."

Rosalind shrugged and mouthed back. "I had no choice."

"I should love a house party," Phaedra said happily.

"Oh no, dear." Cousin Winnie shook her head, graying ringlets dangling at her temples. "You're far too young for such a thing. Only Andromeda and Theodosia." She stopped. "With your permission, of course, Amanda."

Romy's mother stopped picking at her plate. "You have it if the girls wish to attend, which I'm certain they do. I am acquainted with Lady Molsin, though I've not spoken to her in ages."

"She's throwing the house party to celebrate the expected engagement of her nephew, but there will be several eligible gentlemen in attendance, including the Earl of Blythe."

Theo's fork slid from her fingers, propelling a pea into Romy's cheek.

"Theo," she said quietly watching the pea bounce and roll beneath her chair. "Whatever is wrong with you?"

"She's pelted you with peas," Phaedra whispered in a sing-song voice. "Because of Blythe. You don't know because you've been at the modiste's and not the park."

"Not another word." Romy didn't bother to ask how Phaedra knew about Madame Dupree. There were few secrets between the sisters and Olivia. It was a struggle to keep anything quiet. "You will say nothing of that," she hissed under her breath.

Phaedra's attention returned to her plate.

"I should love to attend, Mama." Theo addressed her mother. "If Cousin Winnie is certain of our welcome."

"Yes, of course. You and Andromeda would be graciously received. Don't you think so, Rosalind?"

Rosalind nodded.

Romy glared at her cousin, who refused to meet her eyes. She'd no desire to attend a bloody house party; the family had only just returned to London. At least a dozen new sketches sat in her portfolio upstairs just waiting for Madame Dupree. Now was not the time to dash off to the country, especially since she was now a *silent* partner in a modiste's shop.

"Perhaps Theo should go—" she started, deciding to decline the invitation.

Another pea hit her cheek. This time deliberately.

3

"I can't possibly attend."

Romy paced back and forth, feet dragging against the rug. "Beatrice and I don't get on. If you will recall, I threatened her at Mama's ball."

"When Tony compromised Maggie? Oh, yes, I remember very well. Didn't you suggest you'd have her tossed out by one of our footmen?"

Romy frowned at her sister. "I did. Her and Rebecca Turnbull."

"Lady Carstairs," Theo interjected.

"That she is now married to Carstairs isn't important. What is crucial for you to understand is that my presence at the house party will give Beatrice fits. She and Rebecca might well have me removed. Think of Cousin Winnie's embarrassment, if nothing else."

"Lady Molsin is hosting the house party, not Beatrice or her parents. The Foxwoods can't have you thrown out."

Romy stopped pacing. "That isn't exactly the point, Theo. I shouldn't go."

"Do you not have any feeling for our poor cousin

Rosalind? She *really* needs us there. Cousin Winnie is busy tossing her at Lord Torrington. Who else shall stand beside and protect her? And Miss Waterstone is attending. How often have you told me you should like to be her friend because she has so few?"

It was true. Romy had a soft spot for Miss Waterstone and, indeed, anyone who needed a champion.

"I'm sure her father is forcing her to attend. Poor dear." A concerned look crossed Theo's face. "She's lovely. It isn't her fault she has a small lisp. I can't imagine you'd leave Miss Waterstone to fend for herself."

Theo knew very well Romy wouldn't, which had surely been Theo's point in mentioning her. And Romy *would* like to see Miss Waterstone in the gorgeous gown she'd designed for her. "Granby and I don't get on," she muttered.

"Granby?" Theo fluffed the coverlet on Romy's bed before she sat, her eyes following as Romy resumed her agitated steps across the rug. "I didn't realize you were acquainted with the duke."

"I am. It is an acquaintance I don't care to further. He is *most* unpleasant."

"So is Beatrice. But it doesn't signify. We *must* go. I can't go without you."

"Why not? As you've pointed out, Rosalind will be there with Cousin Winnie."

"I couldn't possibly manage to guide Rosalind on my own. What's more, I can't depend on Rosalind to guide *me*," Theo said in a quiet voice.

"Guide you?" If Romy didn't stop pacing soon, a path might be forged in the rug.

"On Blythe." Her sister's eyes flashed behind the glass of her spectacles, one finger drawing circles on Romy's coverlet.

Romy halted, coming to stand before her sister. "This is

all because of Blythe? You have seen him exactly one time, riding in Hyde Park over a year ago."

Theo looked away. "My observation of him has been much more recent."

"You have *just* come out, Theo. Barely. How in the world would you have become acquainted with him? We've only attended a handful of events, and I don't recall him being at any of them."

"We met briefly as I walked with Phaedra and Olivia." She shrugged, pulling on a loose thread. "In the park, on the path by the river."

"Do not destroy my quilt, Theo. Explain yourself."

"Fine. It was not a proper introduction. He was flying a kite." Her face took on a dreamy look. "Shaped like a large fish. A trout, possibly."

Romy rolled her eyes and asked for patience. "I don't care what his kite looked like."

"The string became horribly tangled in my skirts, so much so I was forced to seek assistance from Blythe."

"Did you intentionally trap yourself in his kite string?" When Theo didn't answer immediately, Romy prompted her. "Theo."

Two spots of pink appeared on her sister's cheeks. "*Possibly.*"

Romy crossed her arms and eyed her usually sensible, calm sister. "Do you mean to tell me you threw yourself at Blythe? At the park? In full view of everyone?"

"Not at Blythe. His kite. He was quite gallant about the entire affair, even while unraveling the twine from around my ankle."

"Dear God." The situation was far worse than Romy had previously assumed if Theo was resorting to such antics. Apparently, she'd missed quite a bit by spending her days at Madame Dupree's. "You could have been ruined."

"I could *not* have been. Besides Phaedra and Olivia, there were scores of people walking along the path. Literally dozens," she emphasized. "Blythe was a perfect gentleman." Another faraway look came over Theo's face. "Even though I wished him not to be."

Theo's infatuation with Blythe had crossed from girlish adoration to full-fledged obsession. Her sister could very well ruin herself over the handsome earl, causing their mother undue embarrassment while she was only just recovering from her grief. Romy had little choice now in attending the house party, if only to save Theo from her own idiocy.

"This is the worst possible time for me to be gone from London, Theo. I'm in the middle of several designs for Madame Dupree." She stopped short of informing Theo of her partnership with the modiste or that Romy herself was now in trade.

I'll tell them all. Just not yet.

"We will be gone less than a fortnight. I swear," Theo said, her face brightening. "The Barrow is said to be beautiful, with lots of woodland for you to wander around. You adore the country. I promise you won't need to spend undue time in Beatrice's presence. You can disappear and sketch for hours on end. I'll tell everyone you're walking. I promise."

"The Barrow?" Dread clawed at Romy's throat.

Theo looked away, picking at a bit of paint stuck to her palm. There was always a splotch of paint somewhere on her sister's skin, no matter how careful she was. "The house party is being held at the Duke of Granby's estate. And before you become angry, I didn't tell you outright because I knew you would have refused immediately."

"His estate is named The Barrow?" A snort escaped Romy. "How appropriate."

"I don't think his ancestral home is actually built on a

burial mound if it makes you feel better. There are just some in the general vicinity."

"No. It does not make me feel better," she snapped. The situation could hardly get any worse, unless Romy dug in her feet and didn't attend, in which case Theo was bound to humiliate herself, Miss Waterstone would be deserted, and Rosalind left to flutter about helplessly.

"Will you design something marvelous for me to wear to the ball? I want to sparkle like the rarest of gems so that Blythe will take notice." Theo flopped back down on the bed, eyes glazing over.

Romy watched her with abject horror. What had happened to her rational, sensible sister? "Of course I will." She could hardly do anything else. "But *you* are in my debt, Theodosia."

"Thank you." Theo sat up. "And the next time Mama asks where you've gone, I will continue to say you're attending to your charitable work, shining example of charitable endeavors that you are. Is it orphans or widows you are assisting?"

"Both." Romy had been spending the better part of her days at Madame Dupree's, sometimes barely arriving home in time for dinner. An entire plethora of excuses had been invented to explain her daily disappearance to her mother. "I also visit the park to sketch, browse for books at Thrumbadge's, and sit in the gardens."

"It's a wonder you have time for the orphans and widows."

Madame Dupree's business had increased significantly of late, especially with Romy designing entire wardrobes. The modiste was inundated with orders and had hired three more seamstresses. She and Madame were also making plans to expand the store to possibly include ready-made clothing for working class women who could not afford the services of an exclusive modiste.

"You must never breathe a word of my involvement with Madame Dupree. *Never*, Theo. I will tell Mama and Tony in my own time." Once the partnership was more established, Romy planned on confessing everything. "I hope Blythe is worth all your efforts."

"He is," Theo said in a wistful voice.

Romy turned away in disgust as her sister mooned over Blythe. She would need to stay as far away from Beatrice as possible. And avoid Granby at all costs.

4

"Your Grace, are you listening?"

David looked away from the painting he'd felt compelled to purchase months ago, a seascape by an unknown Italian artist. The swirl of blues representing the ocean had called to him when he'd seen it. David hadn't realized until now why the seascape held such appeal for him.

"Granby."

He turned to his aunt, resenting Andromeda Barrington and the way she'd invaded his thoughts so quietly and in such an insidious manner. The swirls of lighter and darker blue in the seascape had reminded him of her eyes. He'd been fortunate, after their unexpected meeting at Madame Dupree's, not to cross paths with her again before departing London. His desire for her unsettled him to the point where the mere thought of her dispelled every rational notion in his brain.

The painting was proof of such a weakness. He reached up and tugged at his cravat. His valet had tied the bloody thing too tight again.

"Apologies, Aunt. I was only considering the improvements I need to make to the east wing."

Aunt Pen, short for Penelope, was his paternal aunt, the younger sister of David's father, Horace. Her presence in David's life had been spotty at best and virtually nonexistent while his father had been alive. But Aunt Pen was here now, determined to mother David, though it was far too late for her to do so. He'd needed her more after the Duchess of Granby had abandoned her son and husband to run off with her lover. But Aunt Pen hadn't come, though Horace had begged her to. The scandal, his father had claimed, kept his younger sister away.

Whether to make up for lost time or for some reason as yet unknown to David, Aunt Pen was committed to staying with David and filling The Barrow with guests for a house party he hadn't asked for. Or wanted.

"I sense you've little interest in any of this but most especially in Lady Beatrice," Aunt Pen said, her tone thoughtful.

"Untrue." David didn't care to have this conversation with his aunt, mainly because who he married was none of her concern. "Her lineage is impeccable. The Earl of Foxwood and his family are well-connected. Powerful. His title is even more ancient than my own. Beatrice is beautiful. Accomplished. Well-bred. As a bonus, her dowry contains a parcel of land the Dukes of Granby have coveted for half a century. In short, she is perfect."

His aunt's lips drew down. "How many times have you actually spoken to Beatrice? Three? None alone, I'll warrant."

"Is conversation necessary to sire an heir? At any rate, I assure you Lady Foxwood spoke enough for all of us. Besides, I thought squiring her about was an uncomplicated way to make my intentions known."

"You mean it is easier than courting her." His aunt's face tightened, wrinkling her brow. Aunt Pen was still a handsome woman. Elegant. David often wondered why she hadn't remarried after the death of Lord Molsin.

50

"A courtship would be a waste of time. And pointless. I require a wife of good breeding and unimpeachable reputation. Foxwood would like his daughter to be a duchess. It is a fairly simple trade."

"Have you no affection for her?" Aunt Pen waved her hand. "Don't answer. You've treated this entire affair as if you are merely purchasing a horse from Tattersall's."

David failed to see the cause of Aunt Pen's upset. Choosing a wife was very much like assessing horseflesh. Marriages, David's father had often reminded him, were nothing more than business transactions. The wrong decision could have catastrophic effects on one's reputation and the standing of one's family. A mistake his father had firsthand knowledge of and had cautioned his heir to be amply aware of.

A well-bred wife ensures a well-bred life.

"What is it about Beatrice you find so objectionable?" David countered.

"Don't you want companionship, Your Grace? Affection? Friendship, at the very least?"

"None of those are necessary for a successful marriage. She will do her duty, as will I." Why did it matter whether he spoke to her or not? Once she produced the requisite heir and a spare, David and Beatrice would have little to do with each other.

"I see you've thought of everything." Aunt Pen worried the rings on her fingers, twisting them about.

"Indeed, I have, Aunt Pen."

Beatrice was a logical choice. He liked beautiful women, and Beatrice was stunning. He'd have no problems bedding her. Best of all, she aroused no emotion in him. Not a whit. He didn't expect she ever would. Certainly Beatrice didn't leave him wishing to throw her skirts up and—

David's gaze wandered again to the magnificent swirls of

blue making up the seascape, none of the color nearly as dramatic as that of Lady Andromeda Barrington's eyes. To only say her eyes were blue would be akin to claiming a painting by Titian resembled a crude pencil drawing done by a child. He likened the color to water caught in a shallow pool when the tide returns to the sea, exactly as the seascape depicted. A ring of indigo, so startling against the lighter blue, circled each of the pupils. Unusual and unforgettable. Much like Andromeda.

It was unfortunate she was a Barrington.

The Duke of Averell and his family had been a particular bone of contention for David's father. Horace had always held the family up as an example of the demise of the nobility, claiming the family would come to a bad end with their blood so muddied.

Horace had struggled to keep quiet the secret of the origins of David's mother, while Averell, on the other hand, hadn't even bothered to hide his wife's previous life as lady's companion, as if he were proud of such a thing.

David reached behind him to the small table where a decanter of scotch sat. Grabbing it by the neck, he brought it forward and refilled his glass with the deep amber liquid. He rarely had more than one glass of scotch, two at most, at least not since returning to England. But this conversation merited it.

"I've been speaking for several moments, yet you've long since ceased listening to me."

"How astute of you." David pulled at his collar again, wondering if he should find another valet.

An angry sniff came from behind him. David didn't wish to alienate Aunt Pen. She was the only real family he had left.

A small bit of the wound he carried inside him tore open. The damn thing had never completely healed.

"Aunt Pen, I do appreciate all you've done. I know you

aren't happy with my decision to wed Beatrice, but she is a good choice for Granby. There are benefits for both parties. I anticipate our union will be highly successful."

Aunt Pen's fingers pressed into the back of the sofa cushions, her knuckles going white. "You sound *very* much like your father, touting breeding and business arrangements." There was an odd note to her words. "Horace would be very pleased with the son he raised."

"He would have been thrilled at the choice of Beatrice." David had earned Horace's displeasure any number of times; the last time had, of course, been the worst. "And my father would have approved of the duke I have become."

"A dead man's approval," Aunt Pen said under her breath.

The pads of David's fingers slid along the glass. "If there is something you would say, Aunt, by all means, enlighten me."

"Only that you have a narrow view of the world, nephew. I bid you to remember there are often many versions of the same story, none of which are usually the entire truth."

David took another swallow, allowing the scotch to burn down his throat. "I'll keep that in mind." Aunt Pen liked to speak in riddles, doing so at the most inopportune times.

"Well." She cleared her throat. "Much as I've enjoyed our discussion, there is much to oversee before the arrival of our guests. Owens has been invaluable." At David's look, she said, "Your butler."

"I know who he is." David had thought his butler's name was Bowen. Close enough. Besides, he rarely addressed the man directly, so he doubted it mattered.

"We'll have a few more guests than I anticipated so I've asked that additional rooms be readied. Lady Richardson is bringing her cousins. Two of them. I neglected to inform you earlier."

David didn't care who was going to be sleeping in his guest rooms; he couldn't even recall who Lady Richardson was, so he certainly didn't care about her cousins. "The more the merrier."

"We will be slightly unbalanced at the dinner table."

David wasn't sure what Aunt Pen expected him to do about it. "Invite Estwood, then. I'm sure he'll be happy to drink my liquor and eat my food. I believe he's in London."

Silence from Aunt Pen. She surely didn't care to invite Harrison Estwood, because his attendance was bound to ruffle some feathers. Horace had *detested* Estwood, likening him to a parasite.

"As you wish, Your Grace."

The sound of his aunt's footsteps met his ears before the door shut behind her, and he was finally left in peace.

His eyes lifted again to the painting, appreciating the careful brushstrokes of the artist. Art was something David enjoyed. Like a beautiful woman or a fine glass of brandy. Beauty was what had drawn Horace to David's mother, Emelia Jones. Emelia had been a baronet's daughter. Not up to Horace's standards, but he had pursued her anyway, completely disregarding his own misgivings, so struck he was by her looks. It was only after they were married that Horace found out Emelia's origins were much farther beneath his own than he'd originally thought. Emelia's grandfather had been a farmer.

Your mother's breeding showed itself in her behavior. I raised her up. But in the end, she chose to return to the dirt from which she came.

Emelia fled when David was nine, leaving him to be raised in the coldness of The Barrow with Horace his only companion. The scandal of a duchess abandoning her duke for a common soldier had been enormous. Emelia had never come back. Not once. Hiding with her soldier. To this day, David still had no idea where she was.

As a result, his father drank. Demanded. Instructed. Any respect or scrap of affection from Horace had to be earned.

Even now, the desire to please Horace lingered even though his father was several years in the grave.

The *ton* had spoken of his mother for years. How a lowly baronet's daughter had brought down the arrogant Duke of Granby, leaving him for a man of no wealth or renown. The taunts had followed David to school. Even now, there was always someone whispering at him from behind a fan or gloved hand. He *hated* his mother for what she'd done to his father. To him.

There was no defense Emelia could give which would allow him to forgive her.

5

"I do hope Blythe hasn't begged off."

Romy shook her head, silently praying for patience before turning her attention to the view of the coastline. The journey had been without incident, unless you counted the constant odes to the perfection of Blythe. If Theo burst into song over the manly shape of his legs or the color of his eyes, Romy meant to toss herself out of the vehicle. Her sister had been reduced to nothing more than a giggling schoolgirl in the throes of her first crush. Theo had even chosen not to wear her spectacles, purely out of vanity. A very bad idea. She couldn't see things clearly without them.

"You won't know if he's there or not. You'll be as blind as a mole without your spectacles."

"I doubt I'll need them. Besides, I would know Blythe anywhere. Especially if he is close to me." Theo's voice took on a nauseatingly wistful air. "He is etched on my memory."

"Ugh. Are you addled? You've met Blythe exactly *one* time and not under polite circumstances."

"The *first* time I saw him in the park, before Papa died, I found him vastly appealing. When he was untangling the twine from around my ankles and he looked into my eyes, I was sure."

"Sure of what?" Theo was behaving like an idiot. "Love? You don't even know Blythe. Did he ask to call on you properly?"

"No, of course not. We weren't introduced. And I failed to give him my name during our . . . encounter."

Romy took that to mean that Blythe hadn't *asked* for her name. He'd merely flirted with a pretty girl whose ankle had become intentionally entangled with his kite string. "Blythe could be a complete dolt for all you know. He'd have to be not to have noticed you throwing yourself at him."

"He's not." Theo pressed her lips together. "He's perfect."

"A paragon." Romy thought of the way Blythe had wiggled his backside upon meeting her at Lady Masterson's. She'd never told Theo because it would lead to a host of questions, namely, how Romy had met Granby and Blythe to begin with.

Theo went back to the book she held, pointedly ignoring Romy.

Romy clasped her hands and took a deep breath. It was the worst sort of luck to find herself as an uninvited guest at the home of the Duke of Granby. She would have to spend the entire week avoiding him.

At least The Barrow *was* an enormous estate, according to Cousin Winnie. Her sister hadn't exaggerated in that respect. A multitude of entertainments had been planned for the guests, few of which Romy meant to attend. She could simply stay in the background. Take a tray in her room if the mood struck her. No one would notice.

At least that was her plan.

Romy turned to the passing scenery outside the coach window, which changed dramatically once they turned to head inland. After another hour or so, the scenery became less wild and seemingly more cultivated. Moments later, the coach stopped before a gatehouse made of weathered gray stone. A guard stepped out, speaking in low tones to their driver before the coach lurched forward again.

"Theo, I think we've arrived." Romy nudged her sister's knee, almost dislodging Theo's book. She craned her neck out the window to assure the smaller coach, bearing two more of the Barrington footmen as well as their maids and trunks, followed close behind.

Romy had tried to convince their mother that she and Theo shouldn't go to a house party without her, even if Cousin Winnie would act as chaperone. At the very least, she and her sister shouldn't travel to Granby's estate alone, but her mother had only waved Romy away. "You are both very level-headed young ladies. You'll have trusted footmen, grooms and two drivers who will all be armed. Both your maids will be with you. And there will be dancing and games. You or Theo might even meet a gentleman."

It was far more likely Romy would encounter a duke she didn't like. Regardless, her mother had seemed completely unconcerned about their safety.

Maybe she should have informed Mama of Theo's obsession with Blythe.

"What lovely flowers." Theo peered out the window as they started up an incline. "Goodness, what a massive display. Granby must possess a veritable army of gardeners."

"Can you even see what type of flowers there are, or do you only see splotches of color interspersed with greenery?"

Theo shot her a look. "If everything or anyone," she emphasized, "is close by, you know I see perfectly well. It is only things at a distance."

"Or across a room, Theo. It was a poor idea not to wear your spectacles. How am I to explain when you bump into a wall? Or begin talking to a potted fern thinking it is Blythe?"

"Very amusing, Romy. You are only put out because of Granby." A mysterious smile crossed her lips.

"No surprise there. I've already explained we don't like each other, so the party is bound to be awkward. If you recall, I didn't want to come."

"No, you didn't. I know you and Beatrice don't tolerate each other well, but you failed to disclose why you and the duke are at odds."

He called me a shrub. And he makes my skin prickle rather deliciously. Which is much more alarming.

"I don't think he approves of Leo," Romy said finally. "Or Tony. At least that was my impression."

"Did he voice his disapproval outright?"

Theo didn't sound as outraged as Romy thought she should be. Or as surprised.

"It was implied."

"We Barringtons tend to invite attention, and Granby doesn't care to do so." Theo turned the page of her book with a finger. "I'm sure it's because of the scandal."

"What scandal?" Cousin Winnie hadn't mentioned Granby again during her visit, and Romy's own mother, when asked, had waved her away with the admonition not to gossip. "Mama would tell me nothing."

"Nor I, but Cousin Winnie speaks rather loudly when she has had more than one sherry. I can't believe you didn't hear her voice echoing down the halls during her visit. She recited to Mama all the sordid details of the great disgrace of Granby. Very shocking," Theo said without looking up.

Her sister was impossible. Must Romy drag the information out of her? "Are you going to tell me? We are growing ever closer to his estate."

Theo shut her book with a loud clap. "His mother ran away with a soldier. Granby was only a child at the time. According to Cousin Winnie, the scandal was that much more enormous because her soldier was just that—not an officer of any renown. Terribly embarrassing for Granby's father, the late duke. Although, I don't suppose it would have been better if her lover had been a general or captain of the guard."

"No, I suppose not." Romy returned her gaze to the countryside, thinking of Granby as a young boy.

"It was gossiped about for years, the *utter* humiliation of the Duke of Granby. Everyone said the old duke deserved it for marrying so far beneath himself. He was mocked constantly, and so was Granby. No wonder Beatrice holds such appeal for him."

"I still don't see what any of this has to do with his obvious dislike for our family."

"Do you not?" Theo asked. "Perhaps it will come to you during the course of the house party."

Romy gritted her teeth. Theo had a habit of appearing wise, as if she sensed the truths no one else could see. She *was* incredibly intuitive, though, unfortunately only in regard to others and not herself. Blythe was a perfect example.

"Oh, dear. What a monstrosity." Theo's eyes widened, taking in her first glimpse of The Barrow. "It is so large even I can see it clearly."

The enormous edifice, rising out of the hill as the coach climbed, was made of the same gray, weathered stone as the guardhouse and was as imposing as the cliffs lining the coast they'd traveled. The Barrow was stark, free of adornment, towering over the surrounding countryside, austere, and intimidating, much like the man who resided within. Four rows of windows faced the drive, like a dozen eyes all looking down at the Averell coach with little welcome as the sisters approached.

It was exactly the sort of estate Romy supposed the Duke of Granby *would* have. Or a menacing giant from a child's fable. The only warmth Romy could sense at all in The Barrow was the estate's gardens. The gardens appeared, at a distance, to be nothing more than a disorganized jumble of plants and color, but as they drew closer, Romy could see the beds had been carefully designed to look like fields of wild-flowers. A profusion of colorful vines, some rather exotic-looking for England, cascaded over a low stone wall on one side of the wide drive. The Barrow's bleak facade could have benefited from some of the beautiful flowering vines, but Romy supposed none were brave enough to scale the walls of the house.

Immense gardens weren't unusual, especially not at a duke's home, but the layout here wasn't typical. No head gardener worth his salt would have planned out the gardens of a prestigious residence in such a way unless he had been commanded to do so. Granby, with his frigid demeanor and reputedly exacting nature, seemed an unlikely candidate to have such wildness surrounding him. Perhaps it was the influence of Lady Molsin.

Another vehicle, painted black, sat stopped before the immense set of double doors. Four perfectly matched bays, feet stomping on the gravel and coats gleaming in the late afternoon sun, stood waiting before The Barrow.

"Blythe," Theo whispered, immediately squinting out the window at the coat of arms decorating the coach's door.

"You idiot. You can't see a thing."

Theo swatted Romy's knee. "It *is* Blythe. Look."

Blythe exited his coach dressed in a patterned waistcoat and a coat of peacock blue. The gold in his hair glittered like an old coin as he jogged up the steps. The footmen rushed forward, greeting him with a friendliness that spoke of Blythe having been a guest at The Barrow many times before. He bestowed a smile on all of them, even clasping the tallest footman on the shoulder.

He never once glanced in the direction of their coach.

Theo's entire body arched and deflated in a dramatic sigh. "Isn't he beautiful?"

"Stop it this instant, Theo. Your mooning over Blythe is becoming intolerable. If I didn't know better, I'd assume you've hit your head and lost your wits."

"You don't understand," Theo said. "You've never been in love."

"I think the word you are looking for is infatuation." If Theo started to giggle and blush, Romy might be reduced to smacking her cheeks.

The door of Blythe's coach banged open again, and another pair of booted feet struck the gravel of the driveway with a crunch. This gentleman was taller than Blythe by an inch or so and was not nearly as well-dressed. While his coat must once have been magnificent, the fine cloth showed extensive wear. He stretched his arms upon exiting, exposing loose threads peeking out of the seams. The fine leather of his boots, and Romy could see they'd once been expensive, was dull with wear and even cracked in some places.

Where Blythe bounded up the steps like an oversized puppy, this man sauntered toward the door like some great tomcat seeking a patch of sunlight.

"Who do you suppose that is?" Romy asked.

Blythe's traveling companion turned his shaggy head, catching sight of Romy and Theo observing him. The tomcat analogy was an apt one, for Romy had only ever seen a cat possessing eyes of that color. The mossy green was evident even from the distance separating him from their coach. The ends of his hair, the same color as the horses pulling Blythe's coach trailed along his collar and teased at his shoulders. He gave them a short, mocking bow, before striding up the steps and into The Barrow.

"Haven," Theo said with certainty. "Completely disreputable."

"Have you met him before?" It seemed unlikely, but perhaps he'd been with Blythe in the park.

"No. But Rosalind knows all about him. She thinks Haven quite handsome, though he's poor as a church mouse. His father gambled away everything that wasn't entailed. Cousin Winnie has warned her away from him. He's a marquess prone to dueling and gambling, himself."

"Well, that explains the state of his coat and condition of his boots. The impoverished part, I mean."

Her sister shook her head. "Must everyone be reduced to nothing more than the sum of their clothing?"

"I notice such things. I can't help it."

As she and Theo exited the coach and entered the house, a thin, angular man rushed forward, twin puffs of white hair on either side of his otherwise bald pate. His mustache twitched at them in consternation. "Greetings. I am Owens, His Grace's butler. Welcome to The Barrow. You must be Lady Richardson's cousins?"

"Lady Andromeda Barrington and Lady Theodosia Barrington." Romy inclined her head, smiling at the harried butler.

Theo walked away from her, attempting to sneak down the hall, perhaps in an attempt to catch another glimpse of Blythe. "Theo," she hissed to her sister, waving for her to return.

"My apologies that you've not been greeted properly." The butler's mustache twitched like a small mouse sensing danger. The last word ended on a slight tremble.

The butler was obviously nervous, desperate to ensure Romy and Theo weren't displeased. It spoke volumes about the way Granby treated his staff.

"The other guests are on the terrace enjoying—" Owens started to say.

"You've greeted us *quite* properly, Mr. Owens. I'll make sure Lady Molsin is well aware. Our delay in arrival is entirely my fault. I hope I didn't cause undue worry."

Romy had insisted on stopping at Madame Dupree's before leaving to drop off a series of sketches she'd just finished for Miss Hobarth. Cousin Winnie was probably beside herself with worry. "Can you have one of the footmen," she gestured to a stoic looking youth hovering by the door, "apprise Lady Richardson of our arrival?"

"Immediately, my lady. I shall do so myself. Your rooms have been prepared." He waved forward a maid. "I assume you would like to refresh yourselves after your journey before joining the other guests? Sara can show you to your rooms. I'll ensure your servants are settled."

"Yes, thank you, Owens."

The butler nodded, cheeks pinking as she addressed him by name.

Everyone, no matter their station, deserved to be treated with respect and recognized for their contributions. Romy's mother insisted all the Barrington servants be treated politely and addressed by name.

Romy held tightly to her sister's sleeve. "Come, Theo." They were both dusty and in need of a change of clothes.

"When you are ready, my lady, a servant will show you to the terrace where the other guests are gathered. You are not the only late arrivals," he added.

"Splendid." Romy dragged Theo up the stairs. "Thank you again, Owens."

6

"Christ, Gran. Did your aunt invite every marriageable chit in England?" Haven complained from a leather winged-back chair. "Will I be forced to play charades? Or some other silly game no dignified marquess should be forced to play?"

"You are hardly dignified," Blythe said from his place closer to the sideboard.

Haven scowled in his direction.

"Depends on what you deem beneath you," David answered his friend. "I'm sure there will be charades this evening in the drawing room, and Aunt Pen has arranged a game of bowls on the lawn for tomorrow."

"Just give me a bloody pistol now. I'll go shoot something in the woods to relieve the tedium. Or better yet, I'll shoot myself in order to avoid participating in such nonsense. I can just imagine a flock of young ladies all tossing bowls about the lawn at me."

"Perish the thought, Haven. *None* of them are after you." Blythe gave Haven a smug look. "Not with a duke and a ridiculously wealthy earl who looks like me in residence. Even

Estwood is far more charming when he chooses to be. Or at least his money is."

"You can't have one conversation without mentioning the size of your purse, can you?" Haven snapped.

"I wasn't talking about *my* wealth," Blythe pointed out. "But Estwood's. Where is he, by the way?"

"Estwood will arrive later tonight, hopefully in time for dinner," David answered. "A delay in London. One of his business ventures required immediate attention."

Estwood was involved in all sorts of schemes, some of which David approved of and many he did not. Ruthless and brilliant, Estwood disregarded all obstacles and a great many people in his pursuit of wealth. He'd amassed a great deal, making Blythe look like a pauper in comparison. But it was never enough. All the wealth in the world would never buy Estwood what he sought most.

"You, Haven, will have to settle for one of the plainer girls, though a well-dowered one," Blythe stated in a conversational tone. "Isn't Lady Mildred still unmarried? I think I saw her wandering about as I made my way to your study, Gran."

"Lady Mildred is a bit long in the tooth for my tastes."

"She *is* quite ancient, but also very desperate. Or Lucy Waterstone. Her father is dying to marry her off. The lisp *is* unfortunate."

Haven gave Blythe a chilly look. "You, Blythe, are nothing more than a spoiled dandy with little to recommend him but his looks. You are fortunate I didn't strangle you on the ride here."

David put his hand up before the growing tension between the two resulted in blows. It *was* a miracle they hadn't killed each other on the journey from London. Haven and Blythe argued often, the hostility between them sometimes resulting in long stretches when the pair didn't speak to each other. David had almost sent a coach for Haven's use so he wouldn't be subjected to Blythe's baiting, but Haven, ever sensitive regarding his poverty, would have seen the gesture as the charity it was.

Blythe was unfortunately correct about Haven's circumstances. The estate he'd inherited was rundown, stripped of the former glory it had once commanded. Returning from abroad, Haven had been greeted with a dead father who had passed along his title as well as a great deal of debt. Haven's sister had been reduced to living like a beggar with a distant relation. Everything which wasn't entailed had been sold, leaving Haven very little else. He still struggled to repay the remaining creditors, refusing loans or outright gifts of money. The damage done to his family's reputation was extensive, thus resulting in Haven's propensity to duel. He thought his honor infringed upon regularly.

Blythe, on the other hand, possessed a well-managed estate and an enormous fortune, inherited from a father who had not squandered the family wealth on the turn of a card. His perpetually sunny disposition was in stark contrast to Haven's gloomy outlook. Blythe was charming, well-liked, and fawned over by every woman within his radius, including his mother and five sisters. In short, Blythe had everything Haven did not.

"Are you going to allow him to threaten me, Gran?" Blythe said teasingly. "I should challenge Haven to a duel. Settle things between us once and for all."

David refilled Haven's glass. He had yet to take a sip of the contents of his own, not wanting the scotch to induce him to relinquish even a bit of his iron control, especially when The Barrow was filled with guests.

"I'd be short one friend," he warned Blythe. "I've not that many to begin with and can't afford to lose either of you. That would leave me with only Estwood at the card table."

Blythe was a decent enough shot, but challenging Haven, who was deadly with either swords or pistols, wasn't wise. "Stop antagonizing Haven."

Blythe clinked his glass with the unsmiling Haven's. "Very well. I apologize, Haven. Lady Meredith Claremont is here. She's pretty. *Lovely* bosom. Much younger than Lady Mildred." He wiggled his brows.

"Have you compromised her?"

"No," Blythe said, not the least offended by Haven's question. "And I promise not to steal so much as a kiss if your interest lies in her direction."

"Fine." Haven curled his lip. "I shall consider her and anyone else who has been invited. Perhaps Granby's aunt is seeking to secure more than one match with this party."

"I'm not sure she's eager to secure mine," David said off-hand, receiving a curious look from Haven.

Blythe studied the contents of his glass, remaining silent. A first.

"Lady Richardson seeks a husband for her daughter," David finally said, if only to break the sudden tension in the study. "I met her briefly upon their enthusiastic arrival. Attractive enough. And there's two other young ladies, cousins of Lady Richardson, who were invited at the last minute. I haven't seen them, so I can't speak for their appearance, but perhaps one of them will do. You *are* still a marquess, Haven. Waterstone wants a title for his daughter."

"Waterstone is a bigger deterrent than his daughter's lisp." Haven snorted. "I can't imagine enduring his company for a lifetime."

"We'll leave out Lady Beatrice Howard as a potential match." Blythe swirled the scotch in his mouth before taking a swallow. "I believe she's spoken for, isn't she? Leave it to Gran to put his claim on the most beautiful young lady in

England. But then, Gran likes pretty things. Is fond of collecting them, in fact."

"I do." David declined to elaborate further, though most of London assumed he would offer officially for Beatrice during the house party.

A pair of magnificent blue eyes floated before him. Andromeda Barrington. Far more beautiful, in his estimation, than Lady Beatrice Howard, but so much more unsuitable. She was stunning even wearing the hideous dress he'd seen her in at Madame Dupree's.

Or better still, if she wore nothing at all.

Arousal slipped down his thighs at the thought of Andromeda, naked, beneath him. David's cock hardened. Painfully. Thank God his coat was now the correct length.

"Lady Beatrice will be just another possession for Gran, like those bloody statues he's been collecting. Or those stone paintings." Blythe tossed back his drink with an angry flick of his wrist.

"Frescoes," David corrected him, wondering at Blythe's mood. "Ancient Roman frescoes."

"I do like the new painting, by the way." Blythe nodded at the seascape hanging on the wall. "Fills me with a sense of melancholy. Terribly expensive, I'm sure."

"It wasn't," David said, knowing even if the seascape's cost had been exorbitant, he would have purchased it. The knowledge irritated him.

"Art is a waste of money," Haven grumbled.

"Spoken as a man with little appreciation or funds for it," Blythe said. "*Should* we be expecting an announcement, Your Grace?"

"Foxwood certainly thinks so." David was bothered by his own inexplicable reticence in confirming his plans to marry Beatrice. His decisions were always the result of careful thought. Planning. Logic. Once decided, he rarely deviated from his chosen path.

Which was Beatrice.

His cock, still stimulated by thoughts of Andromeda, disagreed.

"You don't even like her, Gran." Blythe's words bled with irritation. "Shouldn't you at least *like* the woman you'll marry?"

"I don't *dislike* her, if that is your meaning." She evoked no emotion in David at all. Not even a hint of irritation. "Liking your wife isn't relevant in most marriages of our class, is it?"

His gaze landed on the seascape again. Ridiculous to buy a bloody painting because it reminded him of a young woman who had insulted him. He didn't even like seascapes. He would instruct his butler, Bowen, to remove the painting.

"Not an *ounce* of affection," Blythe persisted.

Blythe was a hopeless romantic. He read poetry, for God's sake.

"It isn't necessary. You know that as well as I. Beatrice is eminently suitable," David stated.

"A resounding endorsement, if I ever heard one."

Blythe had never approved of David offering for Lady Beatrice Howard for reasons his friend had never explained, though he claimed not to want her for himself.

A soft knock sounded at the study door.

"Your Grace." His butler bowed, keeping his eyes lowered. "Lady Molsin wishes me to remind you that your guests are on the terrace enjoying a late luncheon."

David set down his glass, still half-full, at the subtle reminder from Aunt Pen that his presence was required. Resigning himself to the remainder of his day spent in bland conversation, he nodded to the butler.

"Please inform Lady Molsin I'll be along directly."

7

Romy scoured the terrace for any sight of her cousin, but Lady Richardson didn't appear to be on the terrace circulating with the other guests. After bursting into her room as Romy was making herself presentable after the journey, her cousin had chastised Romy for her late arrival before departing in a flurry of skirts.

Romy and Theo came down a short time later and were directed outside by a servant, but Cousin Winnie was nowhere to be found.

Nor was Blythe, much to Theo's dismay.

Miss Waterstone greeted Romy warmly, visibly surprised to find her at The Barrow. As were Lady Meredith Clare and Lady Mildred Dresser.

Rosalind took Romy's arm. "I'm not sure where Mama has gone, but she made me promise to make sure you stayed on the terrace so you can be properly introduced to Lady Molsin."

"I still haven't forgiven you for the invitation." Romy leaned over and whispered in her cousin's ear. "But I like the dress, by the way."

"You designed it." At Romy's look, she said, "Phaedra told me. And don't be cross. No one will hear of your secret from my lips. I'm rather proud of you. I lack all but the most basic of talents."

Romy took in her cousin's petite, slightly rounded form. "You've marvelous instincts about dough."

"True." A smile hovered at her lips. "But Mama doesn't allow me to make pastries anymore." She patted a generously curved hip. "At any rate," she nodded at Theo, "you can't depend on me to save her from her own foolishness in regard to Blythe. Not when I've my own problems to deal with. I'm terrified Lord Torrington means to offer for me. He's arriving with Mr. Waterstone tomorrow."

"He's quite an attractive gentleman," Romy offered.

"And twice my age." Rosalind appeared deflated by her mother's determination to marry her off to the older, widowed earl. "He wants more a brood mare than wife."

"You'd be a young widow."

"It isn't funny, Romy, and you aren't being helpful."

"I'm trying to help you see the positives in the situation."

"Hmph." Her eyes widened slightly. "I think I'll fetch a small plate while Mama is occupied elsewhere. Excuse me."

"Rosalind, where are you—"

"Lady Andromeda, I'm surprised to find you here," Lady Beatrice intoned from behind Romy, trying and failing to keep the dislike out of her otherwise dulcet tones.

"No more than I am myself, Lady Beatrice," Romy answered, silently cursing Rosalind for her abandonment. Keeping a serene, composed look on her features, she tried to think of more pleasant things than speaking to Beatrice. Honey on toast, for example. A bolt of fine tulle. The sound of her pencil as she sketched out a new gown.

Strangling Rosalind.

"I confess, Lady Andromeda, I was quite shocked to learn

you would be attending with Lady Theodosia." Beatrice glanced at Theo, who was discreetly squinting, fingers trailing across the stone wall as she moved forward. "Is your sister well? She seems a bit . . . out of sorts."

"Perhaps unsteady from being in a coach for so long." Theo had already tripped over a table leg. Her vision was much more impaired without her spectacles than Romy had been led to believe. "It was very kind of Lady Molsin to include us along with Lady Richardson. She and Miss Richardson are cousins of ours."

"Lady Molsin is kindness itself," Beatrice replied with a small hint of steel, her annoyance at not being consulted on the guest list apparent. "She only neglected to inform my mother and me."

"We were a last-minute addition."

"Apparently."

Romy glanced out over the rolling waves of flowers, broken up by only a narrow gravel path which disappeared into the gardens. Now that the required pleasantries were over, she and Beatrice had little to say to one another, each searching for an excuse to end this awkward but necessary greeting.

"Does Granby have an orchard?" she said to Beatrice, searching for something to say. Romy could just make out what appeared to be apple trees at the edge of the immense lawn.

"I've no idea." Beatrice drummed her fingers against her skirts, lips pursed, the thin veneer of politeness beginning to fray about the edges.

I should tell her I designed her ballgown. Just to give her fits.

A smile broke across Beatrice's lips, turning her from merely beautiful to absolutely stunning as she waved excitedly at someone behind Romy.

"Rebecca." She brushed past Romy without a second

thought, obviously relieved at having been rescued from conversing with Romy further now that she'd done her duty. "How good of you to come." Beatrice took her friend's hands with affection.

The new Lady Carstairs greeted Beatrice warmly, spinning about to show off her plum-colored ensemble before her joy halted upon noticing Romy. Brow wrinkling in consternation, she nonetheless bobbed politely. "Lady Andromeda. What a pleasure to find you here."

"Isn't it?" Just imagining the tedious conversation she'd be forced into with Lady Carstairs was enough to send Romy sprinting across the lawn.

"A late addition to the house party," Beatrice said. "Lady Richardson begged an invitation for Lady Andromeda and her sister." A gloved hand waved in the direction of Theo, who winced as she stubbed her toe. "Lady Theodosia."

Begged an invitation? She opened her mouth to object.

Rebecca observed Theo. "I thought Lady Theodosia wore spectacles."

"Broken," Romy bit out. "During the journey here. Very unfortunate." The last thing Theo would appreciate was these two nitwits gossiping about her vanity.

"Rebecca," Beatrice cooed to her friend. "My gown, the one I told you about, was finished just in time. You'll have to come to my room later to see it. Madame Dupree has outdone herself. I confess, she is a marvel. There are even tiny clips for my hair to match the dress."

Rebecca clapped her hands. "How splendid."

"The clips resemble small suns," Beatrice continued. "I shall *outshine* every woman in the room."

"As you should," Rebecca giggled, Beatrice's pun more than her tiny brain could comprehend. "Granby won't be able to take his eyes from you."

Had she known the gown was going to Beatrice, Romy

would have created tiny snakes instead of suns. A small snort left her thinking of Beatrice as Medusa.

Beatrice and Rebecca shot her twin looks of annoyance before proceeding to ignore Romy completely and exclude her from their conversation.

With a sigh, Romy cast a glance in the direction of the gardens, meaning to excuse herself for a stroll when she caught sight of Cousin Winnie beckoning to her with a wave. She stood next to an older woman who was busy directing one of the servants. Lady Molsin.

"Excuse me. My cousin bids me to join her."

Neither Beatrice nor Rebecca bothered to acknowledge her departure.

Head shaking at their rudeness, Romy hurried to Cousin Winnie's side, discreetly observing their hostess. Delicate and fine boned, with refined patrician features and ash-blonde hair, Lady Molsin bore little resemblance to her nephew. Powder blue eyes sparkled with warmth at Romy's approach, her hand reaching out in welcome.

"Penelope," Cousin Winnie said, "may I present my dear cousin's daughter, Lady Andromeda Barrington. Andromeda, dear, this is our hostess, Lady Molsin."

Lady Molsin took Romy's hand. "Lady Andromeda. A pleasure. I regret I could not greet you upon your arrival. I'm afraid the other guests were demanding their luncheon, and I dared not leave the staff without direction. I hope Owens took good care of you?"

"Andromeda and Theodosia arrived much later than anticipated." Cousin Winnie sent Romy a pointed look. "And you had other guests to see to, Penelope."

"Indeed, Lady Molsin. I would not have wanted you to desert your other guests on our account. Owens was very welcoming and is a credit to His Grace's household," Romy said. "My apologies if our late arrival caused any undue concern."

Lady Molsin waved away her apology. "Not at all," she said, her grip on Romy's hand firm as she studied her. "Quite beautiful, aren't you? Like all the Barringtons. I am acquainted with your mother, though it has been some time since I've seen her. How does Amanda fare these days?"

"She is well, my lady. And in London, enjoying her grandson, Lord Welles."

Lady Molsin nodded. "Good. I was saddened to hear of your father's death. He was a lovely man. Quite the rogue, before marrying your mother. Caused quite a stir. I remember it well."

At Romy's questioning look, Lady Molsin only smiled broader. "Forgive the ramblings of an elderly woman."

"Where has Theodosia gone?" Cousin Winnie said, clearly agitated. "She was right there only a moment ago." Shrewd eyes scanned the terrace. "She should greet our hostess properly."

"I'm sure Theo will turn up, Cousin," Romy assured her, pondering Lady Molsin's comment. "If you will excuse me, I feel the need to stretch my legs after our journey. I was thinking of a walk before dinner."

"But dear," Cousin Winnie turned back to Romy, "you haven't yet met the duke."

The very *last* thing Romy wished to do was reacquaint herself with Granby.

"Nonsense." Lady Molsin batted away Cousin Winnie's concern. "My nephew has yet to appear, and Lady Andromeda won't be gone long, I'm sure. The gardens *are* lovely. Very wild. The best thing about The Barrow, in my estimation. The gardeners took all their direction from the duke. His Grace is very exacting."

And arrogant. Rude. Snobbish. It was one of the few times

Romy didn't voice her opinion. But she was surprised that the gardens were the purview of Granby and not his aunt.

"Many of the plants are not native to England but have been coaxed to grow here all the same. The roses at the far corner"—Lady Molsin pointed to a spot hidden from the terrace—"are in bloom."

"Oh, there she is." Cousin Winnie waved.

Theo had reappeared on the opposite side of the terrace. She was leaning over, peering in Cousin Winnie's direction, one hand shading her eyes from the sun.

"Perhaps Lady Theodosia can't see us?" Lady Molsin offered gently.

A puzzled look appeared on Cousin Winnie's face. "She usually wears spectacles."

Before her cousin could question her as to Theo's eyesight, Romy took a step in the direction of the stairs leading down into the gardens. She had no desire to run into Granby, at least at present, and especially not after being subjected to Beatrice.

"I think I'll take your suggestion, Lady Molsin." Bobbing politely, Romy hurried across the terrace and down the broad stone steps leading into the gardens. She took a deep lungful of fresh air. Trees. Flowers. The chirping of birds. All of it was so much better than being subjected to the conversation filling the terrace behind her.

As her feet touched the gravel of the path, she heard Lady Molsin say, "Ah, there's Granby now."

8

avid stepped outside, taking in the guests busily eating his food and ordering his servants about. House parties, as a rule, required a certain amount of forced intimacy between host and guest. He eschewed such informality. David neither cared nor wanted to know most of these people any more than he already did. Which was to say, not at all.

He stretched his neck, hoping to loosen his cravat.

Aunt Pen had made the guest list, but he was sure Lady Foxwood had had input because of the presence of Lord and Lady Carstairs. Carstairs was a pleasant sort, but he and David were only slightly acquainted. It was Beatrice who was close to Lady Carstairs, which made him seriously consider the intelligence of his future duchess.

If Lord and Lady Carstairs were in possession of one brain between them, it would be a miracle on par with a virgin birth. Attractive and wealthy, the newly married couple seemed to exist in their own world where intellect wasn't noted or required. He wasn't even sure what to call such a match. A marriage of equals?

Doubtless due to the influence wielded by Lady Foxwood, the other young ladies in attendance were all lovely, but not so attractive that Lady Beatrice's beauty would be eclipsed. His eyes were drawn to the odd movements of a willowy brunette, seemingly oblivious to a servant carrying a tray of poached chicken. She shuffled forward before nearly upending the tray. Smiling, she apologized profusely to the shaken footman.

David's lips formed their usual scowl. No one should have to apologize to a servant. It wasn't necessary. His father had assured him it wasn't appropriate when David had made the mistake of apologizing to a groom at the age of ten.

There was something vaguely familiar about the young lady, yet David was positive they'd never met. As the brunette gingerly made her way over to Aunt Pen and a woman he recalled to be Lady Richardson, David was struck by how lovely the girl was.

Lady Foxwood had certainly not approved this guest.

His observation was interrupted by the arrival of Lord Foxwood, who came toward David while rubbing his hands together, likely already contemplating his daughter's elevation to duchess.

"Your Grace." He bowed.

Foxwood was a trim, neat gentleman clothed in a coat of walnut brown. His lean features and narrow nose spoke of centuries of refinement. The air of superiority hovering about his compact form had been honed from inheriting a title which was one of the oldest and most prestigious in England. Though close in age to David's late father, Foxwood appeared years younger.

Horace and Foxwood had been close acquaintances, sharing many of the same interests. It had seemed logical to seek him out when David determined he was ready to wed. But it didn't mean he and David were friends. They weren't.

"Lord Foxwood, welcome to The Barrow. I trust your journey was without incident."

"Indeed, Your Grace. And informative. I can see why your father sought the small parcel of land just to the south of your estate. It would be much easier to build a bridge spanning the river at its narrowest point than to go around and build an entire stretch of road."

How like Foxwood. David did not need to be reminded of every benefit to wedding Beatrice, as he'd already decided to offer for her; he just hadn't done so yet. He found it amusing to watch Foxwood and his wife twist in the wind, breathlessly awaiting the announcement. David felt no need to reassure Foxwood nor explain that he meant to build a bridge suitable for a locomotive, with a great deal of rail, complete with a station. The idea had been Estwood's, and it was a good one. Estwood was rarely wrong when it came to investing in industry. The parcel of land which was part of Beatrice's dowry included the area where the river narrowed.

"A bridge is preferred." David decided to toy with Foxwood. The man was far too sure of himself and his daughter's charms. "But not necessary."

Foxwood's perfect little mustache quivered at David's noncommittal response. "Of course, Your Grace." A charming smile, one patently false, broke across Foxwood's lips. "I quite agree."

"Your Grace." Lady Foxwood floated to them in a cloud of luxurious silk and floral perfume. "I see Foxwood has found you." Her hand slid easily down her husband's arm with practiced affection. The silvery-blonde hair twisted atop her head was a shade lighter than her daughter's, but otherwise Lady Foxwood could easily be mistaken for Beatrice's older sister. Her sophisticated golden beauty was a perfect foil for her husband. The two reminded David of a matched pair of

Pomeranians, carefully styled and coiffed to hide their calculating nature.

David detested small dogs.

"I must thank you again, Your Grace, for your escort as Beatrice and I perused the shops the other day."

"It was my pleasure, Lady Foxwood." The 'other day' had been a month or so ago, and Lady Foxwood had already thanked him numerous times. Her intention was to remind David he'd since neglected to call on Beatrice. In his estimation, calling on Beatrice would not only be unnecessary but a test of his patience. An entire afternoon with Lady Foxwood and her daughter had been an incredible waste of time.

Except for seeing Andromeda Barrington.

His eyes drifted from Lady Foxwood to the less-than-graceful young lady he'd noticed earlier. She was still conversing with his aunt, hands clasped politely. There was something about her that reminded David of Andromeda. The young lady's hair was a shade darker, her bosom more generous. And Andromeda didn't stumble like a blind man while hurling insults at dukes, but still—

Beatrice was suddenly thrust before David by her mother, demanding his attention.

She dipped into a graceful curtsy, moving her shoulders forward so the valley between her ample breasts deepened. A practiced move meant to draw a gentleman's gaze to her bosom.

While David could only see the tops of her breasts rising above her neckline, he assumed her bosom to be as perfect as the rest of Beatrice. The sun hit the golden strands of her hair, giving the appearance of a halo around her stunning features.

Her lashes fluttered gently against her cheeks, like the wings of a tiny bird, as she straightened. Pink rose petal lips held just a hint of a pout. He'd spoken to her exactly three times before her arrival yesterday, most of which had been during their conversation at Madame Dupree's.

"Lady Beatrice, you look lovely."

"Thank you, Your Grace." She cast her eyes down in a demure fashion.

Blythe appeared, sidling up next to David with little warning, shining like a brilliant gold guinea. Teeth, even and blindingly white, showed as he smiled broadly at David and the Foxwoods.

Blythe always knew how to make an entrance.

"How nice to see you again, Lord Foxwood, Lady Foxwood." His voice lowered just a shade. "Lady Beatrice."

"Lord Blythe." Foxwood gave a sharp jerk of his chin to Blythe.

Lady Foxwood's tiny mouth puckered instantly. "My lord."

Beatrice, apparently immune to the charms of Blythe, moved back a pace, away from his golden form, deliberately pulling back her skirts. "Lord Blythe." Her greeting was coldly polite.

"I didn't realize you were acquainted." David glanced at all four of them. Clearly Blythe knew the Foxwoods, although it didn't appear to be a friendly association.

Foxwood's lip curled, not bothering to hide his displeasure at having to converse with Blythe. "I didn't realize you'd be attending, Lord Blythe."

How odd. *Everyone* liked Blythe. Even Haven, at times.

"The duke and I are old friends."

Beatrice's features remained composed, her gaze floating over Blythe with little interest before returning to the perusal of her clasped hands.

Blythe's agreeable smile faltered. "A moment of your time, Your Grace?" he said in a low voice. "There is a matter requiring your attention."

"If you'll excuse us." David nodded and followed Blythe

some distance from the Foxwoods so they wouldn't be overheard.

"Why didn't you tell me you know Foxwood?" he said before Blythe could speak.

Blythe ran a hand through his close-cropped hair, causing the ends to stand up. "I beat Foxwood soundly at whist during Lady Ralston's ball last year," he replied, avoiding the larger question. "Won quite a tidy sum. Embarrassed him, I'm afraid, by bringing his poor playing to the attention of the rest of the table. Later, in the ballroom, he was quite rude to me in front of his wife and daughter. Our discussion may have become heated."

"I see." It didn't quite explain the strange tension he'd witnessed, but David didn't question him further. Whatever had occurred between Blythe and the Foxwoods had been well before David decided to wed Beatrice. He glanced at Blythe, trying to conjure in himself a hint of jealously or possessiveness over the possibility that his friend might desire Beatrice and found . . . nothing. There was only a lingering sense of annoyance that Blythe hadn't told him he knew the Foxwoods. He and Blythe had been friends nearly their whole lives. There wasn't anyone David trusted more, even when Blythe deliberately withheld information, as he was doing now.

"Foxwood is a poor loser. Don't ever play cards with him, Gran. He holds a grudge."

"Now you've told me." He started to walk away, but Blythe took his arm.

"That isn't what I needed to discuss." He pointed to the young lady David had observed earlier, still speaking to Aunt Pen. "I need to make an introduction. Wait a moment."

Blythe strode over and bowed to her before tilting his head in David's direction. She nodded, with little enthusiasm, but followed Blythe, her adoration of him apparent.

As the young lady neared, David studied her exquisitely sculpted features. Where had he seen her before?

"Your Grace, may I present Lady Theodosia Barrington."

She lowered her head, immediately dropping gracefully, the skirts of her gown billowing out around her. "Your Grace."

David was staring at her. Not *exactly* her, but—

Barrington.

Lady Theodosia was obviously Andromeda's sister, both daughters of a low-born mother who thought naming her children after characters in Greek mythology would obscure the fact she'd once been a lady's companion.

Andromeda's sister raised her eyes, glancing at Blythe with absolute worship before looking at David. Theodosia's eyes were the same spectacular blue, the distinctive indigo ring unmistakable around the darker pupil.

"You are related to Lady Richardson are you not?" he said, watching as Theodosia struggled to pull her attention from Blythe. The poor girl was besotted *and* half-blind, though no less beautiful for either affliction.

"Lady Richardson is our cousin, Your Grace. My sister Andromeda accompanied me to The Barrow. She is," Theodosia looked across the terrace, doing her best not to squint, "somewhere. Taking a turn about the gardens, I expect. She adores the country."

Theodosia, much like her sister, wasn't the least impressed with David. Not his size nor the fact he was a duke. She had the same self-possessed manner and confident way of speaking as Andromeda. Obviously being raised by a lady's companion resulted in a lack of the modesty required of young ladies.

"I'm sure she'll turn up, my lady." Blythe stayed by Theodosia's side, flattering her with his attention. "If not, we'll go in search of her."

Theodosia blushed, likely at the thought of her own ruin should Blythe lead her into the gardens, before her brow wrinkled in consternation at the arrival of Lady Meredith, who also seemed intent on adoring Blythe.

Excusing himself, David found his way to Haven, who was sitting at a table alone with an enormous plate of tiny finger sandwiches and cakes in front of him. From this vantage point, David could see most of the gardens.

Desire lashed him at the thought of that gorgeous, annoying creature roaming about his beds of hollyhocks and peonies. Alone.

"Cucumbers." Haven ate a sandwich in one bite. "I was hoping for something a bit more robust. There isn't any more chicken left. Or ham. And I *like* ham." He resolutely bit into another sandwich of cucumber.

"Dinner is not far off," David said absently, his gaze once again drawn to the gardens. Instead of staying on the terrace with the rest of the guests, as a proper young lady should, Andromeda had set off to explore on her own. It was an obvious attempt to avoid him and one that would ultimately fail.

"My aunt has created a spectacular menu, Haven. I'm sure you'll be pleased." His friend was always starving as if he could never get enough to eat.

"She's quite pretty." Haven gestured with the crust of his sandwich in the general direction of Lady Beatrice.

"She's suitable." It seemed the only compliment he could bestow on her. Suitable. It sounded very trite.

"No, not Lady Beatrice." Haven discreetly pointed his finger in the direction of Blythe, who stood just to Beatrice's left with Theodosia Barrington. "Her. The one who is giggling over Blythe and keeps running into things."

"That is Lady Theodosia Barrington. She's quite taken with Blythe. A sister of the Duke of Averell."

Haven raised a brow. "He's more than one?"

"Apparently," David said absently, watching as a breeze ruffled through his rose bushes, looking for any sign of Andromeda. His patience was rewarded when a flash of mauve skirts fluttered into view.

"Excuse me, Haven. I'm going to take a turn about the gardens. Enjoy a cheroot." If she was going to start tossing insults in his direction, David thought it best she do so away from curious eyes so as to avoid a scene.

At least, that's what he told himself.

Haven reached into his coat, pulling out a small flask, dribbling some of the contents into his teacup. "I don't care for tea," he said when David raised a brow. "I've asked for wine. Enjoy your stroll, Gran."

David slipped off the terrace, feet crunching on the perfectly maintained gravel path. He paid his gardeners a sinful amount of money for the upkeep of the grounds. Horace hadn't cared much for the gardens other than insisting the hedges be subjected to weekly trimmings. A small palette of tea roses, deemed acceptable, had once been the only splash of color in the dreary landscape of The Barrow.

When he'd returned to England from his time abroad, David had made sweeping changes to the grounds. Horace, confined to his sickbed, deemed David's plans a waste of money. But by that time, his father was in no position to stop him.

David's steps faltered on the path at the memory before resuming his pursuit of Andromeda.

It had taken him three tries to find a head gardener who understood his vision. Experimenting with different plants, some of David's suggestions had been complete failures while others grew but did not thrive. While the weather here was milder than in other parts of England, some of the cuttings and flowering bushes could not tolerate the winters. At least outdoors. More than one fountain had been installed among the wild beds and small, charming alcoves created by stone and thick hedges. There were days when David would sit and listen to the sound of water flowing in his fountains, turn his face to the sun, and inhale the sweet smell of jasmine hovering in the air, all while pretending he wasn't in England.

He stepped quietly once he grew closer to the roses, listening for the slightest sound.

A rustle of skirts came from the direction of the rose bushes, and David turned.

Andromeda was bent over a profusion of blooms, one hand gently pulling a bud toward her. The red gold in her otherwise dark hair sparked like bits of copper thread in the late afternoon sun. She was humming, though the tune was so soft, he couldn't make it out.

He stayed silent, content to admire the curve of her hips and graceful line of her back, trying to recall why he found her so incredibly annoying and unsuitable. Because at that moment, with the bees buzzing and the sun glancing down the delicate skin of her neck, David found Andromeda anything but flawed.

She straightened abruptly, sensing his presence. Her spine and shoulders took on a tightness, steeling herself to face him. When she turned, there was resignation lurking in the magnificent blue of her eyes, along with trepidation. "Your Grace." The mauve skirts puffed out gracefully around her as she curtsied.

Andromeda was not as well-endowed as Beatrice, or her sister, but the small glimpse of what he imagined were exquisitely rounded breasts caused his cock to throb painfully. He hated the loss of control Andromeda's presence brought, the way his desire for her leached out of him whether he willed it or not.

"Lady Andromeda Barrington. What an unexpected pleasure."

"Is it?"

Why must every word she uttered in his presence be fraught with challenge? He took her hand as she straightened.

"Welcome to The Barrow."

❧ 9 ❧

Oh, bloody hell.

Maggie, Romy's sister-in-law, claimed cursing, even if you didn't do so out loud, was a great way to calm emotions which otherwise might grow out of hand. And Romy knew a great deal of vile words, thanks to her brothers. Leo, in particular, had a colorful vocabulary.

Granby was alone, sneaking up on her while she admired his gardens. She tilted her chin upward to meet his gaze, refusing to appear the least intimidated because he probably wanted her to be. A warm prickling sensation moved slowly up her arms and down across her chest, causing a soft flutter above her heart.

Romy tried to pull away, startled when his fingers curled more firmly around her own. She stared at their clasped hands, his so much larger, dwarfing hers.

She forced her gaze to the edge of his coat. The hem was perfect.

"Does everything meet with *your* approval, Lady Andromeda?" The low, caramel-tinged words wrapped softly around her.

She snatched her hand from his. "The gardens do. Meet with my approval, that is." Her heart floundered about inside her ribs, beating out an uneven rhythm. "Your gardens are magnificent. I have a marked preference for roses."

"Because of the thorns?"

Ebony waves blew against his cheek and fell over one eye. Granby possessed beautiful, *wild* hair. Too long and not carefully trimmed like his friend Blythe's. The dark strands matched the rambling expanse of his gardens but little else about him. Admiring his hair led naturally to the curve of his cheek and rigid line of his jaw. There was an unearthly beauty about Granby, a rawness to his looks which was absent in most of the gentlemen she knew.

"Especially the thorns," Romy answered.

"Seems fitting. After all, you are not without your own."

Granby's lips were full and sensual, much more noticeable when he wasn't scowling. Consumed with observing his mouth, Romy at first didn't acknowledge the thinly veiled insult.

Dragging her gaze from his lips, she drew herself up. "I have a preference for roses because, despite their looks, they are surprisingly hardy. Though I suppose if a rose dared to defy you, Your Grace, you would instruct your gardener to rip the entire bush out by the roots. *Sacked*, as it were."

It was gratifying to see the slight flare of his nostrils as her words hit their mark.

Point in my favor.

"I must confess, Lady Andromeda, I am relieved to find you."

"Are you?" He was standing much too close to her, the breeze shifting. She caught the scent of trees and shaving soap as a delicious heat wafted off his much larger body in her direction, tendrils caressing against the tops of her breasts and across her arms.

"Relieved?" The word was unsteady on her lips.

"You very nearly disappeared after rounding a cluster of hawthorn bushes. My gardeners could easily have mistaken you as a *shrub* and accidentally wielded their pruning shears in your direction. It would have ruined the house party." He tilted his head to peer down at her. "And your dress."

Romy had the distinct impression that he was admiring her bosom, a curious sensation which sent another ripple of heat down her body. "I doubt I was ever in any danger," she said through her teeth. "I'm sure your *staff* is quite observant." Not bothering to add the implication that Granby himself was not.

"I must ask, Lady Andromeda." The silky rumble drifted over her skin. "Are you angry with me because I thought you a servant at Madame Dupree's or that I asked to have you sacked for your impudence?"

"That? I'd forgotten all about your arrogant behavior that day, putting it from my mind as I do most things which I find unpleasant."

His beautiful lips disappeared into another scowl.

Romy should bid him good day and return to the terrace. It was poor form to stand and throw petty insults at her host, but she seemed unable to help herself. Granby was such a deserving target. One that sent her pulse racing with his very presence.

"I picture you marching about different establishments," she continued. "Ordering the proprietors to dismiss their loyal employees for any minor infraction you deem offensive."

"You are the most annoying creature I've ever met," he said in a casual tone. "You've not an ounce of self-preservation in addition to your other arrogant, insulting behavior."

Romy hissed, preparing a scathing speech with which to bring him low, but when she glanced up at him, there was no chilly dismissal as he looked at her. Not a hint of disdain.

Instead, his eyes resembled the embers of a fire which had burned for hours, full of banked heat.

"You weren't angry about my arrogance," he murmured softly as the ebony locks of his hair danced against his cheek, buffeted by the breeze. "At least, not completely."

"I wasn't?" Romy found it difficult to breathe as it seemed Granby had sucked up all the available air around her.

"You were upset, Lady Andromeda," he leaned down from his great height, the scent of pine, leather and trees invading her nose, "because you didn't think I remembered you from Lady Masterson's garden party."

The buttons of his coat were mere inches from her. If he moved, even slightly, he would brush the tips of her breasts.

Romy told herself to step away from him, but her feet refused to move, shocked by his words.

"But I do remember you." His voice grew husky. And annoyed. *Very* annoyed. "You are hard to forget." The dark gaze dropped to her lips. "Impossible, it seems."

"You should seek a new valet," she stuttered, horrified to find her nipples were growing taut beneath the fabric of her dress.

"Should I, my lady?"

Her mouth must be fascinating. Granby hadn't taken his eyes from her lips.

"Your hair touches the collar of your coat," Romy said, wincing at the outlandish and improper observation.

"What a thing for you to notice, my lady." A hungry look crossed his face, his gaze dipping to her breasts again before returning to her mouth.

Attraction, powerful and sharp, spiraled into the small space separating their bodies. It sparked between them like tiny bolts of lightning releasing from a summer storm, the force of it sending a shiver down to Romy's toes.

"I notice many things." There was a seductive quality to

her reply, surprising Romy almost as much as did the overwhelming need to touch him. What would Granby do if her hands splayed across his chest, testing the muscles beneath the fine lawn of his shirt? "I was right about your coat, Your Grace. Surely my advice should be followed."

"You have an argumentative nature," he purred, so close his breath ruffled her hair. "It infuriates me. A young lady should be demure. Obedient."

Romy's lips parted, her entire body arching toward his in invitation. "I've never been considered . . . biddable."

Granby's fingers skimmed the line of her jaw before tilting her chin up. "I don't suppose you have." The husky octaves of his words pulsed against her skin.

He was going to kiss her. And Romy was desperate to have him do so.

Their breath mingled in the rose-scented air as the pad of his thumb ran gently over her bottom lip.

The sound of breaking glass echoed through the stillness of the afternoon, disturbing the silence cocooning them in the garden.

His thumb stilled before jerking back from her, hand falling to his side. His dark eyes flashed with savage, thwarted hunger and then faded to their usual chilly flatness. Granby took a deliberate step back from her, regarding Romy with both desire and dislike.

She blinked, slightly dazed, willing away the intoxication of Granby. Looking down at her feet, Romy focused on regaining her senses, her breath coming in short bursts, shocked at what had nearly occurred.

A curse drifted toward them, along with a string of muttered apologies.

Romy lifted her gaze, careful to avoid looking at Granby, and walked down the path until she had a clear view of the terrace. Theo was apologizing profusely to Lord Haven while he pushed her hands aside, wiping furiously at his coat.

"Not that it is any of my affair," Granby's cool words came from behind her, "but does your sister have some sort of affliction? In the last hour, she's run into the balustrade, nearly tripped a servant, and now ruined Haven's coat."

"Vanity, Your Grace. Our physician suggested spectacles last year, but she chose not to bring them to The Barrow." Romy took a cautious step in the direction of the terrace.

The scowl once more crossed his lips as he surveyed her with a frosty glance. Had Romy truly been a shrub, she might have merited more interest.

"If you will excuse me, Your Grace. I should go to my sister's aid." Her legs were unsteady as she moved forward, still trying to understand what had nearly happened and her own reaction to it.

"It would be best if you did, Lady Andromeda." His broad shoulders dipped, effectively dismissing her. He reached inside his coat, pulled out a cheroot and proceeded to ignore her.

"Agreed." Romy fled to the terrace without looking back.

"I SEE YOU'VE REACQUAINTED YOURSELF WITH LADY Andromeda Barrington."

David flicked the ash from his cheroot and saw Blythe on the path before him, his own cheroot clutched in one hand. Lighting the end, Blythe took his time before speaking, seeming more concerned with enjoying his smoke. Finally, he said, "Did she have anything to say about your clothing this time?"

"No." The word snapped from his lips. *Christ*, he'd nearly kissed her. Which wouldn't have been nearly enough to satisfy the unwelcome hunger David had for her. He wanted to *devour* Andromeda. Swallow her impertinence and taste every inch of her luscious peach-toned skin.

"Impudent little thing, isn't she? Her sister is much the same. I get the sense the Barrington sisters are all quite bold, though I have only Theodosia and Andromeda to base my observation on."

David would have said confident. Opinionated. But he declined to correct Blythe. "You knew who she was, didn't you? Not at Lady Masterson's, but surely before now."

"I made the acquaintance of Lady Theodosia in London." Blythe stretched his shoulders. "I was flying a kite in the park for my nephew. She managed to entangle herself in the kite string. On purpose." He shot David a cocky wink. "Which I allowed her to do. She's bloody stunning. I knew from the moment I saw Theodosia in the park she must be related to the girl who had insulted you at Lady Masterson's. There's no mistaking those eyes."

"You neglected to tell me." Blythe seemed full of secrets of late.

Blythe shrugged, blowing a series of smoke rings over the roses and up into the sky. "Theodosia didn't give me her name that day in the park, and I neglected to ask. I never heard her full name until today. Besides, even if I had known, what would have been the point in telling you? I'd no idea you even remembered the chit."

"I suppose you didn't."

"Exactly," Blythe continued. "Besides . . ." He laughed. "Lady Andromeda is the Duke of Averell's sister. A gentleman as well known for his sexual exploits as he is for his association with Elysium. Which he owns with his *bastard* half-brother. The entire family is rife with all sorts of imperfections you detest. I suppose if you'd known she and her sister would be here, you would have asked Lady Molsin to rescind her invitation to Lady Richardson."

"That would have been prudent." David's fingers tightened over his cheroot, nearly snapping it in half. Blythe's pretty speech didn't fool him. His friend often found David's inclination to disassociate himself from the baser aspects of society to be nothing short of ridiculous. Blythe didn't understand the damage such deviations could produce, having never been the victim of such things. Perhaps if he had, his perspective would be different.

"Were Horace not already in the ground, the sight of two Barringtons inside The Barrow would have put him there." An edge crept into Blythe's words at the mention of David's father. "But I'm sure he would have been proud of your choice of Beatrice."

"He would applaud it."

"Imagine, applause from the grave." Blythe pursed his lips to blow out another string of smoke. "I've yet to feel the approval of my own father's ghost. Perhaps it is only something the Duke of Granby can manage."

David's teeth gnawed on the end of his cheroot. "If there is something on your mind, Blythe," he bit out, "by all means, feel free to speak." First Aunt Pen and now Blythe.

Blythe shook his head. "Only making an observation." Tossing the cheroot at the ground, he smiled, but with a tautness to his lips. He bowed. "Enjoy your walk in the gardens, Your Grace. I'll see you at dinner."

☙ 10 ☙

"**A**ren't you even going to guess?" Romy said to Theo as Lady Mildred contorted her angular body, jerking wildly before the guests gathered in the drawing room. "Or can't you see what she is desperately attempting to pantomime?"

"Spasm? Seizure?"

Romy laughed discreetly into the palm of her hand. "I would have guessed apoplexy. I detest charades. Phaedra is the only one of us who has ever been any good at this game. So, did you converse further with Blythe?"

"You mean after I made a cake of myself and ruined Lord Haven's coat? No. Nor at dinner. Poor Lucy Waterstone required all my attention. She speaks quietly so as not to offend anyone with her lisp, which makes carrying on a conversation with her challenging. I find the lisp hardly noticeable the longer you speak to her. But her father has made much of the impediment, blaming it for her lack of husband."

"Having Mr. Waterstone as a father-in-law has much more to do with her lack of husband than anything else. I fared much better. My dinner companion was Mr. Estwood," Romy said. "A most interesting gentleman, to say the least."

"Would you *call* him a gentleman?" Theo made a show of shielding her eyes as Lady Mildred became tangled in her skirts while trying to give the clue. "Oh, dear. Mildred's legs are quite exposed from her thrashing. Why doesn't someone put a stop to this?"

"He's a bit rough around the edges." Romy found Mr. Estwood nothing short of intriguing, especially when his upper crust accent slipped, as it had during a rather impassioned recital of a trip to Egypt he'd taken. Estwood was fascinated by everything old. People. Pottery. Jewelry. Weapons.

"But he's highly intelligent," she continued. "I know he's a businessman, though I'm not sure exactly what sort of business he engages in. Mr. Estwood's true passion seems to be archaeology."

"Really?"

"Don't act so surprised, Theo. He spoke at dinner of stopping his coach on the journey here to examine a rock which may have contained a fossil of some sort. I believe everyone noted his interest."

"I only meant it makes more sense to me now, his friendship with Granby. Haven't you noticed that Granby has filled this place with antiquities? The frescoes are Roman. Perhaps that is how they became friends—through a shared mutual interest."

It was true. The Barrow resembled a cold pile of cut stone from the outside, but the interior was filled with all sorts of treasures. The paintings in the drawing room alone were surely worth a small fortune, based on the way the Foxwoods reacted to them.

"The Foxwoods seemed impressed," Romy whispered,

shielding her eyes from Lady Mildred, who was now twisting her arms about.

"As they should be. I'm fairly certain there are several Caravaggios hanging on these walls. The one closest to the window—"

"The one depicting a satyr?" The painting, while beautiful, gave off a bleak, joyless feeling. Romy had noticed it immediately.

"Is by Gentileschi," Theo finished. At Romy's look of confusion, her sister gave a tight shake of her head, frustrated at Romy's lack of knowledge in regard to Italian artists. "Artemisia Gentileschi? Mama has studied her works. She isn't at all popular, at least if you are collecting Italian art, which Granby appears to do. Gentileschi is not what a typical duke would have in his home. Such angry brush strokes. And she's a woman. Most unusual."

Theo was also a female artist, though she tended to focus solely on miniatures. She'd done only one full-size portrait. Romy thought she needed to branch out.

"Estwood's interest seems confined to items of the archaeological variety, not art. Apparently, there is a site of moderate historical significance nearby for which Granby's estate was named. We're to have a picnic there. A series of barrows where bits of weaponry have been found."

"Sounds dreadfully boring." Theo gave a deep sigh. "I've little interest in barrows and the bones they may hold." She discreetly glanced at Haven, who was wearing an expensive coat the color of burnt toast, probably borrowed as it didn't quite fit him and appeared far too fine to be his. "I feel as if I should purchase poor Haven a new coat. Look, he's had to wear one of Blythe's."

"A terrible idea, Theo. And one that would only serve to remind him of his financial difficulties. It would make him angry, I think." Haven didn't strike Romy as the sort of man who would appreciate such a gesture.

"I know, but I do feel awful I ruined his coat. How was I to know the glass I broke contained a healthy amount of ratafia? The stains will never come out. I tried to apologize, but he only glared at me and stomped away. Incredibly rude. Blythe told me not to be concerned." She looked across the room at the Earl of Blythe who stood, handsome and solid, against the far wall, conversing with Lady Meredith Clare and her aunt. "I suppose I will try to gain Blythe's interest tomorrow on the lawn. We're to play bowls."

"How are you going to play bowls if you can't see? Really, Theo. If Blythe finds you attractive, he will do so whether you are wearing spectacles or not. I don't see why it should matter. Granby even asked me if you had an affliction of some sort."

"I thought you were avoiding Granby." A tiny smile crossed Theo's face. "Oh, but he followed you into the gardens."

Romy bit her lip. "How would you know? You can't see well enough from such a distance."

"Oh, *I* didn't see you, Romy. Blythe mentioned going to enjoy a cheroot and said quite distinctly, '*I think I will join your sister and Granby, though I hate to interrupt their conversation.*'"

Romy's fingers plucked at the fold of her skirt. "He was checking to ensure I didn't become lost in his massive gardens. Nothing more. Something any polite host would do, even Granby. Really, Theo, the man isn't the least amusing and lacks even the basic tenets of a pleasing personality."

"Yet he was concerned for your welfare. Shall I tell you what else Blythe said?"

Romy wasn't sure she wished to hear it. "Go on."

"'*Perhaps they aren't conversing, and your sister is sketching Granby's backside again.*' He drifted off before I could question him further. So how *did* you meet Granby? And don't tell me it was at a ball or the opera, especially with Blythe claiming you were drawing."

Damn Blythe.

"I was definitely not sketching any part of Granby's person. And Blythe asked *me* to sketch *his* backside, if you must know. That is what sort of gentleman you've become fixed on. A total rogue."

"Don't change the subject. I know Blythe borders on impropriety, which is why I find him so appealing. We are talking about you and Granby. What sort of encounter did you have with him which inflamed you with such dislike? And you were sketching? A large event of some sort. Lots of gowns to tempt you, I imagine. I'm certain your fingers wouldn't have strayed far from a pencil."

With a sigh of resignation, Romy said, "Lady Masterson's garden party. It was some time ago."

"Before Papa died?" Theo's voice caught for a moment. "You went as a plant of some sort."

Absolutely no one had seen her vision for the costume she had worn to the garden party; it was very frustrating. "I was a *tree nymph*. At any rate, I was sketching. Miss Cummings had on the most unusual dress. There were honeybees —"

"I don't care about Miss Cummings. Get to the part where you met Granby." Her eyes widened briefly, taking in Lady Mildred who was now prancing around. "Someone please put an end to this display." She elbowed Romy. "Do go on."

"I happened upon Granby and Blythe."

"You didn't tell me." Theo frowned.

"Because it would have meant telling you of Granby. Didn't you ascertain Blythe must have been there from his comments?" Romy shook her head. "Never mind. Granby was blocking my view of Miss Cummings. And I noticed the length of his coat was far too short for a man of his height."

"Oh, good Lord, Romy. Please tell me you didn't."

"I'm afraid I did." She looked down at her hands, struggling to remember her outrage at the way he'd spoken to her at Lady Masterson's and again at Madame Dupree's; all she could recall with any clarity was the velvet sheen in the depths of his eyes when he'd nearly kissed her. "He was incredibly insulting. And dismissive. I merely suggested he should seek out another tailor."

Theo put a hand to her lips, whether in horror at Romy's bad behavior or in an attempt to stifle her own amusement, Romy wasn't sure.

"I never saw Granby again until we returned to London. He was escorting Beatrice to Madame Dupree's. We became reacquainted and had a rather unpleasant exchange. I may have told him at that time his cravat was the color of tepid bathwater."

Her sister shook her head. "I'm sure he didn't appreciate your helpful observation."

The room suddenly erupted in applause.

Romy looked up, watching as Beatrice, smiling as if she'd accomplished something of great magnitude in correctly guessing Lady Mildred's riddle, stood up.

She supposed, considering the way Lady Mildred had looked as if she'd been in the midst of a fit instead of playing charades, the applause was justified.

"Well done, Lady Beatrice," someone said. "Well done."

"Granby and I don't care for each other in the least," Romy said in a low tone to her sister. "We engage in mutual hostility."

Beatrice smiled at the guests in the drawing room before gracefully clasping her hands, taking a small bow in acknowledgement of her achievement. "I'm afraid I'm not very good at this part." Beatrice had a lovely speaking voice when she wasn't being snide. "I beg you all for patience." She dipped her head in pretended shyness.

"Is that why he's staring at you?" Theo nudged her again, tilting her head in the direction of the window near where the painting by Gentileschi hung.

"Who?" Romy pretended indifference.

"Him. Granby. Don't act as if you don't realize it."

There had been a curious prickling against the back of her neck during Lady Mildred's performance, but Romy had put it down to a chill caused by the open doors at the far end of the room, though she didn't feel the least cold.

Pushing her chin down, she tilted her head slightly, not wishing Granby to see her observing him.

He was indeed looking at her, studying Romy with a grimace as if wondering how she had come to be in his drawing room. Unlike most of the other gentlemen and some of the ladies, Granby didn't have a drink in his hand; instead, his arms lay on top of the chair before him.

Romy shifted, ensuring her entire back was to him.

"Do not antagonize him further, Romy. I don't want our stay revoked. I've just begun to make progress with Blythe."

"I shall do everything I can to avoid him." The entire length of her back tingled in awareness, much worse now since she was certain the cause was Granby.

"Good. It shouldn't be terribly hard, outside of dinner. You can avoid most of the amusements. Make an appearance on the lawn tomorrow and then disappear. I'll tell everyone your head aches from the sun or something." Theo turned her attention to Beatrice. "Just look at her. Do you think she practices before a mirror to confirm she looks smashing from every angle? She's trying desperately to gain Granby's attention, I'll merit, just as she did in the dining room."

"I hadn't noticed," Romy lied. She'd spent most of the

meal keeping her eyes averted from the head of the table to avoid watching them interact. The entire house party knew of Granby's interest in Beatrice. Cousin Winnie had even declared an announcement would be made here.

"Fluttering her lashes and giggling as if someone were tickling her feet with a feather. I nearly tossed a potato at her to make her stop but was afraid I'd hit Granby instead. That would assure us of an early departure."

"How could you make out what Beatrice was doing without your spectacles? She was some distance away." Theo usually wasn't prone to embellishment, unlike Phaedra. But she had been behaving unlike herself since becoming infatuated with Blythe.

"It was quite blatant. Granby seemed not to notice, though, and ignored her. She finally gave up her antics after the main course was served."

"I'm sure he noticed. What gentleman could not? Beatrice is stunning." Romy's eyes ran over the young lady spinning about and pouting prettily. She had to admit Beatrice and Granby made an attractive couple; her, all shimmering gold, and him, large and darkly savage. The entire room viewed Beatrice with rapt attention while she pantomimed the next clue.

Except one person.

Romy could almost feel the touch of his fingers against the base of her neck or trailing along the slope of her shoulders.

His rude perusal was unwelcome. She turned, glaring right back at him.

The scowl left Granby's mouth, easing the hard slant of his lips. He didn't look away from her, nor was he the least bothered to be caught staring. He deliberately took in her neck and bosom before returning to her mouth.

Romy's fingers dug into the cushion of her chair. She'd

never in her life been so blatantly assessed by a gentleman, especially one who also regarded her with so much disdain. But there was no hostility in Granby's eyes now. Nothing lingered in the velvet depths but a sort of predatory hunger. An intensity which was unsettling and somewhat arousing.

"Romy? Are you well? You're very flushed."

"Just a bit of a headache, Theo. And I didn't care for the soup. I fear it may have upset my stomach." The bothersome attraction to Granby had resurfaced, filling her mind with all sorts of improper images.

"Because your constitution is so delicate?" Theo added sarcastically.

"Exactly. I think I'll retire." She needed to get away from Granby's presence and the resulting confusion. Standing, Romy made her way quietly across the room to the door. Everyone's attention was focused on Beatrice. It was likely no one would see her slip away.

Except for Granby.

ANDROMEDA BARRINGTON WAS UNSUITABLE IN EVERY single way that mattered to David.

Even if she hadn't been sired by a duke who'd elevated tupping to a sport and a lady's companion, Andromeda's immediate family consisted of a bastard half-brother, another brother of dubious reputation who'd compromised his wife at a ball before marrying her, and a sister who, from what David could see, was intent on ruining herself over Blythe. There was also the family's ownership of Elysium, a place David had visited often enough and to great pleasure, but it wasn't the sort of establishment that should be associated with a titled family. Her legitimate brother, the duke, was the only Barrington with a somewhat respectable pedigree.

Yet David's desire wasn't dimmed by such a list of unacceptable qualities. Instead, his hunger for Andromeda continued to grow and evolve, immune to his dislike of everything she represented. The better part of his evening had been spent studying the graceful line of her back and the fascinating curve of one delicate ear.

While the game of charades went on in his drawing room, David watched her instead. To his great shame, he'd gone out of his way to find the location of her guest room. It was for the best David didn't overindulge in spirits. Horace endlessly preached control, especially if The Barrow was full of guests, as it was tonight. A duke should never become foxed in the company of wolves.

The slightest drunken misstep and you'll be labeled a sot. Or worse, father a bastard.

David's finger slipped between his skin and collar. Every bloody shirt he owned was too tight around the neck. He dragged his eyes from Andromeda to glance at the painting beside him. It was of a satyr chasing a young woman, the satyr's hands grasping at her clothing, attempting to tear the wisp of material trailing off her back.

It matched his mood exactly.

David had thought of little else but relieving Andromeda of her clothing since nearly kissing her in the garden. He had observed her discreetly during dinner while Estwood tried to charm his way beneath Andromeda's skirts by spouting nonsense about ancient tribes and fucking shards of pottery. The struggle not to leap from his chair and toss Estwood out of The Barrow had been so unlike David's usual controlled manner, he was certain he'd gone mad.

He had forced his eyes away from Andromeda for the remainder of the meal.

When the gentlemen had joined the ladies in the drawing room, she had drawn his gaze immediately. No one else existed for him. The roof could have come tumbling down or the house caught on fire. Not even the strange gyrations of Lady Mildred merited his attention.

David told himself it was because Andromeda was beautiful, nothing more. He liked pretty things. But when she turned to face him, challenge and obstinance in her eyes, lust for Andromeda bled deep into his core. He wanted her. All of her.

The wisest course of action would be to send her and her sister back to London before the situation spiraled out of control. Had Haven's very timely curse not interrupted them, David wasn't certain his friend's coat would have been the only thing ruined.

Andromeda stood with a nod to her sister and silently floated from the drawing room, lavender skirts teasing at her ankles.

The mere thought of her ankles inflamed him.

His father would have said that Andromeda's bold behavior was consistent with other persons of low breeding. The Duchess of Averell, Horace had insisted, was little better than a harlot.

Your mother was poorly bred as well, but at least she wasn't a paid companion of dubious, unknown origin.

As the sound of Andromeda's skirts faded, David turned his attention to the woman meant to become the Duchess of Granby. Beatrice held court in the middle of the drawing room, reminding him of a well-dressed porcelain doll.

She caught David's eye on her and blushed prettily, giving him a modest, ladylike smile of acknowledgement.

Lord Foxwood, seated behind her with a glass of David's scotch in his hand, nodded in approval of his daughter's behavior.

Christ, she's like a trained lapdog.

A very well-bred, well-pedigreed one.

11

"Lady Andromeda, you're looking lovely."

"Good morning, Mr. Estwood," Romy said to the attractive gentleman watching her from the bottom of the stairs. "I overslept, I'm afraid."

She'd slept terribly, largely due to her host. How like Granby to wedge his enormous, arrogant form into the privacy of her bed, invading her thoughts with a host of improper ideas. Romy already possessed a vivid imagination and needed no assistance on that score. Curiosity about such things was fed by her knowledge of Elysium and what went on behind the confines of the velvet covered walls.

"You came down just in time, my lady," Estwood assured her. "I slept late myself. Have you had breakfast?"

"A tray in my room."

Estwood stood waiting. "Then shall I escort you out to the lawn? The first game of bowls has already begun."

"I would be happy for your escort." Romy liked Mr. Estwood, as did several of the other ladies in attendance. Only the Foxwoods seemed dismayed at his presence.

"Splendid." He held out his arm with a grin.

Lord Foxwood, in particular, had been rude to Estwood. The earl had gone out of his way to exclude Estwood from the conversation flowing about the dinner table the night before, intentionally making comments to rile him. Through it all, Estwood had maintained a determined politeness, refusing to allow Foxwood to goad him into losing his temper and perhaps prove Foxwood's point that Estwood wasn't a gentleman.

"Are you a player of bowls, Lady Andromeda?" Estwood had lovely eyes, like pale gray mist on a spring morning, except for the ruthlessness gleaming about the edges. But Romy would ignore that for now. She often saw the same look in her brother Leo's eyes. A determination to succeed at all costs despite the Foxwoods of the world.

"I do," she replied. "My father taught me when I was no more than a child. It was a favorite pastime of his. We even had teams composed of the staff of Cherry Hill, our estate in the country, though it was against the rules." She gave him a sideways glance. "Don't tell on me, Mr. Estwood."

"I would never, my lady," he assured her, patting the hand tucked securely in his arm.

"I found it all perfectly normal when I was a child. We Barringtons are a bit eccentric. Do you play bowls, Mr. Estwood?"

"Marginally. It isn't a game I played as a child. I'd no time for such things."

Romy had overheard Lady Foxwood whispering to Mildred after the ladies left the table for the drawing room. Estwood's father had been a village blacksmith. Lady Foxwood, in a horrified voice, could not countenance why a duke would invite such a person to dine at The Barrow. If he were ever to approach her, Lady Foxwood cautioned, she must cut him directly, no matter how rude it might seem.

Romy thought Lady Mildred, quickly approaching thirty and plain of face, would be fortunate to snag Estwood.

"Perhaps you can offer suggestions on improvement, should I choose to play, Lady Andromeda? I promise to be a good student." His voice lowered flirtatiously, his pale eyes gleaming back at her like the surface of a mirror.

"I would be delighted to show you the finer points of bowls, Mr. Estwood." She had no qualms about Estwood not having a proper pedigree. He was attractive. Intelligent. But there was no humming against her skin when he touched her. No delicious sensation curling around her spine. Not even a modest display of the feelings Granby invoked in her.

Most troubling.

Holding Estwood's arm, Romy followed him off the terrace to an area set some distance from the house. A great expanse of lawn greeted her as well as a perfectly maintained green for bowls.

"I didn't realize the duke had such a proper green. I think you must be teasing me, Mr. Estwood. You are obviously a frequent visitor to The Barrow. Surely you play much better than you've led me to believe. You seek to take advantage of my good nature."

"Am I succeeding?" The friendly glint in his eyes shifted, deepening into something Romy didn't wish to encourage.

"Not in the least." Romy lifted a brow.

Estwood laughed softly. "I find you very direct, Lady Andromeda. It is a trait I don't often see in young ladies."

"So I've been told. A fault of mine. Now, I think you must confess as to your abilities in regard to the game before us."

"I never played until recently. The old duke wouldn't have allowed such a thing." He hesitated, the small brackets on either side of his mouth deepening as a frown crossed his lips. "We didn't get on," Estwood said slowly, choosing his words carefully. "He was very particular regarding the guests who came to The Barrow."

Granby's father hadn't approved of Estwood despite his friendship with the man's son. "I'm sorry if he treated you poorly, Mr. Estwood."

A light flush crept up Estwood's neck; was he embarrassed by her show of empathy?

He gave a careless shrug. "I was one of many, my lady. There were those who suffered much more." Estwood's gaze was focused on the far side of the green where Granby stood.

"How unfortunate." It was all she could manage under the circumstances.

Estwood turned with a grin, his mood once again pleasant as he led her to Theo and Lord Carstairs, stopping any further conversation. She suspected Estwood had said more than he'd meant to and was now embarrassed about it.

Carstairs seemed intent on displaying for Theo the correct posture necessary to roll the bowl down the length of the green. He explained how one side was weighted heavier than the other, which influenced which way the bowl would land, as well as how to cup the bowl, placing your fingers properly while using the correct stance.

All of which was wasted effort on Carstairs's part.

Theo knew perfectly well how to play bowls, though she would be hampered today by her inability to see properly. Her sister pretended ignorance of the game in order to gain Blythe's attention and have him assist her. Theo's plan wasn't working. The earl was engaged elsewhere.

Blythe laughed, clearly amused by Lady Meredith who pouted up at him coquettishly, and it echoed across the green. Meredith, propriety be damned, apparently, spun about, giving Blythe a glimpse of her shapely calves. Rosalind stood off to one side, gamely pretending to enjoy herself.

Theo squinted, glowering at Meredith, who, Romy was convinced, her sister couldn't clearly see.

Miss Waterstone strolled along the side of the green, parasol in hand, showing little interest in a game of bowls. Her skirts trailed along the grass as her chin dipped, watching her feet. She looked forlorn, like the heroine of a tragic gothic novel, especially with the foreboding backdrop of The Barrow behind her.

"Lady Andromeda, Mr. Estwood." Carstairs nodded his head in greeting, eyes kind but vacant.

"Lord Carstairs," Romy greeted him warmly.

Carstairs was a good sort, and he'd been a friend of the Barrington family for as long as Romy could remember. Far from brilliant, Carstairs made up for his lack of intelligence with his unfailing kindness and good nature. His interests seemed to revolve around hunting, fishing and other outdoor pursuits, though Romy supposed Carstairs had now added his wife, Rebecca, to that list. Romy liked Carstairs because he wasn't complicated.

She glanced in the direction of Miss Waterstone, plodding along with resignation.

Carstairs was regaling Mr. Estwood with the story of a large trout he'd caught while Estwood tried to appear interested.

Romy was positive he wasn't.

Lady Mildred arrived, glancing with interest at Estwood. Apparently, the guidance of Lady Foxwood had little effect on the spinster. It appeared Mildred had designs on Estwood.

"Mr. Estwood," Mildred cooed. "I'd be much obliged if you'd partner with me?" She fluttered her lashes and pursed her lips in an imitation of Lady Beatrice.

Estwood's brows drew down in consternation; he was clearly uncomfortable and looked as though he would refuse.

If Mildred wished to court scandal by flirting with Estwood, who was Romy to deny her? The poor thing probably needed a little excitement in her life. Taking pity on the plain-faced older woman, she said, "Please excuse me, Mr. Estwood. I need to have a word with Miss Waterstone." Romy nodded to the melancholy figure at the edge of the green. "Do partner with Lady Mildred." She gave Mildred a discreet wink. "She is an excellent player."

Mildred took a step in Estwood's direction. She was a tall, robust woman, almost masculine in appearance.

Estwood shot Romy a look of terror.

"Fine, fine." Carstairs nodded. "It's already been decided that the winner of our match will have to play Granby and Lady Beatrice." He nodded to Beatrice, who circled Granby like a lioness trying to determine the best way to take down an elephant.

Since avoiding the elephant—in this case, Granby—was at the top of Romy's list of things to accomplish today, it was nothing short of fortuitous that Mildred had set her sights on Estwood. She did feel terrible about leaving him in Mildred's tender clutches, but evading Granby took precedent over Estwood's feelings.

Her host stood at the edge of the lawn, his commanding form surveying the green as if he were a general about to order his troops to charge. The day was warm, and Granby had discarded his coat. As Romy watched, a light breeze blew the fabric of his shirt against his arms, the outline of the bunched muscles beneath clearly visible. He reached up and tugged at his collar as if his valet had tied his cravat too tight.

Blythe said something, and Granby turned his face into the wind, the air sifting through the ebony waves of his hair to toss them over one eye. He brushed the thick strands back with one hand and caught sight of her.

The air grew still and quiet, the laughter of the other guests muted to whispers. Romy heard nothing but her heart, beating like a drum in her ears. His harshly carved features were remote. Detached. But not his eyes. They blazed with a heat which scorched Romy from across the green. The attraction to Granby pulled and tugged at Romy's skirts before settling low in her belly with a delicious rustle.

Intent shimmered across the green to her, accompanied by disapproval. Reluctance. His hands curled into fists at his sides, probably restraining himself from chasing her off the lawn.

Romy jerked her chin away from him and made her way to Miss Waterstone. Granby could go hang. If she were the source of his discomfort, he had only to ask her to leave. She *also* found the attraction between them unwelcome.

She focused her attention on Miss Waterstone, who was staring unhappily at the area where tables laden with an assortment of fruits, cheese, and small sandwiches along with other refreshments were manned by Granby's servants. Miss Waterstone's chaperone, an elderly cousin, was seated with Lady Meredith's aunt. Both women shot Miss Waterstone twin looks of pity.

Romy frowned and hurried to Miss Waterstone. Here was a young lady in dire need of a friend. She regretted not calling after seeing her at Madame Dupree's. At the least, Romy would have realized they were attending the same house party that much sooner. And possibly found a way out of coming to The Barrow.

"Miss Waterstone." Romy reached her side. "I thought I was the only one not interested in playing bowls."

"Lady Andromeda." Miss Waterstone bobbed politely with a shy smile. "It appeared you would partner with Mr. Estwood." Her lovely features took on a wistful look as she glanced in his direction.

Romy took note of her interest. "I'm not yet in the mood for a game, and Lady Mildred was eager to play." She took Miss Waterstone's arm. "Shall we walk for a bit? The day is fine, and the duke's gardens are oddly magnificent."

"Oddly?"

"I only meant, based on first impressions of the duke, His Grace doesn't seem the sort of gentleman to harbor such a wild display of flora. I pictured neatly trimmed hedges and constrained vines. Possibly a small maze with a Minotaur lurking in the middle. His head gardener—"

"Oh, His Grace has had several. He's *very* particular. I understand his father was much the same."

"That is exactly my point, Miss Waterstone. This profusion of blooms seems out of character for Granby and far more exotic than I would have imagined." Romy peered closer. "I've no idea what that particular bush is, for instance." She pointed to a cluster of bright, papery pink flowers.

"The name escapes me." Miss Waterstone tapped her lips with a forefinger. "The duke has a greenhouse which contains all manner of flowers, shrubs, and vines used to much warmer climates. A hobby of his, I think."

Miss Waterstone appeared to have a great deal of information about the Duke of Granby.

"How unusual."

"Greenhouses are fairly common, my lady."

"Of course." It was Granby's penchant for growing things which confused her. Clawing, half-dead vines filled with thorns seemed more in character. "How would you come by such knowledge?" Surely Granby didn't spend an inordinate amount of time with Miss Waterstone.

Romy bristled at the thought.

"His Grace has business dealings with my father, so this is not my first visit to The Barrow, my lady." She paused. "I think at one time my father thought to make a match between myself and the duke, which is preposterous. Granby has much higher expectations for his duchess."

Romy mulled the comment over, thinking it accurate. "Is that how you met Mr. Estwood? At The Barrow?" She squeezed her arm. "I noted your interest earlier."

Miss Waterstone's cheeks bloomed pink. "Mr. Estwood advises the duke on his investments, some of which involve my father. Much to my father's displeasure, Estwood sees fit to accompany the duke to business meetings and the like. He finds Estwood beneath him." Miss Waterstone placed a hand on Romy's arm. "Not the duke," she rushed to assure Romy. "I meant my father."

Miss Waterstone's lisp became less pronounced the longer she spoke and relaxed in Romy's company. Romy wondered if her new friend had ever spoken to a physician about her speech problem. "A title doesn't make a man."

"No, but breeding does. It is the only thing I think the duke and my father have in common, outside of business."

"Yet, Granby is friends with Estwood. Doesn't that strike you as contrary, Miss Waterstone?"

She nodded slowly. "I was surprised to find Mr. Estwood attending the house party." Her eyes lifted to the green where Estwood stood with Mildred.

"You should speak to him." Romy inclined her chin. "Mr. Estwood."

"Oh, I couldn't." Her lisp increased. "I'd only embarrass us both and possibly anger the duke, which I certainly do not wish to do. I find him," she lowered her voice, "intimidating. Which isn't surprising. Miss Eddison says I am afraid of my own shadow."

Romy looked over at Miss Waterstone's chaperone, who resembled nothing so much as a mushroom with her rumpled dress of gray wool puffed out about her sallow, wrinkled cheeks.

"A toadstool," she said aloud. "Not you, Miss Waterstone. You're lovely."

"You are very kind to me." Her lips trembled slightly. "I wish I was braver. More like you, Lady Andromeda. I think you quite fearless, and you have excellent taste in clothing."

"Me? I grant you my fashion sense." Romy grinned. "But I am not brave; I am only the victim of an awful temper which, once unleashed, loosens my tongue. That is not bravery, Miss Waterstone, but stupidity."

"I esteem you nonetheless, Lady Andromeda."

"I would be honored if you would call me Romy. At least when we are together. We are friends, are we not?" Romy truly liked this shy, reserved girl.

"We are. And it would please me, my lady, if you would call me Lucy. Romy is short for Andromeda, I take it? From the myth?" Lucy, when she smiled genuinely, was quite lovely. Beautiful, even. She only needed the proper incentive to relax and step out of her shell.

"And a constellation. When my father was alive"—she hesitated slightly, feeling a tiny press of grief over her heart—"he and my mother were great admirers of the night sky. It was an interest they both shared. There were many mornings my sisters and I would find them on a blanket together on the lawn. They'd fallen asleep, you see, watching the stars together."

Lucy stopped and took Romy's hand. "You miss him very much."

"I do. My father didn't subscribe to the notion that children of dukes should be raised by nannies and governesses, at least once he married my mother. He taught me to play bowls." She waved at the green where Carstairs, Theo, Estwood, and Mildred were competing against Beatrice,

Granby, Blythe and Meredith. "Among a great many other things."

He told me I should find a way to practice my art. And I have.

Lucy was silent, the only sound the gentle rustle of her skirts. She hugged Romy to her. "You are fortunate, Romy, to have had a father who cared so much for you."

Romy knew Lucy's father was often unkind to her, even ridiculing her in front of others. She vowed to help her new friend navigate London and perhaps assist her in finding the sort of gentleman who would appreciate her gentle soul.

"Think how pleased your father will be that you've garnered the friendship of a duke's daughter."

"Pleased?" An odd look flitted across Lucy's face. "Yes, I'm certain of it." Her eyes found Estwood again. "Lady Molsin tells me most of the duke's neighbors have been invited for the dance at the end of the week. No one eligible *and* titled, unfortunately, which is bound to make my father unhappy, but she's assured me several nice gentlemen will be in attendance."

"There's always Haven. He's a marquess."

Lucy shook her head. "My father doesn't approve of him, title or not."

Romy leaned in. "Do not allow your father to dictate your future, Lucy. Neither who you are nor who you wish to be. Your life and choices are your own." Theo claimed this to be one of Romy's best and worst qualities, the way she interfered at times when she shouldn't. But Lucy didn't deserve to be browbeaten by her father.

"The duke watches you, Romy." Lucy looked over Romy's shoulder.

"He dislikes me." Romy shrugged as if it were of no consequence, all the while feeling the press of his eyes against her skin.

Lucy gave her a sideways glance. "His disdain is quite apparent."

"He may even ask us to leave. Theo and I weren't actually invited."

"Oh, dear." Lucy looked up at her, eyes innocent. "That would be unfortunate."

❧ 12 ❧

After speaking to Lucy for a few more moments, Romy left her friend to the dubious care of Miss Eddison before making her way to Theo. Her sister tossed the bowl in the direction of Blythe, who had his back to her. He was on the green, pointing to the cluster of bowls, probably determining which had been closest.

Theo's bowl tapped him on the heel and Blythe jumped. Meredith nearly tripped over a bowl.

"I beg your pardon, Lord Blythe." Theo waved, pretending distress. "I'm only just learning."

Romy raised her hand, covering her mouth to stop from laughing. "Fairly good aim," she whispered in her sister's ear, "considering you can't really see at that distance."

"I was aiming for Meredith." Theo fumed. "She's taken all of his attention since coming to the lawn. I was hoping to bruise her ankle and compel her to sit on the sidelines. He's barely noticed me at all today. It's very discouraging. I've spent the whole afternoon acting as if I've never played the game, hoping he would offer his assistance."

"Perhaps it is time to give up this foolish pursuit of

Blythe."

It was the wrong thing to have said. Theo was immensely stubborn.

"The house party hasn't even ended. I've several more days to garner his attention. I'm not going to lose to Meredith, of all people."

Mr. Estwood had stopped playing and was leaving the green. The scent of a cheroot floated in Romy's direction, and she caught sight of his lean form striding into the trees at the edge of the lawn.

Lady Mildred, who had been partnered with Estwood, left the game as well, staring wistfully after him.

"I hope she doesn't go running into the woods to find him," Romy said more to herself than to Theo. "But at least if she does, no one will notice your behavior."

Theo's mouth thinned.

Carstairs was speaking to his wife, who blushed and giggled like a schoolgirl, oblivious to anyone watching them. Since the previous game had ended, Carstairs was showing her how to properly toss the bowl, which required quite a bit of close contact. Lady Carstairs squealed in delight as her bowl knocked against Meredith's.

"Keep practicing, Theo." Romy's stomach grumbled. "I'm going to seek out something to eat. Check on Rosalind."

Her sister waved her off, eyes still focused on Blythe, or perhaps she was only trying to determine how best to injure Meredith.

Romy wandered back to the area where the food had been set out. Lady Molsin, Lady Foxwood, and Cousin Winnie sat at one table sipping tea while Lord Foxwood reluctantly conversed with Haven. Lucy and her chaperone were making their way back to the house. Mr. Waterstone was due to arrive today in the company of Lord Torrington.

Rosalind appeared at her mother's elbow, popping up

from beneath the table.

"Hiding already, cousin?" Romy whispered after greeting the three older women.

"The tablecloth isn't nearly large enough to cover me. I lost one of my earrings." Rosalind held up a tiny bit of amber attached to a gold thread. "The catch keeps coming loose. Mama wants me to wear these tonight." She stole a glare at Cousin Winnie's back. "Torrington adores amber. And I am supposed to care."

"I might be able to fix it." What she could not fix was Cousin Winnie's determination that Rosalind wed Torrington. "Come to my room before dinner. I'll see what I can do."

"Help me flee the premises?"

If Romy could accomplish that with no fanfare, she would already have done so.

She wandered over to the largest table and picked up an apple, declining a footman's offer to peel and slice it for her. Instead, she tossed it up in the air a few times, mainly to annoy Lady Foxwood, who was watching her with disapproval, before taking a large bite.

"Have you misplaced your parasol, Lady Andromeda?" Lady Foxwood called to her over the short distance.

"Not at all." Romy sailed back past their table, deliberately crunching loudly on her apple. She winked at Rosalind. "But I appreciate your concern, Lady Foxwood."

Cousin Winnie shook her head, stifling her amusement behind a gloved hand.

Lady Molsin sipped her tea, pretending not to take note, but her eyes gleamed with merriment.

Romy walked back along the edge of the green, considering whether she should grab her portfolio and work on some of her sketches in the garden, when a shadow fell over her. Much too small to be Granby. And there was no skin prickling.

"You don't care to play bowls, Lady Andromeda?" Blythe, smashing as usual even with sweat dampening his hair, greeted her. Romy had to admit, any woman would be enamored of Blythe, no matter their age; even Miss Waterstone's ancient chaperone eyed him when she thought no one was looking. He was glorious. The picture of health and masculine vigor, shining like a ray of the sun.

Poor Theo.

Though Romy and Blythe had finally been properly introduced before dinner the previous day, they hadn't yet conversed. And while he knew who she was, based on the conversation he'd shared with Theo the previous day, Blythe hadn't acknowledged their previous acquaintance directly.

"Not at present, my lord." She took another bite of her apple, allowing the tartness to slide over her tongue.

Blythe watched the movement with a look which probably drove most young ladies into his arms but did nothing whatsoever to Romy.

How bloody disappointing.

"I thought I would come to ask if you will be sketching my backside today. Or are you still focused on Granby's?"

"You are shameless, my lord. Truly." She wasn't angry at Blythe for his improper comments. "I did wonder if you would mention our previous acquaintance to me." Casting a sideways glance at his mischievous grin, she said, "As you have to my sister."

"You are quite unforgettable, my lady," he replied flirtatiously, but there was no real interest, only practiced flattery. She doubted he could speak to a woman any other way.

"And I was not sketching anyone's backside, as you well know, my lord. Though I do apologize for eavesdropping. It *was* purely accidental."

"I confess, I'm disappointed to find you were not sketching me, Lady Andromeda."

"Somehow I doubt that."

Blythe's eyes sparkled. "What *were* you sketching at Lady Masterson's, if I may ask?"

"The dress a young lady was wearing," she said, trying not to reveal too much. "A habit of mine. So that I can show my modiste. The design struck me as original and different. Fashion interests me."

"That explains your interest in the length of Gran's coat."

Romy said nothing, only chewed her apple.

"I'd mentioned the length of his coat to Gran before," Blythe continued, "but he brushed me off. I, on the other hand, pay much attention to such things."

He would. She took in his impeccably tailored waistcoat with its splash of vibrant blues and greens. Blythe was mere steps away from becoming a dandy.

"The fault was his tailor, as you surmised. Granby inherited the tailor from his father, and the poor man's eyesight was failing. He struggled to measure Gran properly, as you can imagine. Had to stand on a box to do so. Forty years of service to the Dukes of Granby and then asked to leave The Barrow." Blythe shook his head. "He lived here most of the time but traveled to London with Granby when required."

"Forty years?" The taste of the apple turned foul in her mouth.

"Once Granby confronted the elderly man concerning the incorrect cut of his clothing, of which you'd so kindly advised him, he had the tailor put out to pasture." Blythe sounded mournful. "He wept when he was told to leave The Barrow. The tailor, not Granby," Blythe said.

Romy struggled to swallow the piece of apple now lodged in her throat. She was aware of the duke's exacting nature and his adherence to status. Many titled gentlemen of his station likely felt the same way, but that didn't excuse his behavior.

She hadn't thought him intentionally cruel. "I can't believe the duke would do such a thing."

Or rather, she didn't want to.

"Ask Granby yourself if you don't believe me."

Romy took another determined bite of the apple, righteous indignation warming her cheeks. The tailor's dismissal was her fault. And now she must correct the situation.

"His father didn't tolerate imperfection either," Blythe added casually with a shrug, as if the callousness of his friend was of no great consequence. Perhaps to him, it wasn't. "I must confess, though, I was shocked to see you and your sister here, given how rigid Granby can be in his thinking."

"We weren't actually invited but were included at the behest of my cousin, Lady Richardson," Romy said absently, mind already working on how best she could help the elderly tailor. It had been over a year ago since she'd insulted Granby. The poor man could be dead. Was he buried in a pauper's grave? Because of her?

She turned to Blythe. "Shocked? Because we weren't actually invited but tagged along with my cousin? Is his dislike of me so obvious?"

"Another thing you can ask Granby about."

"Ask me what?" Granby stood just behind Romy, looming over both her and Blythe.

She hadn't even heard him approach. Sneaking up on his guests should be impossible for such a large man. Romy added it to the ever-growing list of things she didn't like about the Duke of Granby.

Damp curls clung to Granby's temples, his cheeks colored pink from the sun; he stood before her looking more appealing than ever. The sleeves of his shirt had been rolled back to reveal muscular forearms dusted with dark hairs, the material of his shirt so fine, Romy could see the curves of sinew across his chest and shoulders. Long, elegant fingers drummed lightly against his thighs as she stared in fascination. She'd never seen him without gloves. What would it feel like to have those massive hands move across her skin?

A rush of heat flew up her chest at the mere thought.

What *was* wrong with her? Granby was an unlikable wretch.

"Our match is next, Blythe." His eyes never left Romy. Nor did Granby bother to hide his apparent admiration for her bosom.

"I'm afraid I'll have to beg off. I've promised Lady Meredith a turn around the pond. But Lady Andromeda might wish to play you." Blythe shot her a look. "I've an idea she may want to challenge you. Perhaps even make a wager."

She was too outraged at the fate of the tailor and her continued reaction to Granby to give more than a passing thought to the knowledge that Blythe was subtly manipulating her. He'd given her a way to possibly help an elderly retainer, which was much more important.

"Do you even *play*, Lady Andromeda?"

Granby's coldly dismissive tone infuriated Romy. She was very close to tossing her half-eaten apple at his head. Blythe hadn't even demurred when she'd said Granby disliked her. Well, he was going to detest her a great deal more after she trounced him in bowls. Perhaps then this unsettling attraction they had for each other would finally dissipate.

Romy snorted in derision. "Of course, I play bowls, Your Grace. Rather well, as it happens. My father, the Duke of Averell, taught me. *We* Barringtons like to wager when we play." It seemed the appropriate time to remind the giant block of ice before her that her brother owned a gambling hell.

"A wager?" There was a deceptive softness to his reply. "What do you have I could possibly want?"

Romy bit back the urge to stomp on his foot. He'd not

feel it anyway. She doubted Granby ever felt anything. "Afraid you might lose to me, Your Grace? The humiliation will be difficult to avoid."

Romy meant to see that Granby properly pensioned off the old retainer. If the man were still alive, which she prayed he was. She would see things made right. Beating Granby soundly would merely be an added bonus.

He leaned down, just enough so that she caught his scent, the slight aroma of pine and shaving soap mixing with his sun-warmed skin. Granby always smelled as if he'd just arrived from a stroll in the woods, which angered her further.

"I don't lose, Lady Andromeda. *Ever.* I'll even spot you two points."

"There is no need."

"I insist."

Bloody tyrant.

"Fine. We must each make a wager on the outcome."

"Agreed." The word rasped lightly against her skin. He waved her forward.

Romy marched in the direction of the green. Granby's nearness had a habit of muddling her thoughts, and she needed all her concentration for the game before her. A servant passed her with a tray, and she tossed what remained of her apple atop it.

"Thank you." Her skirts were flapping wildly around her legs in agitation.

A disgruntled noise came from her host.

"I merely thanked him, Your Grace. He is not beneath *my* notice."

"His very employment demands that he remain beneath notice." He'd caught up with her easily; after all, his legs were much longer.

But she was *angrier*.

Her body refused to stop being aware of his, sparks flying

up her skin when he drew closer to her, as he did now. Romy stopped to face him so abruptly, her skirts whipped around both her ankles and his. Papa had cautioned her from the time Romy was a child to control her temper. He would be disappointed in her behavior today.

Granby cocked his head, chilly regard firmly in place. "Something distresses you, Lady Andromeda. Perhaps you've changed your mind about challenging me."

"Perish the thought, Your Grace. When I win—"

"I am not the only one guilty of arrogance, it seems." Granby's lips twisted into a small frown. "What is it you want, if you should win?"

Romy bit the inside of her cheek, struggling to retain the string of insults she wished to hurl at him. Now was not the time to do so. "You will settle upon your former tailor a tidy sum for his retirement. And a cottage. If he is still living," she added, making a great show of pulling her skirts away from his boots.

Confusion crept along the sharp edges of his face. "A sum? On my ancient, inept tailor? The one you told me emphatically to sack?" His mouth relaxed into something resembling amusement.

The ebony strands of his hair were spilling wildly around his cheeks, tickling the line of his jaw in a way that was incredibly distracting. "Yes."

"He left my employ several months after you suggested I find a new tailor."

"Even so."

He pressed a finger to his lips. "But you suggested I rid myself of him, did you not? He is still alive, by the way."

"I did not think you would take my advice."

"Then why did you give it?" The wisp of a smile broadened.

"Blythe told me everything, Your Grace. I imagined your

tailor to be in London with a stable of clients, not an elderly retainer of your family who, after many years of service, would be tossed out on a whim. The poor man—"

"Silas," he added helpfully. "His name is Silas."

"Very well. I'm certain Silas suffered often under your employment—"

"Tormented every day."

—Given your exacting nature." She took a deep breath, not wishing to say more lest Granby pitch a fit and refuse the wager.

Bits of black ice glared down on her. "I can see Blythe has told you everything. It is a shame, for I did so enjoy the *suffering* of Silas, but I was left with no other alternative. I couldn't go about with a coat the incorrect length, could I? Given my exacting nature."

"As you say, Your Grace."

"Very well. I agree. If you win our match, I will settle an indecent sum on Silas, enough so that he may live the remainder of his days a wealthy man. And a cottage, should he wish it."

A weight lifted from her heart, along with a great deal of guilt at the situation she'd inadvertently caused. "Thank you, Your Grace." She walked to the designated spot at the edge of the green. Theo stood with Carstairs while Lady Carstairs talked with Beatrice. All four of them turned as she and Granby approached.

Romy ignored them all.

"Are you not curious," Granby's words hovered close to her ear as he bent forward, "what I will ask for should I manage the impossible task of beating you at bowls?"

Romy was confident of her victory. Her father had taught her well. "I've no intention of losing."

A low rumble came from his chest.

"No one ever intends to lose, Lady Andromeda."

13

Romy lost.

By one *bloody* point.

The game had dragged on much longer than anticipated. The sun was already low in the sky, and most of the other guests had either moved to the terrace to enjoy tea or gone up to their rooms before dinner.

Blythe strode past them on his way to the house, escorting Theo. He took Romy aside, whispering in her ear to pursue justice. Someone, he said, must put Granby in his place.

Haven appeared next, a smirk on his handsome face. He waited until Granby took his turn before murmuring cryptically to her, "He is already beat, Lady Andromeda. Only he doesn't know it."

No amount of goodwill, however, gained her the final crucial point she needed. When Granby knocked her bowl, putting him closer to the jack, she blinked stupidly in shock. The shot shouldn't have been possible, given the distance and—

"The green is uneven," she stated with assurance.

"I see you are prepared to accept your loss graciously," came his sarcastic reply. "What a poor loser you are, Lady Andromeda." The breeze was ruffling his hair again, making the dark strands drag against his collar.

Romy pulled her eyes away, refusing to allow the sight to distract her. Why didn't he cut his hair? Like the gardens, the thick waves had been left to grow wild in blatant contradiction to the rest of Granby.

"It is rude to gloat, Your Grace."

"I am a duke. I don't need to gloat."

The worst part of her loss was not Granby's pleasure, which was considerable, but the fact that now Romy could not help Silas. He was destitute and homeless because of her.

Distraught over her loss, she walked back and forth along the green, looking for the flaw the carefully manicured lawn hid from view. So intent on her task, Romy neglected to inquire what Granby would demand for winning. Maybe an apology for insulting him. He'd probably enjoy watching her grovel. Or perhaps Granby would request that she and Theo leave The Barrow and return to London.

Theo would be furious.

Romy swallowed her pride, dipping low before him. "Thank you for the game, Your Grace," she said as politely as she could, though the words choked her. "I'm sure you'll inform me in due time what it is you require from me."

"Undoubtedly," he said quietly. Bowing to her, Granby turned on his heel and strode back to The Barrow, leaving Romy alone on the lawn with her thoughts.

HAD HE NOT LEFT HER ON THE LAWN, DAVID WOULD HAVE kissed her senseless.

Annoying, *exquisite* creature.

An afternoon spent watching her athletic grace and bold determination to vanquish him left an ache stretching across David's chest. Every swish of her skirts pulled him closer to her warm, lavender-scented, female skin, teasing his nostrils and causing his cock to twitch.

His desire for Andromeda existed in blatant defiance to the very ideals David had been raised to believe.

Once he reached the steps leading to the terrace, he paused, looking back at her. The sway of her skirts whispered to him, drawing his attention to the delicate line of her back.

Andromeda was pacing back and forth at the edge of the green, pausing at the point where a small, barely noticeable slope began. She hunched down, running her fingers over the grass.

Clever girl. David had never appreciated a woman's intelligence the way he did Andromeda's.

She'd been bloody magnificent during their match, openly triumphant with each point she picked up, never willing to concede his victory until the final moment. Andromeda displayed a bold confidence in her ability. There was no demure batting of lashes or false shows of modesty in her dealings with him. No blatant compliments to salve his masculine ego. None of the behavior young ladies were admired for. Instead, Andromeda openly challenged him over the fate of an elderly servant, bristling with the indignity she assumed David had bestowed upon him.

Silas had indeed been released from David's employ, but not in such dramatic fashion. Blythe had deliberately left out some important facts. In contrast, David's father, Horace, would have sacked poor Silas without a thought.

Unfortunately, the change in tailors hadn't resulted in an improvement in the size of David's collars, though Smithfield, the man he now employed, assured him the measurements were correct.

David glanced out once more at Andromeda. She'd started pacing back and forth again. He could almost hear her muttering to herself that he'd swayed the game in his favor.

He had.

The wager he wished to collect from her was completely improper, especially given that he meant to officially offer for Beatrice. He'd decided on it the moment Andromeda had challenged him, her plump lips pursing in outrage.

Andromeda had a temper.

Every time her rounded bottom had come into view while she bent to toss one of her bowls, it had inflamed him beyond reason. And the smug grins she'd given him when she scored only served to make David imagine her naked and pliant beneath him. Even the copper sparking in her hair drove him mad. He'd had to turn away from her several times because her nearness aroused him to a painful extent.

As it was doing now. His cock throbbed between his legs, instinct making him want to grab her from the lawn and spirit Andromeda away. A soft groan left him.

The scandal would be insurmountable.

"Shit."

"Your Grace?" A footman appeared next to him, holding his coat, face full of anxiety as if he were responsible for David's mood.

He took his coat from the footman and flung it over his shoulders, grateful he wouldn't have to stand on the steps to regain his composure before joining the few remaining guests on the terrace.

The coat would cover the worst of his condition.

14

Romy grabbed her portfolio, tucking it securely under her arm. She checked her pockets again to ensure she had several pencils and exited her room, grateful that the house was completely still and quiet. Most everyone had left a short time ago to attend a fair in Upper Granby, the small village about half an hour's ride away.

Last night, Rosalind had come to her room shortly before joining the other guests for dinner, her damaged earring clasped in one hand. After retrieving the small pliers from her trunk, Romy had fixed the broken wire holding the amber. She had been absorbed in her task, forgetting she'd left out the sketch of a day dress she'd been working on.

Rosalind had taken the earring, hugging her in gratitude before placing it in her ear. Her gaze had run over the sketch, then back to Romy. "Someone will guess eventually." Rosalind's eyes had grown concerned. "You frequent Madame Dupree's shop far too often. Even Mama has commented."

"I've a headache caused by too much sun. I won't be at dinner." Romy had evaded the unspoken question.

Once her cousin had departed, she'd rung for Daisy, asking her to procure a tray as she wouldn't be going down to dinner. If, rather, *when* she received Granby's note, requesting she and Theo cut their stay short, Romy meant to leave privately, without the eyes of the other guests upon them. It was the only thing she could conceive of him requiring of her. Granby found her unacceptable. Opinionated and insulting. She thought him a heartless beast, one whom she was shamefully attracted to.

Romy shoved the portfolio more firmly beneath her arm.

Each day, though she didn't wish it, Granby became more beautiful to her, like a savage landscape which, upon closer examination, revealed small details which drew her interest further. She seemed powerless to stop it.

Granby didn't wish to be attracted to her, either. His gaze on her was filled with both desire and regret. Disdain and longing. It was a confusing combination and one that she was certain would lead to her imminent departure.

She could sense his discomfort and knew he blamed her for it. Granby likely wasn't capable of any true emotion. Affection, and the like. The cold detachment with which he viewed everyone, including Lady Molsin, was evidence of such lack of feeling. Status was of primary importance. She knew Foxwood shared his views.

Which begged the question of Estwood.

Estwood is like the coat. The hair. The gardens.

Lost in her contemplation of the contradictions of Granby, Romy meandered through the garden, searching for the path she'd spied from her window while drinking her morning tea. It had been easy to beg off from today's excursion by claiming her headache from the previous evening had not abated. Theo, as promised, held up her end of the bargain in explaining Romy's absence.

Finding the path, Romy strolled at a leisurely pace. She was in no great hurry. The path curved, circling the pond where yesterday she'd seen Blythe and Meredith walking. She followed the trail into the expanse of trees where it continued around a large yew tree.

Another young lady, one raised primarily in London, might have been more cautious about venturing into such wilderness without escort, but Romy had been raised in the wild expanse of trees and fields bordering her father's estate, Cherry Hill. The idea that harm would come to her on land owned by the Duke of Granby was ridiculous. Everyone for miles must be terrified of him.

As she rounded another bend, a girlish giggle broke the silence, followed by a splash. Slowing, Romy climbed up a small incline, careful to keep herself hidden in the thick bramble. Brushing aside the leaves and twigs catching at her cheek, she peered through an opening and caught sight of a large boulder.

And a great deal of Lady Carstairs.

Lord Carstairs and his wife were fishing; at least, that seemed to originally have been their intent, Romy guessed, catching sight of the two poles propped up and secured by a pile of rocks. But she doubted they were interested in catching anything but each other. Their bare feet dangled in the water below while Carstairs kissed his wife, simultaneously cupping her naked breast. She moaned softly, arching back as his mouth trailed along her neck before bending lower, taking a pert nipple into his—

Romy blinked, straining for air and thankful that much like Lady Carstairs, she'd neglected to wear a corset today. She had intentionally designed some of her day dresses to be worn without such constraint. Because—

Another moan came from Lady Carstairs. "Please, Douglas."

She found herself unable to look away from the scene before her. Unbidden, an image of Granby, large hands splaying across her own body, invaded her thoughts. Would he elicit the same sounds from her? Caress her in such a way? The sensation of Romy's nipples peaking sharply beneath the fabric of her dress forced her to suck in a breath.

Good Lord.

She quickly averted her gaze so as not to see what Carstairs was doing to make his wife pant as if she couldn't catch her breath.

Romy backed up the way she'd come, careful not to make a sound, a distinct throbbing between her legs making her unsteady. The scene had unnerved her, both because of the intimacy she'd unwittingly stumbled upon, but also because watching them had aroused her. And made her think of Granby. Specifically, Granby doing such a thing to *her*.

Romy pushed such thoughts firmly aside. Chilly block of ice that he was, she doubted Granby possessed an ounce of passion. Certainly not enough to do something as shocking as making love to a woman atop a boulder, as Carstairs was apparently doing. She was imbuing him with attributes he didn't possess.

"Bollocks," she said, startling a wren from its perch above her.

Romy had been raised with two parents whose love for each other was apparent to any who saw them. They'd never hidden their affection from Romy and her sisters. As a child, it had been an embarrassment to hear her parents speaking in low tones and hearing the rustle of fabric behind a closed, locked door. Her parents remained passionately attached to each other until her father's death. A true love match, rarer in the *ton* than a flawless emerald.

I want you to find affection, for little matters in life without it.

Thinking of her father's words, Romy knew he had left

instructions for Tony regarding his expectations. Unlike so many titled men, her father had placed a great deal of value on his daughters, never failing to remind Romy and her sisters how precious they were.

I miss you, Papa.

Romy pressed a palm against her chest to still the ache. Wiping at the small tear which escaped one eye, she forced a smile to her face, remembering how she and Papa had often walked in the woods. On one occasion, he'd taught her to whistle. It had been sunny that day as well, the light bursting through the trees above their heads.

Pursing her lips together, Romy whistled a few notes, trying to remember a particular song he'd taught her. The tune was ribald and incredibly improper. Papa had instructed Romy she was never to whistle it in front of her mother, or he'd be punished.

Skipping and whistling, nine-year-old Romy had found it marvelous that she and her beloved Papa had a secret. It had made her feel special. Loved.

Whistling the tune, Romy stayed on the path for another quarter of an hour until the sound of water rushing over the rocks broke through the quiet of the forest. Moving farther down the path, Romy came to a footbridge spanning a bubbling stream. A slope, bare of trees and covered with wild-flowers, merged with a pebble-strewn beach. A perfect spot for skipping rocks. Another skill her father had taught her.

Bees buzzed around her head as Romy made her way down the slope to find the perfect spot. There had been no way to procure a blanket without raising suspicion, but Romy did have her shawl, which she spread across the ground. Opening her portfolio, she placed the sheaf of papers containing her designs out in a semi-circle around her, so she could look at everything at once. Beatrice's cream and gold gown sat alongside the sketch of the hair clips she'd created to complete the ensemble. Lucy Waterstone's was next, as well as the gowns she'd created for Theo and herself. Lady Molsin's ball was actually little more than a dance. There would be no more than fifty guests or so, those attending the house party and Granby's neighbors. The ball would be held on the final night of their stay at The Barrow.

Romy wondered if she and Theo would still be here.

An assortment of day dresses followed. Two for Miss Hobarth which needed a bit more work. Perhaps a bit of piping along the sleeves. The half-finished sketch of a riding habit for Lady Benbridge had been put aside before leaving London. She'd start there.

Romy got down on her knees, re-sketching the outline of the shoulders on the riding habit. Uncaring about grass staining her dress, she flopped down on her stomach, her pencil moving across the page until the correct shape took form.

Whistling, she made notes next to her drawing. Lady Benbridge was fond of excessive embellishment, as many ladies were, but the newer styles were more about the fabric, though Romy thought gold braid would be lovely. Lady Benbridge might balk, but once she saw the finished product, Romy was confident she'd be pleased.

Romy propped her chin up with one elbow as a bird trilled somewhere to her left. Her spirits lighter than they'd been in days, she hummed and whistled as she worked on Lady Benbridge's design. It was peaceful here by the stream, far from the house party.

A large shadow fell over her and her sketch, blocking the sunlight.

Her pencil halted in the outline of the riding habit. She glanced around her, searching for a rock or large stick should she have need of a weapon, although her position in the grass put her at a disadvantage. Romy was sprawled on her stomach, skirts hitched up, her feet in the air. Whoever stood behind had an excellent view of her legs and possibly her bottom.

"I almost mistook you for a blade of grass," a voice growled softly, "except for the whistling."

❦

WHEN ANDROMEDA'S SEAT AT THE TABLE HAD STAYED vacant at dinner last night, and after hearing the ridiculous excuse that she'd had too much sun, David had known it was merely another one of her attempts to avoid him. Besides, anyone admiring her lovely, unfashionable peach-tinted glow could surmise Andromeda spent a great deal of time outside without a bloody parasol.

He spent the remainder of the meal desiring her presence and then chastising himself for it.

After breakfast this morning, David had gone to his study, pretending complete immersion in his account books. When his butler had come to the door to remind him of the excursion to the village, David had jotted out a short note to his aunt, apologizing for being unable to join the group. An urgent business matter required his attention, he informed her. One that he must see to personally. It was a terrible breach of conduct.

Foxwood and Waterstone, both attempting to curry David's favor for different reasons, would have to keep each other company today. He didn't spare a thought for Beatrice.

All he *did* think of was Andromeda and the way her skirts had fallen about her hips while she'd demanded David take care of an elderly man she didn't even know.

And her mouth. He spent a great deal of time considering the plump curve of her lips.

Once the sound of the carriages departing met his ears,

David finally stood, deciding a walk would help him regain some semblance of control over his thoughts. He needed to clear his head.

I've decided on Beatrice.

Andromeda was wrong for David on every level.

He found himself headed in the direction of the stream where he'd spent hours as a child. It was where he'd first happened upon Blythe, whose estate was less than an hour's ride from The Barrow. They'd been on opposite sides of the water, skipping rocks, when Blythe had tossed a large stone at David, hitting him in the cheek.

Their relationship hadn't changed much from those days.

Giggling floated in the air from a large pond as David rounded the bend followed by the low timbre of a man's answer. After a cursory glance, David kept walking. He didn't care to see whatever Lord and Lady Carstairs were doing, half-naked, with fishing poles between them.

Deeper into the woods he went, but the silence except for the birds and the breeze rustling through the trees didn't fill him with the usual sense of peace. The walk had done nothing but agitate him further. Turning, he meant to head back the way he'd come when the strains of a ribald tune met his ears. David stopped.

The air around him remained silent, except for the nuthatches chirping above his head.

Thinking he was hearing things, David took a step forward, only to stop again when the tune floated into the air. It was a song sung mostly in taverns or brothels. The story of a baker's wife who passed out her favors to every man she met along with hot cross buns.

A poacher, perhaps? Or a villager?

He strained his ears as another verse sounded.

The tone was light. Feminine. A woman. Out in these woods. *Alone.*

David hurried down the path in the direction of the sound. The reputation of the Duke of Granby was well-known to everyone in the area, and he doubted anyone would dare tread on his land without permission. Even so, a woman should not be in these woods alone.

He slowed as he approached the footbridge spanning the stream, head cocked, waiting for his whistler to resume her tune.

The third verse floated up from a patch of tall grass covered with wildflowers. The grass swayed, the tune halting as a mild, feminine curse came from a spray of forget-me-nots.

Andromeda's dress was pale blue, the exact color of the blooms surrounding her.

He moved across the grass, making no effort to disguise his presence, because he didn't wish to frighten her.

Christ.

Andromeda was on her stomach facing away from him, scratching away at a piece of paper, a pencil grasped in one hand. The roundness of her delicious bottom was visible from where he stood, the very same backside which had taunted him during the entire game of bowls. He'd thought of her bottom quite a bit in the privacy of his room last night, envisioning how her skin would taste as he nipped at one plump buttock. His imagination had forced him to fist his cock, growling out his release into a handkerchief before he'd felt composed enough to go down for dinner. A loss of control he hadn't experienced since he was a lad.

She never once looked up as he approached or paused in her sketching.

He could have been *anyone*. A poacher. A brigand with evil on his mind. Hell, even one of his guests. Estwood came suddenly to mind.

David's gaze left the rise of her lovely ass to roam over the curve of one thigh, down the line of a slim calf, watching as she tossed her foot back and forth. It took every ounce of restraint David possessed not to pounce on her like a wild animal.

"I almost mistook you for a blade of grass, except for the whistling."

Her foot stopped swinging. The tune halted.

"Shrubs don't often whistle, Your Grace." She rolled over to face him, lovely features displaying only moderate interest at his unexpected appearance. If anything, she looked irritated to have been disturbed.

"You don't seem surprised to see me."

The blue of her eyes fairly glowed among the forget-me-nots. A thick braid hung over one shoulder, a few strands of her hair, spiked with copper, having come free to float around her temples.

David thought her the most beautiful thing he'd ever seen.

"I'm not." She gestured to the area around them, completely at ease. "This is your estate, is it not?"

He wanted to kiss the tart reply from her lips. Devour every inch of her, starting at her ankles and only stopping when he reached the apex of her thighs where he would kiss her again.

"Were you expecting someone else?" He struggled to keep the jealously suddenly surging through his veins at bay, thinking of her rolling about in the grass with Estwood. "Or were you hoping to be set upon by passing gypsies?"

"I didn't realize there were any gypsies at The Barrow," she replied. "Haven't you scared them all away by now? If they'd been so bold as to come into your woods, of course." Andromeda shot him a smart look, proud of her little insult.

David's eyes dipped to her bodice. He imagined her

nipples to be the color of a pomegranate. "You could have become lost or set upon by someone less appealing than me."

A feminine snort left her. "I am perfectly capable of taking care of myself, Your Grace. I'm sure you are eminently aware my brother *Leo* runs a gambling hell. As a Barrington, I've come into contact with all sorts of disreputable persons."

The words were a challenge, flung at him as a reminder of all the reasons he shouldn't want her even as the space between them grew charged with sexual tension, sparking to life among the bees and wildflowers.

"He's taught me how to handle certain situations," she continued. "I'm certain I could outwit a vagrant or a gypsy. Or even you, Your Grace, should it come to that."

Andromeda was so absorbed in her disdain of him, she'd yet to acknowledge the wanton display she presented. David pointedly looked at the lower half of her body where her silken clad legs were so fetchingly displayed. His father would have said Andromeda's lack of breeding was clearly apparent. He would have reminded David that Andromeda's mother had once been a lady's paid companion. Only a step above a maid.

At his look, her cheeks pinked, and she came to her knees in one graceful movement, fluffing out her skirts around her in a neat circle to hide her previously exposed limbs. Her luscious mouth parted, as if she wanted to speak but didn't trust herself.

If Andromeda had *any* inkling how erotic David found her current position, she would flee in an instant.

No, he reconsidered. *Andromeda wouldn't run.*

She would stand and fight, use some of those tricks her mongrel brother had taught her and possibly pummel him with the large leather portfolio he saw laying to the side.

She sat back on her heels, unaware of the torrent of lust

she'd unwittingly unleashed and, thankfully, ending the worst of his lascivious thoughts.

"What are you doing here, Your Grace?"

"I thought we had only just established that this is my estate, my lady."

Her lips tightened; she obviously did not care for his reply. A long-suffering sigh came from her as if he were too simple to understand the question. "What I mean, Your Grace, is that the other guests have gone into the village for the festival today."

"Not all of them. I passed Lord and Lady Carstairs as I came this way."

Andromeda turned the color of a beet. He wondered what she'd accidentally seen on her way to the stream. Had she watched? Possibly become aroused herself?

The thought caused his desire to sharpen. She'd soon make him into a lustful, babbling idiot.

"And not you," he pointed out. "I was told you were suffering from a headache brought on by too much sun yesterday; that, and the blow to your ego."

Her spine stiffened immediately, her beautiful mouth pursing. He adored her anger. It meant she wasn't unaffected by him. David didn't want to suffer alone.

"As our host, I assumed you escorted your guests to the village." Her voice took on a politely modulated, conde-scending tone. "As any *good* host would do."

"The village puts on a fair or festival at the drop of a hat. I'm sure the occasion isn't for anything special other than word spread my aunt was hosting a house party at The Barrow. Every tradesman between here and London will be hocking their overpriced and inadequately made wares to my guests. I saw no reason to subject myself to such nonsense."

A flower petal was stuck in the dark strands of her hair.

Another clung to the bit of lace on her bodice, hovering above the small valley between her breasts.

A soft groan escaped him as his cock twitched painfully.

She narrowed her eyes at him. "Did a bee sting you?"

"No," he replied, much sharper than he'd intended.

"You've no idea if either of your assumptions are true," came her tart reply. He wasn't surprised by her defense of a group of unknown tradesmen.

David found Andromeda's ability to champion others an admirable quality, though misplaced at times. "How many festivals have you been to in the village of Upper Granby, my lady? I've been to many. I speak from years of experience."

"So you object to them making a bit of coin?"

"Not in the least."

A light, feminine scent came off her skin, wrapping him in a ridiculous cloud of lavender-scented desire David found impossible to escape, mainly because he didn't want to.

"I happen to enjoy a good fair now and again," he said. "Living in Italy, there was a fair almost daily. The Italians like to celebrate every obscure saint imaginable with a festival or feast."

"You lived in Italy?" She nibbled at her bottom lip, studying him with a look of disbelief.

Apparently, cold monsters such as himself couldn't possibly have survived in the warmth of Italy. "I did."

"I'm not sure I believe you."

Such a carefree existence was unfathomable now. A brief act of rebellion intended to save what was left of his soul. He had lived abroad for nearly a year, mostly in Rome, away from the duty of Granby. The constant bitterness of Horace, his contempt for David's mother and the bastard son she'd borne after she fled, had nearly suffocated him.

"Italy is a wonderful country. I was drawn to the beauty to be found there," he said quietly, thinking of his reluctant return to England after receiving word of his father's collapse. His father's letters had become increasingly scornful to David, at turns threatening and cajoling. Filled with contempt for David in one paragraph, only to plead with him to come home in the next. His disappointment in his only child would ease, Horace wrote, if only David would be the son he needed and return. Then Horace had fallen ill, and what David wanted no longer mattered. Granby did.

David tugged at his collar, trying to loosen his cravat. "You seem very surprised, Andromeda."

Her magnificent eyes followed the motion of his fingers against his neck. "I am only hard-pressed to imagine you in Italy, of all places. It seems a . . . frivolous destination for you."

It had been. Marvelously frivolous.

David had gambled, drank and fucked his way around Italy with abandon. A bloody spectacular experience. There were times he thought his father had purposefully planned his stroke. It had been the only sure way to bring David back.

"I lived in Rome. And Venice. I finally managed to make my way to Florence, where I studied for a time. I returned to England when my father became ill."

"What did you study?" She stared at David with open interest.

It was rather wonderful to have all of Andromeda's attention solely on him. His gaze fell to the slender threads of copper shining in her braid. She had beautiful hair, a lovely shade that was neither brown nor red, but some amazing color in between. He wanted to wrap the thick braid around his wrist and pull her lips to his.

David's fingers twitched against his thighs.

"Architecture, mostly." At her obvious surprise he said, "I was obsessed by the building of the Colosseum and the mastery of those who built it. The design fascinated me. Did you know the Romans would flood the main floor of the Colosseum and hold boat races? The engineering involved in such an enterprise is astounding." David had spent hours roaming the levels of perfectly cut stone, marveling at the feat built so long ago.

"My father told me once, but I thought he was teasing, for I couldn't conceive of such a thing." The corner of her lips drifted upward in a smile, perhaps the first one she'd ever truly bestowed upon him. She was looking at David as if he were the most fascinating human being in the world.

A pressure built inside his chest, squeezing gently above his heart.

"My mother," she continued, "is obsessed with Greek culture, as you can probably guess, Your Grace."

The lady's companion. The familiar stirring of distaste welled up inside him, warring with the desire he had for her.

"My father loved ancient Rome," she said. "It was a passion they both shared, ancient civilizations. They toured Greece before I was born. A dream of my mother's. I have a younger sister named Phaedra. Andromeda, Theodosia and Phaedra. We also have a cat named Theseus and a stable full of horses all named for Greek gods."

The force of her smile warmed David from the inside out. "Your mother should have named you Athena. Is she unaware of your combative nature?" He could easily imagine her as the warrior goddess, ready to do battle with the hideous gorgon.

I am the gorgon. The thought tore at him.

A small laugh bubbled from her lips and she closed her eyes, holding her face up to the sun. "Athena? She changed a poor girl into a spider which I am incapable of doing. But Athena is the goddess of crafts and weaving, so I suppose that, at least, is appropriate."

He wondered at her comment but didn't question her, not

wanting to disturb the sense of intimacy invading the grass. "Closing your eyes will not make me disappear."

"Oh, Your Grace," she said in a saucy tone, "if only that were all I had to do." Another soft laugh came from her as her lashes fluttered open. "I was trying to imagine you in Rome, carefree and walking about, attending a festival. I can't picture it. Seems an impossibility, though your love of art is everywhere in The Barrow. Theo claims the paintings in your drawing room show the discerning eye of a collector. She's an artist and has studied the Italian masters," she added.

"But not you?" He looked down at the drawings scattered behind her, trying to make out what had her so absorbed that she'd not heard him approach.

"No." She slid her body, successfully blocking his view of whatever she'd been sketching. "I know only enough to sound intelligent. For example, the fresco installed against the far wall of the garden. Very impressive. One of the labors of Hercules, isn't it? Something to do with golden apples." Another smile. "My bedtime stories were all Greek myths, you must realize."

He'd purchased the fresco from a dealer outside of Venice who was eager to rid himself of it. The fresco wasn't perfect. The tiles were chipped, the once vibrant colors faded. A large crack bisected one of the nymphs. But the dealer would have destroyed the fresco had David not purchased it. "The Apples of Hesperides. It's cracked."

"Indeed, it is. Imperfect." A question hovered in her eyes. The orbs were such a luminous blue, a hue, until recently, David had only seen in paintings. "Italy and broken stone seem somewhat out of character for you, Your Grace," she said, her voice light.

"Perhaps you don't know me as well as you think." Andromeda made David doubt the truths of his life. The duke Horace had demanded warring with the young man he'd been in Italy. He'd been so certain of his destiny until a beautiful shrub had insulted his coat at a garden party. Andromeda had no idea what she'd done to him. What she was still doing to him.

"I don't know you at all, Your Grace. This may be the first conversation we've had in which we haven't expressed our mutual dislike for each other." She waved her hand. "There is no need to give me a polite excuse that it isn't the case. We got off to a bad start, and it has only continued. Especially after cheating me yesterday in bowls. Don't bother to deny it."

He hadn't cheated, exactly. More a sin of omission. "I spotted you two points, which put you ahead before the game even started. How is that cheating?"

"The green slopes on one side. Very hard to see. Only someone familiar with the green, a person who plays there often, would know of it. I'm sure your other guests weren't aware. It should have been disclosed at the beginning of the game because knowing of such a flaw on the green gave you an unfair advantage."

A chorus of birds started in the trees above them.

David gave a careless shrug, knowing how much his indifference would irritate her.

"Do you admit it?" She clasped her hands and looked at him patiently, not the least concerned she'd just accused a duke of cheating, something no man would even do. "Does no one ever question you, Your Grace?"

"Not usually." He sat down across from her, folding his larger body into a crouch until he was within a hair's breadth of her slender form. "You are the first."

The beast inside him howled, urging him to just press her into the grass.

She gave him a curious look as he lowered before her, her brows lifting slightly.

Andromeda was very certain of his dislike, evident from the lack of concern she showed at his nearness. She was a small hare being circled by a wolf, convinced the wolf preferred lamb.

"You stalked away from our game," he said in a low voice, marveling at the gold flecks swimming in her eyes, "before I could even declare what I wish from you. There's nothing wrong with the green," he continued, watching the way the gold flecks sparked as her temper flared. "I think you are only a poor sport."

"I am not usually, Your Grace. But you deliberately stacked the odds in your favor by your omission."

Burnished leather. That was the color of her hair.

"Your Grace, I cannot live with myself knowing I am the cause of your tailor's unwelcome banishment. He was an elderly man. Surely you could have been kinder in your dismissal."

Blythe deserved to be strangled for telling her such a thing.

"I understand why you felt it necessary to send him away," she continued in a worried voice. "I'm sure you were distressed to find that your attire was not as impeccable as you wished it to be. Given your exacting nature." The last bit was said with no small amount of sarcasm.

David did demand perfection from his valet and his servants. It was habit. Something which his father had ingrained in him from the time he was a child. But he hadn't with Silas.

"He likely served your family faithfully for many years."

"He did," David answered, not wanting to discuss the tailor. He was far more interested in nuzzling the slope of Andromeda's neck.

"Please, Your Grace," she implored him.

Oh, how David wished to please her, not just in the

matter of the tailor, but in all things. Pleasure her. With his hands. His cock. His mouth.

"I would like to make sure he is well taken care of. I have an acquaintance who owns a dress shop. She had been thinking of making shirts for gentlemen. Perhaps—"

"Stop."

Silas had been going blind for years, and though David had known the tailor his entire life, the man had been too afraid to tell him.

Because Horace *would* have tossed him out.

David had not. He had pretended not to notice his tailor's increasing infirmity or the damage to his wardrobe. It wasn't until Andromeda had insulted the length of his coat that David had realized he must do something about Silas. The old man's lips had quivered as he'd explained to David how he could no longer see to sew or measure properly. He hadn't been dismissed but pensioned off as a loyal retainer should be. Silas had wept tears of joy as his daughter had come to collect him. It was a kindness David had felt compelled to offer the man who'd secretly taught him how to fish.

David wasn't his father. Not entirely. Not yet.

"A pity you didn't win." His fingers touched the edge of her dress, rubbing his finger over the fabric. Sliding his finger beneath the edge.

"But you did cheat. I am owed my forfeit," she insisted.

"Yes," he admitted, watching her eyes narrow into slits, her determination to save Silas nearly breaking what he thought might be his heart. Andromeda possessed such passion for others. David only wanted some of it for himself.

"It's very honorable of you to wish to care for someone you don't know," he said. A lovely pressure started over his chest, like fingertips pressing against the folds of his heart. He wanted to curl himself around her. Inhale her. Bury himself in her. The longer he was with her, the more intense the feeling became.

I've gone mad.

"Will you promise to care for Silas properly?" she asked. "Or at least allow me to do so?"

Andromeda Barrington was dangerous to him in ways she couldn't possibly fathom. His lust for her made his entire body ache, but it was what else he longed for that left him bruised and unsure as how to proceed.

I'm to marry Beatrice. I've decided. She's perfectly suitable.

"I vow to ensure he lacks for nothing again," David finally said, determined to keep the truth from her until he collected his wager. It was why he'd not told her about the incline of the green. Why he'd allowed her to challenge him to begin with. "But you must honor our wager in return."

He was that much of a monster—at least where Andromeda was concerned.

She didn't want to. He could see it in her face. But her need to ensure the welfare of Silas was far stronger. "Very well. I already know what you will ask for."

"You do?" That surprised him.

A pained look came over her lovely features. "And I completely understand, Your Grace."

"You do?" he murmured.

"You wish Theo and me to leave the house party. It is unfortunate you and I have formed such a dislike for each other."

"Is that what you are calling it?"

"I'll make an excuse that I'm ill or that I'm concerned for my mother so we may return to London with all haste." She turned away from him and bent at the waist, giving him another lovely view of her backside, glaringly apparent through the folds of petticoats she was encased in. Her hands flew over the papers spread out across the grass to gather them up.

Andromeda assumed, incorrectly, that he wanted her to leave The Barrow. The very thought created a hollow sensation in the middle of his stomach.

"No. I would never suggest such a thing." His voice sounded chilly even to his own ears.

"You don't need to, Your Grace. I take your meaning."

Andromeda hadn't the slightest idea how badly David wanted her. He looked over her shoulder as her hands began to stack the papers neatly together. Not drawings of the stream and woods as he'd thought. What most young ladies with a mediocre talent for sketching would draw. But gowns. Dresses. One with a motif of butterflies across the skirt. There was even a sketch of a riding habit.

I have an acquaintance who owns a dress shop.

Andromeda, already fascinating, became more so.

"I don't wish you to leave the house party," he said to the trim line of her back.

"My presence clearly annoys you, Your Grace."

Indeed it did, in so many ways, David had stopped counting. "A correct assessment."

"Then Theo and I will leave in the morning."

"No," he said roughly. "You will not."

Andromeda's hands stilled on her drawings, stiffening with what he could only assume was anger at his commanding tone.

David stared at the line of buttons running down her spine. Could he bite them off with his teeth? The dress would fall away from her shoulders, exposing all her glorious skin.

She turned back to face him, angrily tying a piece of leather around the portfolio to keep it closed. "What else could you possibly want, Your Grace? An apology for the insult about your coat? How petty; it was well over a year ago."

His head fell forward, nose gliding up the slope of her neck, inhaling the soft lavender scent lingering on her skin.

A soft gasp of surprise left her, but she didn't move away. The portfolio slipped from her hands.

"I want this," he whispered. David nuzzled the bit of skin just beneath her ear before catching her lips with his.

❧ 15 ❧

Oh.

Granby's lips on hers were soft. Persuasive. The barest brush of desire against her mouth. There was no urgency in his kiss, only temptation, a quiet coaxing for her to surrender.

Romy arched against him as coherent thought fled. She'd dreamt of his kiss. Of him.

When his tongue trailed across her bottom lip, she opened without hesitation, her own curiosity and the impatience she sensed in Granby guiding her. The small globes of her breasts grew heavy and heated as they strained against her bodice, trying to make contact with the planes of his chest. When the very tips of her nipples chafed against his coat, bright jolts of sensation burst down across her stomach to fall between her thighs.

A low sound came from Granby's chest, the vibration echoing across her skin.

"I do not dislike you, Andromeda," he murmured. "That is rather the problem."

He nipped at her bottom lip before his tongue sank back

into her mouth, tasting her. With a groan, his fingers sunk into her hair, sliding over her scalp before he fell back into the grass, bringing her with him.

Granby kissed her as though nothing else existed but their mouths and the stream bubbling away beside them. When he slowly sucked on her tongue, Romy pushed herself more fully against him. She didn't care how improper this all was. All she wanted was him, solid and warm beneath her fingertips. She sunk her fingers into the ebony waves of his hair, letting the thick strands trickle across her hands, wiping everything else from her mind but Granby.

When at last he pulled his mouth from hers, Romy cried in disappointment, finding that somehow one of her hands had curled into his shirt, holding him to her. He was nuzzling the side of her neck, his breath wafting over her skin.

"I find you incredibly disagreeable, Your Grace," she whispered, happy in a way she had never been before.

"I know." As he looked down at her, his lips curled up at the ends in a genuine smile.

Romy's heart beat violently beneath her ribs. Granby was savagely, *wildly* beautiful when he smiled.

One large finger reached out to trace the line of her cheek. "I fear you will always find me so. Disagreeable, that is." His finger trailed over her jaw before moving across her shoulder, lingering on the skin of her chest. The dark eyes caught and held hers, watching her reaction as he touched her, perhaps waiting for her to tell him to stop.

His touch continued along her neckline, pausing briefly to dip below the tiny row of lace, the pad of his finger brushing against the very tip of her nipple.

A small noise came from her throat.

Coal-black lashes fell down to brush his cheeks. "Jesus," he whispered.

Immediately the finger retreated as if burned by a flame.

"We should go."

Romy blinked at the cold, icy words. She could practically see the bits of frost gathering around his mouth. Refusing to meet her eyes, he helped her to her feet before bending over to hand her the leather portfolio.

Romy allowed it, though she was wounded by the sudden change in his mood.

When Granby's gaze finally met hers, the aloof mask was once more firmly in place, a slight scowl tightening his lips. He'd closed himself off without warning so quickly, Romy hadn't had time to object.

Romy's fingers reached out, willing the lover of moments before to return, wanting some sort of assurance from him. A declaration that the kiss they'd shared had affected him as much as it had her. But just as quickly, her fingers retreated, knowing instinctively *this* Granby wouldn't welcome such contact.

"Come. I'll walk you back." Granby made no effort to take her hand, as if he couldn't bear to touch her.

"It isn't necessary, Your Grace." Her pulse wobbled as she tried to pull her own emotions back under control. Her anger toward him resurfaced; not for his arrogance or cold manner, for that was never in short supply, but for disregarding her as if she meant nothing. As if *this* had meant nothing.

And Romy was very certain it had. "You needn't concern yourself. I'm quite capable of finding my own way back. I'll hardly become lost." She pointed to the clearly marked path.

"Nonsense. There could be unsavory creatures in these woods, myself among them." He waved her forward. "Besides, we can have a rather awkward stroll back to The Barrow. You will ask me questions seeking to understand why I kissed you when it's assumed I'll offer for Lady Beatrice Howard."

"Possibly." She kept her gaze forward, not wanting him to

see how much the idea of him marrying Beatrice hurt her, especially now.

"I will refuse to answer you," he continued in a detached tone, "which, in turn, will stoke your anger and general dislike of me."

He *wanted* her to dislike him. Hate him. It would be better for Granby if she slapped him and announced she'd be leaving tomorrow.

"Why will you refuse to answer me?" she said quietly. "Because it is far easier if I dislike you, isn't it?"

His lips tightened, but he didn't look at her. "How perceptive of you, Lady Andromeda."

Granby said not one more word to her as they traveled through the woods together, the silence so deafening, Romy wanted to scream. Or kick his shin. Anything to shatter the chilling blandness he forced between them.

As they passed the pond, Lord and Lady Carstairs appeared on the path, carrying their fishing poles. Rebecca was flushed, her hair tangled. When her shawl slipped, Romy could see the back of her gown was buttoned incorrectly. Her eyes, full of ill-concealed malice, darted between Romy and Granby.

"Lady Andromeda, what a surprise to see you out walking." Her lips lit with a sly grin, perhaps hoping for a scrape of gossip she could circulate.

"I walk often," Romy stated, focused on getting away from all of them as quickly as possible.

"As do I," Granby intoned. "One of my tenants reported a gypsy encampment in my woods. I thought to seek it out and found Lady Andromeda instead. Sketching." He nodded to the leather portfolio. "I've reminded her to stay closer to the estate."

Carstairs nodded, satisfied with the explanation.

"How good of you to do so," Rebecca said, glancing once

more at Romy, her eyes searching for any sign of torn lace before focusing on Romy's swollen lips.

"I checked the pond first." Granby looked directly at Rebecca until she blushed up to the roots of her hair and took a step closer to her husband. "Best fix your wife's dress, Carstairs, before you reach the house. You know how guests talk at a house party. I *abhor* gossip of any kind."

His implication was clear. Granby expected them both to not repeat seeing him and Andromeda together. Romy thought Carstairs would comply. The same could not be said of Rebecca, once the shock of Granby's threat wore off.

"Of course, Your Grace." Carstairs shot his wife a mean-ingful glance before bowing, allowing Romy and Granby to pass.

🥀 16 🥀

Two *more days of this bloody house party and we can return to London.*

Granby hadn't spoken one word to her since kissing her in the woods. The remainder of their walk back to The Barrow, after running into Carstairs and his wife, had been completed in an awkward, extended silence. Just as he had predicted. He'd waited until they had arrived at the fresco of Hercules in the gardens before discarding her with a polite bow, then jogged up the steps to greet Haven, who was sitting on the terrace.

Romy had flopped down on a stone bench, staring at a shrub with waxy leaves, one hand pressed to her stomach, trying to stanch her ever growing confusion over the situa-tion. Theo found her there, worried she was still wandering about on the lawn somewhere, sketching a day dress. She'd hurried her in the side entrance of The Barrow, asking why Romy had grass stains on her skirt and where she'd left her shawl.

"I suppose the gypsies have my shawl now," she had answered as Theo shook her head.

The shawl had been left back at the stream. Perhaps if any gypsies were bold enough to invade the land of the Duke of Granby, they would find it.

She blamed Granby. Not just for the shawl, but also for the ache in her heart which refused to go away. It was worse now. Because he'd kissed her.

The source of Romy's confusion had spent each of the last few days squiring Lady Beatrice Howard about, politely listening to Lady Foxwood and, in general, blatantly ignoring Romy's presence. If she stepped into a room, a few moments later, he gave an excuse and left. At breakfast, he lifted the paper in her direction so he wouldn't have to look at her. His eyes never made it as far down the dinner table as she sat.

She was very close to disliking Granby again. Romy dug in her heels.

Theo, meanwhile, was enjoying herself immensely. Blythe divided his attention between Meredith, Theo, and the very thrilled Lady Mildred, who had apparently given up in her pursuit of Estwood. He squired the three women about, spouting off amusing stories and telling jokes. Mildred's laughter, reminiscent of a braying mule, filled the halls of The Barrow.

Blythe *was* incredibly charming.

Lucy Waterstone avoided her father, floating about the edges of the drawing room begging to go unnoticed. Rosalind sulked and tried to pretend the disinterest of Lord Torrington didn't bother her.

Romy thought the earl was playing things smartly. She'd caught him admiring Rosalind when her cousin wasn't looking.

Haven grumbled about, a glass of scotch clutched in one hand keeping him company. Romy noticed he wore yet another new coat, a bit snug in the shoulders just like the first; it was likely also borrowed from Blythe.

It was all so bloody civilized.

On the second day, unable to tolerate another snide look from the Foxwoods or ignore Waterstone's treatment of Lucy, Romy had taken a walk, after which she meant to take a tray in her room. She took the path once more, unsurprised to find herself back at the stream where Granby had kissed her. Luckily, her shawl was still there, sitting amid the flowers. She had bent to pick it up, then promptly flopped down in the grass, her mind filled with all the ways one kiss could change a person, namely her, in such a profound way.

Now, today, with the end of the week in sight, Romy bestowed a smile at Lucy as the carriage lurched forward on the last of the excursions planned by their hostess.

Lady Molsin had arranged for the guests to be taken to the site of a line of barrows which had been the attention of much scientific speculation some years ago. The very same area Estwood had spoken of to Romy during dinner the first night. There was to be a picnic and then the guests could explore, admire the view, or converse for the better part of the day.

Or avoid guests whom you had kissed, as Granby was certain to do to her.

She pushed away the longing she felt for him, determined to enjoy the brilliant sunlit day and the company of Lucy Waterstone. Enough time had been spent reliving the kiss by the stream. There were other things which required Romy's attention, namely assurance that the tailor, Silas, had been taken care of. And dear Lucy, who had wilted under her father's oppressive presence.

Romy shared the carriage not only with Lucy, Lady Mildred and Mr. Estwood, but with their hostess, Lady Molsin. For the entire duration of the house party, Lady Molsin had been in the constant company of either Lady Foxwood, Cousin Winnie, or Lady Meredith's aunt. When

Lady Molsin had climbed into the carriage, she'd taken the seat directly across from Romy.

Theo, Lady Meredith, Rosalind and Beatrice were in the carriage behind them, sitting across from Blythe, Granby and Haven. Lord Torrington shared the final carriage with Lord and Lady Carstairs and Lord and Lady Foxwood.

To everyone's relief, Mr. Waterstone declined to attend the picnic.

The passing scenery of rolling hills was lovely as they traveled the short distance from Granby's estate. Mr. Estwood, who was an expert on such things, informed the group in the carriage of the difference between round barrows and long barrows and their use as burial mounds. Estwood went on to explain that many scholars had once believed the Vikings were responsible for the barrows, or possibly the Romans, but more recent exploration pointed to a much earlier origin. It was thought the area they approached had held some religious significance to the ancient tribes who'd once inhabited this part of England.

"Is the Duke of Granby's estate, then, actually built on a grave?" Lady Mildred's brows raised. "It is called The Barrow, after all."

"I think it the proximity to such places which gave His Grace's estate the name," Mr. Estwood assured her. "There was a keep there, built during the time when England faced all sorts of invaders. Our ancestors were a superstitious lot and would not have placed their castle on any sort of burial mound."

"A pity," Romy said without thinking.

Estwood grinned at her. "How so, my lady?"

"It only seems fitting, Mr. Estwood, for His Grace to actually live *on* a barrow." Romy bit her lip, hoping she hadn't offended Lady Molsin.

"I quite agree," Granby's aunt said.

Estwood chuckled. "As do I."

The carriage erupted into laughter, even Lady Molsin chuckling into one gloved hand.

When Romy looked up, she could just see Granby in the carriage behind them, regarding both her and Estwood with frosty intensity as if he knew their merriment was at his expense.

Romy ignored him. He could go hang.

"Lady Andromeda, how are you enjoying your stay?" her hostess inquired, eyes sharp on Romy.

"It has been delightful, my lady. A most welcome escape from London. I thank you again for being so kind as to include us."

"You are most welcome, my dear. Lady Richardson has been concerned for your welfare and that of your sisters since your father's passing." She lightly touched Romy's hand as her cheeks reddened. "Forgive me for reminding you of it. Sometimes I speak without thinking."

"Please don't distress yourself, my lady. It has been well over a year." Romy thought for a moment. "Closer to two, in fact."

Lady Molsin nodded. "When my own husband passed, I felt lost for a time. One day, I woke up and realized it had been three years." A faraway look entered her eyes. "It was a difficult adjustment, but I am fortunate. As is your mother. In our stepchildren." Granby's aunt leaned forward. "Your brother taught me to play faro. I'm quite good." She cast a sideways glance at Lady Mildred, who was thankfully engaged in conversation with Estwood. "I refer to Mr. Murphy. Not the duke."

Romy had difficulty hiding her surprise. The very idea that Leo had taught this elegant older woman how to play cards was rather scandalous.

"Handsome scamp. He and the duke could be twins. They both favor your father."

"Yes." Romy nodded, slowly aware that Lady Molsin was attempting to make some sort of point in mentioning that she knew Leo, but she wasn't sure exactly what it was. Lady Molsin shouldn't *want* to admit knowing Leo. Her brother being a bastard typically meant his very existence would be ignored by a lady of Lady Molsin's status. The very *last* person in all the world Romy envisioned inside Elysium was Granby's aunt.

Lady Molsin smiled, ending their conversation, and turned her attention to the passing countryside.

The carriages slowed and finally stopped before a vista of green grass waving under a patch of clear blue sky. Small mounds sat in a semi-circle around the area which Romy knew from her conversation with Mr. Estwood had to be barrows and not hills. The area bustled with activity as they approached, Granby's servants having arrived earlier to set up a place for the guests to picnic. A short distance from the picnic area lay a collection of rectangular stones sat strewn about the field. Estwood claimed the arrangement of the stones was significant and held a special meaning due to their placement.

Romy studied the stones as the carriage grew closer, seeing no discernable pattern. Maybe Estwood was incorrect and the rocks were just that. Rocks.

Blankets and cushions littered the ground meant for the more adventurous guests, though a table and chairs had been set up as well for those who didn't wish to sit on the ground. The smell of roasted chicken hung in the air along with fresh grass and a hint of honeysuckle.

"Goodness. Here already," Granby's aunt said. A footman opened the carriage door and Estwood jumped out, offering his assistance to Lady Molsin. "Ladies, I do hope you've all brought your parasols. The sun can be quite warm."

Romy had brought her parasol today. Cousin Winnie had been in a lather that she'd been going about without one. She tucked it under one arm as Estwood assisted her from the carriage.

"Some stones are half-buried, so watch your step," Lady Molsin cautioned.

"May I escort you, Lady Molsin?" Mr. Estwood said politely. The light flashing in his pale eyes told Romy his offer was more a challenge, daring her to reject him.

Lady Molsin didn't hesitate, her gloved hand floating above Estwood's forearm before she gingerly placed her fingertips on his sleeve. "That would be most welcome, Mr. Estwood. Over there." She pointed to the lone table.

Estwood inclined his head and led her forward, his steps slowing to match hers, as Lady Mildred followed closely behind. She'd conversed with Estwood the entire ride and now followed closely behind him and Lady Molsin.

Estwood paused and gallantly held out his other arm which Mildred took immediately, beaming at the attention.

Blythe sailed by Romy, who stood with Lucy, Theo on one arm, Meredith on the other.

Theo waved. "Come along, Miss Waterstone."

Lucy took several steps to catch up, giving Blythe a shy smile when he greeted her.

Romy started forward, glad to see Lucy smile. She hadn't done much of that since her father's arrival at The Barrow. Mr. Waterstone was a tyrant and barely tolerable.

"A wise decision on Estwood's part," Haven murmured in her ear as he came up alongside her, extending his arm.

"What is?" Romy placed her fingers on his coat. "Oh, you mean in escorting Lady Molsin? I would have to agree, Lord

Haven. It is always advisable to further ingratiate yourself with the hostess of the house party you are attending."

"No," he said, leaning closer; she caught a whiff of spice. "In not escorting *you*." He jerked his chin discreetly at Granby who had Beatrice clinging to one arm, Lady Foxwood on the other.

"I'm sure you are mistaken." Romy's heart thudded at Haven's words. "His Grace and I do not get on."

"No, not in the least, from what I've observed," he said solemnly.

There had been just a touch of mockery in his reply, which Romy chose to ignore. "I do apologize about the destruction of your coat when we first arrived."

Theo, who was just ahead, giggled madly at something Blythe said while she hugged his arm.

Haven's gaze fell on her sister. "It's clear she needs spectacles." His voice had a raspy quality. Very unlike the deep rumble of Granby.

"She has spectacles. But vanity has kept her from wearing them."

"Foolish." Haven's gaze remained on Theo.

"Because she cannot see?" Romy said. "I too grow weary of watching her stub a toe or wave to one of Granby's guests only to realize, upon coming closer, she is greeting a statue."

"No." The rasp deepened as the muscles beneath her arm grew taut. "Because she is beautiful either way."

Romy gave Haven a sideways glance. "I would have to agree."

He led her to the blanket where Lucy and Mildred had already settled, nodding politely to both women as he deposited Romy in their company and headed straight toward the food-laden tables. She'd never seen a gentleman in her life eat so much, not even Granby. It was a wonder Haven wasn't round or portly with his appetite.

Haven was still watching Theo as his plate was loaded down by an agreeable servant.

"Mr. Estwood seems to be very informed about the area," Lucy said. Her friend's lisp was barely noticeable now that her father and his constant judgement remained at The Barrow.

"I find his intellect to be stimulating." Mildred tilted her parasol slightly to avoid the sun hitting her face.

"I'm sure he'd be delighted to escort both of you about the stones after lunch and discuss the things that have been found here. I fear his knowledge is wasted on me." Romy leaned in. "I've little interest in such things."

"Oh, no, I couldn't ask," Lucy demurred, looking back at Estwood.

Estwood and Haven's heads were together, Estwood speaking while Haven tore into a chicken leg.

"Then I most certainly will," Mildred stated firmly. "Gentleman or not, I like Mr. Estwood very much. He is wealthy and well-connected." She stood and strode over toward Estwood and Haven, uncaring at her boldness.

"You should speak to Estwood," Romy said to Lucy.

Lucy only nodded, plucking at her skirt.

A servant appeared at Romy's elbow, asking if she and Lucy would like lemonade or perhaps some cheese or a roll.

"Yes to everything," she replied. "I'm quite starving." Maybe she shouldn't be so quick to judge Haven's appetite when her own was stronger than most young ladies she knew. Once the servant returned with their plates, Romy dove in with gusto.

Beatrice wandered over and settled herself on the blanket next to Lucy, without asking if she could join them. Placing a pillow at her back, she smoothed out her skirts. Beatrice was overdressed for a picnic. The pale green frock was more appropriate for paying calls rather than sitting in the grass.

KATHLEEN AYERS

Her eyes took on a calculated gleam as she looked at Romy.

Romy took a bite of her chicken and glared right back. Obviously, Lady Carstairs, true to form, had gossiped to someone about seeing Romy and Granby in the woods.

"Are you enjoying the house party, Lady Andromeda?"

Romy munched as loudly as possible on her chicken, hoping to drive her away. "Very much, Lady Beatrice."

"I confess, I was surprised to see you joining us today. Picnics don't seem to be your style. You much prefer wandering about with your portfolio, sketching away. I do *wonder* what interests you so that you feel compelled to put the image to paper."

Romy's chewing slowed, considering Beatrice's words. Surely the other girl was only being snide. Beatrice couldn't possibly know about Madame Dupree.

"Do you wander with a purpose? Hoping to become lost, perhaps?" She shook her head. "And require rescue?"

If she tossed the chicken in just the right way, with a flick of her wrist, the bone should land right in the center of Beatrice's forehead. What sort of nitwit was Beatrice to suggest Romy had deliberately gone into the woods in the hopes Granby would decide she needed rescue and come looking for her? The timing alone would take far more patience than Romy possessed.

Dabbing at her lips with a napkin, Romy set the remainder of the chicken on her plate. Lady Molsin might object to having one of her guests pelt the other with a chicken bone.

"I do like to sketch." Less than fifteen minutes in Beatrice's company and already Romy had reached her limit.

"That is my understanding," Beatrice answered.

Romy looked away. Part of her wished she could shake Beatrice and ask if her presence was the result of Granby or

170

because she'd somehow, impossibly, figured out Romy was secretly designing gowns for Madame Dupree. She didn't really want the answer to either question.

She'd had quite enough of Beatrice.

Granby had joined Estwood and Haven, towering over both his friends and stealing a piece of fruit from Haven's plate. He looked in her direction, his gaze passing over Romy as if she were merely part of the landscape.

And more than her fill of Granby as well.

"Won't you excuse me?" Romy balanced her plate on one hand and stood, holding on to her skirts, deliberately leaving her parasol. She cast an apologetic look at Lucy for deserting her. "I think I'll go for a walk."

Beatrice waved. "Don't get lost lest we be forced to leave without you."

Romy bit back her reply. After handing a footman her plate, she started out across the expanse of grass, glad now, after Beatrice's odd comments, that she hadn't brought her small notepad with her.

✣ 17 ✣

A quarter of an hour later, Romy found herself a good distance from the rest of the group. Their conversation no longer broke through the grass waving gently in the breeze. Even if she screamed, she doubted anyone would hear her.

And she did feel a good scream coming on.

Several people had walked away from the picnic area and headed in the direction of the stones. She could barely make out Estwood from this distance, but Romy thought Lucy walked beside him.

Romy flopped back on the ground, hidden from the rest of the world by the tall grass surrounding her. She supposed someone might come looking for her after a time, or not. Perhaps she'd be stranded out here among Granby's bloody barrows.

"Damn," she said to herself. "Not a cloud in the sky." A pity. Conjuring animals out of clouds was a hobby of hers.

Estwood's voice lingered on the breeze, though Romy couldn't make out what he was saying. Probably something gruesome. He'd started a tale of human sacrifice during the carriage ride, only stopping when Lady Molsin had shot him a pointed look.

Romy watched the long strands of grass wave in the wind, thinking of Granby. He'd kissed her endlessly by the stream. Even now, warmth crawled up her limbs at the remembered feel of his mouth on hers and the touch of his finger across her breast.

A slow curl of longing wrapped firmly around her midsection.

She'd wanted so much more than that kiss. She'd wanted to press her lips against his skin, see the muscles only guessed at beneath his coat. Last night, Romy had run her fingers across her breasts and down between her legs, dreaming of Granby, dark and savage above her.

"Thank goodness you moved, else I would have mistaken you for a blade of grass." The words rippled across her already heated body.

To her credit, Romy didn't lift her head or even sit up, not wanting him to see how his presence affected her. "So you've said before, Your Grace. I suppose it is an improvement over being labeled a shrub. You seem to have wandered from the main group. I believe Lady Beatrice is over there." She waved her arm up in the air.

A noise came from Granby's throat. Probably one of annoyance.

"You're blocking the sun," she informed him.

"You should thank me. You've forgotten your parasol."

That was true. Romy may have intentionally neglected to bring it on her walk. She imagined Beatrice holding it aloft in triumph as a sign Romy had been vanquished.

Granby stared down at her from his great height, hair blowing against the slash of his cheekbones. There was a savageness stamped on his features, as if this ancient spot called to the blood of his ancestors flowing through his veins. And hunger. A great deal of it.

If she hadn't already been so aroused by the mere thought of him, Romy might have taken a moment to be afraid.

As she gazed up at him, a deep ache started across her chest to match the soft throb between her thighs. A longing she'd thought never to feel for another person; one that was not returned.

"I have something I must confess."

"There is no need for you to confess anything, Your Grace," she said into the wind. "If you have come to voice your regret over what transpired at the stream, there is no need." It pained her to know he found her so unacceptable.

His lips twisted in annoyance. "You've no idea what I wish to say."

"Stop scowling at me. I grow weary of it." Her heart had only begun to sort through her muddled feelings for Granby, and here he was, stomping about in his arrogant way, determined to undermine her progress. "The incident is forgotten. We shall never speak of it or endure an awkward walk again. You may continue to dislike me. I shall return the favor."

The grass whipped about as Granby sat next to her with a grunt. He looked as if he wished to strangle her with his cravat. Which was expertly tied.

"Stop looking at my cravat," he growled, "to see if it meets with your approval."

"I was only going to say it is a lovely hue."

"Like tepid bathwater," he snapped, before stretching his long body out in the grass beside her.

They lay there together, only mere inches separating them, staring at the sky for the longest time until Romy's hand crawled across to his, her fingers gently caressing the crease of his thumb.

"Andromeda." Her name choked out of him. He rolled to

his side and brought her wrist to his mouth, pressing his lips against her pulse. Dark eyes flashed across her face with the sheen of brushed velvet.

The merest touch emboldened her. Brazenly, she pulled his mouth down to hers, thinking only of being close to him. The confusion spiraling inside her settled as a sense of contentment enveloped her. Wrapping her arms around his neck, Romy notched her body against the hard length of his.

Granby gave a sharp, ragged breath, the wall of ice around him shattering enough to leave small fissures for Romy to crawl through.

His palm brushed against one breast with a groan, cupping the underside, squeezing gently until her nipple peaked.

"*Christ*. You aren't wearing a corset." He pulled away from her lips.

"No, I—" Romy almost told him she'd designed several day dresses specifically so she wouldn't *have* to be constrained by a corset. It was difficult to walk or try to picnic in one, let alone lay in the grass to be kissed by a large male. "You see—"

"I don't care." His mouth fell on hers, ferocious and urgent, cutting off the rest of her explanation.

Romy was falling, surrendering to the intoxication of Granby. His mouth ravaged hers, exploring her with his lips and tongue while the low hum between her thighs spread across her entire body. She could even feel it in the tips of her toes. All Romy wanted was to be closer to him, her hips tilting upward, offering herself to Granby.

His hand left her breast, moving with purpose down her skirts, tracing the outline of her legs beneath the layers of fabric. When his hand reached her ankle, his fingers tightened.

The pulsing of her body robbed every other coherent thought from her mind, including the fact that the remainder of the house party was roaming about a stone circle some distance away. She struggled to press her lower body closer to his, desperate to ease the growing ache inside her.

Granby threw a leg over her, stilling her movements. "No," he whispered.

The hand climbed up inside her skirts.

"Granby." Her breath hitched as the warmth of his fingers touched her knee. "You've avoided me for days." Her head fell back with a sigh at the gentle caress her thigh received. "Don't you think—"

He ignored her, his mouth catching hers once more while his hand continued its journey, pausing to stroke the skin of her inner thigh. He paused there, waiting.

Romy's legs fell apart, permission for him to go further, gasping as the tip of his forefinger trailed along the opening of her underthings. Moisture spilled, encouraged by his touch, welcoming his exploration of her flesh. A voice at the back of her mind screamed that anyone could come upon them. She'd be ruined or worse.

A moan left her as his finger dragged along her slit, sliding through her now wet flesh.

"Someday," he murmured against her lips, "I'll kiss you here." His finger teased at the small bit of flesh which ached for him.

The very thought of him doing such a thing sent another rush of moisture between her thighs. Romy twisted, forcing herself more fully against his questing fingers as Granby gently teased at her flesh, sinking two fingers deep inside her. His thumb brushed softly back and forth, the fingers thrusting inside her until she lay panting beneath him.

He tore his lips from hers, cupping the side of her cheek, dark eyes burning against her skin. His thumb pressed down, breaking a damn of sensation free inside her.

Romy arched back, a cry leaving her mouth before Granby's lips met hers again to swallow the sound. She was floating in a cloud of bliss inspired by clever fingers and the yearning of her own heart.

Granby pressed a kiss to her temple. "Beautiful, beautiful."

"Your absence has been noticed." The words floated across the grass, wiping away in an instant the last of the pleasure trembling from her body.

Granby's fingers stilled, his breath coming in short bursts.

"You wandered off to enjoy a cheroot some time ago. I joined you over the hill by a strand of trees. You didn't wish to offend the ladies," Haven said before moving off.

Granby abruptly pulled his hand from beneath her skirts and rolled away, a thick sheaf of ebony hair falling over his eyes.

Another tremor shook her, the shock at being discovered by Haven overriding the intimacy she'd just shared with Granby. What had possessed her to allow such a thing?

I think I might be in—Romy refused to finish the thought.

"This must cease," he stated calmly, as if they'd only been sitting together discussing the weather.

She was still on her back, tugging her skirts down. "Because of Beatrice?"

"No. Because of *you*." He shook his head. "You are everything I *do not* want."

Romy flinched, letting the pain of his words settle deep in her chest. "I see." She sat up, miserable and sick to the very core of her being. "Why?" They were fortunate it had been Haven who'd come across them and not someone else.

"I have taken care of Silas. He has a lovely cottage near his daughter and a fortune to spend."

"Answer me," she snapped. "I deserve to know why I am so offensive to you, considering what has just occurred."

"Will you cry ruination then?"

"I refuse to make things so easy for you, Your Grace."

"There are rules, Andromeda. Dictates that must be followed. There are elements I cannot allow the Duke of Granby to be associated with." He still wouldn't look at her; he only tugged at his collar.

"I see." Except, she didn't, really. It was not the first time Granby had implied she was somehow lacking in suitability by some stupid measurement only he was privy to. She was the daughter of a bloody duke. "You are the only one who feels I am deficient in some way."

"Not the only one," he said, barely above a whisper.

"Estwood certainly doesn't find me wanting," she said, lashing out at him. "He finds me *incredibly* suitable." She drew her knees up to stop the trembling of her legs.

"Stay away from Estwood."

"I'll listen to Estwood and his stories anytime I wish. If I choose to sketch Blythe's backside, as I should have done at Lady Masterson's, I will." Her words turned snide. Raw. "The service you've just provided me doesn't bestow upon you any right to dictate the company I keep."

"Service?" The word cracked across her coldly, like the snap of a whip.

"What would you call it, Your Grace? It certainly wasn't an act done with an ounce of affection. I've already determined you aren't capable of such emotion."

An ugly, wounded sound came from him. "None of this is easy."

"Haven is waiting for you. I will take my time and return to the picnic area from the opposite direction." Romy stayed perfectly still, her eyes focused on the view before her, and refused to look at him. Her insides felt torn and damaged. As if he'd ripped out the seed of something before allowing it to take root.

The grass rustled around her as he stood.

Romy struggled to keep the moisture gathering behind her eyes at bay. He was right. This situation *must* cease. Her emotions were in disarray, overriding all caution when it came to Granby. The last hour was proof of that.

Finally daring a look behind her, she saw that Granby was gone.

❦

DAVID STRODE TO THE SMALL GROUPING OF TREES AT THE edge of the field Haven had directed him to, reaching into his pocket for a cheroot to complete the charade. Andromeda's scent lingered in his nostrils. Her sweetness clung to his fingers. If Haven hadn't come upon them, David would quite possibly have taken her virtue. The loss of control he'd shown was nothing short of shocking.

Andromeda was a terrible weakness. Bits of him unraveled whenever she was near, and he couldn't stop it.

"Have you lost your bloody mind?" Haven stepped from around one of the trees, hand out. "We'd both best go back reeking of tobacco if the tale we tell is to stick."

David reached into his pocket for another cheroot and handed it to his friend. "I appreciate your intervention. Thank you."

"You're a bloody fool." Haven lit a match, lighting the tip of his cheroot. "You *want* her because she *isn't* Beatrice. No one gives a fig but you, and possibly the ghost of Horace, that Andromeda's mother was once a lady's companion; she's *still* the daughter of a duke."

A familiar chill clawed at David's chest, nearly restricting his lungs. Haven didn't understand. He couldn't. "Breeding is of the utmost importance."

Haven snorted. "You sound just like him. One wonders how you tolerate Estwood. Your father certainly didn't."

179

"Breeding *always* shows, Haven. As evidenced by the fact she was willing to roll about in the grass with me. Didn't even think twice about it. Beatrice would never have done that." David cringed, hearing how condescending he sounded.

Haven's gaze on him grew ugly. "I find it says more about *you* than Andromeda, you pompous ass. I don't know what Horace did to you, Gran."

"He did nothing but raise me to be the duke I am." The words fell smoothly from his lips, but the usual duty he felt toward Granby was absent. He'd been thinking quite a bit about his father lately, also Andromeda's fault. Things David had long avoided, he'd been examining too closely.

"I don't claim to know what your upbringing was like being raised by that cruel prick. Or why you seem so determined to emulate him. You were never happier than when you were in Italy."

David tossed down the cheroot, grinding the tip beneath his boot, wishing it were Haven. "I don't wish to make the same mistakes Horace did. There are certain rules which *must* be followed. My mother—"

"Has nothing to do with Andromeda. If you don't want her bastard brother in your house because it offends your sensibilities, then don't allow him to visit. You don't need to drink scotch with Averell or have tea with the dowager duchess. Live at The Barrow and avoid the Barringtons if you can't stomach their eccentricity."

"What a polite way of putting it. You act as if I'm the only one who feels that way."

Haven shook his head in disgust.

"And even if I could overlook the aspects of Andromeda which I find unappealing, there is an expectation in regard to Beatrice. A scandal is bound to erupt."

"Are you some fragile milquetoast who can't weather such talk?" Haven threw down his own cheroot in disgust. "You're an idiot. Frankly, I hope Andromeda comes to her senses. She deserves better."

Haven marched off without another word, coat flapping as he made his way back to where the guests were milling about the carriages being readied to leave.

A slender form made its way up the incline from the opposite side of the field. Andromeda's steps were confident as she waved at her sister who came to greet her. Miss Waterstone joined them. There was nothing in her manner which would indicate how the world had shifted dramatically beneath her feet. And his.

David slowly made his way to the carriages, in no hurry to join his guests. The longing for Andromeda pierced him the closer he came, never once abating, not even when he assisted Lady Foxwood and Beatrice into the carriage, apologizing for his absence.

Cheroots, Lady Foxwood claimed, giving both David and Haven the benefit of her unsolicited opinion, were a dreadful habit.

Andromeda, in the carriage ahead of him, shimmered in the late afternoon sun, gleaming like a rare and precious jewel. The sound of her laughter filled the air, reflecting her amusement at something Miss Waterstone relayed to her.

David had never wanted anything so badly in his life.

𝕾 18 𝕾

Romy sipped her tea, watching as Daisy bustled about the room, packing the trunks to be loaded on the Averell coach for their departure tomorrow morning. The only items of clothing left out were her ensemble for tonight and the traveling dress she would wear back to London tomorrow.

The ball, finally putting an end to their intolerable stay at The Barrow, was tonight. A shame Romy couldn't find it in her heart to enjoy all of Lady Molsin's efforts, especially since four of the guests, including herself, would be wearing creations of Romy's own design. One of those spectacular gowns would be draped over Lady Beatrice Howard as she eagerly anticipated a proposal from the Duke of Granby.

Sticking a finger into her tea, Romy stirred the liquid about in her cup, thinking of Granby and her feelings for him, all of which were destined to remain unresolved. She refused to regret one moment of their time together. Not the kiss by the stream and certainly not yesterday as she had climaxed with him looking down upon her.

Her finger trembled, and she pulled it abruptly out of the tepid tea.

Romy didn't blame Granby for what happened. She'd wanted him to touch her. If such a thing made her unacceptable to him, so be it.

Lady Beatrice, on the other hand, was a perfect example of English womanhood. She *never* would have rolled about in the grass with Granby or allowed him to stick his hands up her skirt. The very thought would make her faint.

Her maid paused in her packing. "Are you well, my lady? Its nearly time to dress."

"I'm quite well, Daisy. Just not looking forward to the journey back to London. I detest being confined to a coach for any length of time."

Daisy nodded. "I quite agree."

Beatrice, if she were Granby, made much more sense as a wife. Her sense of superiority was firmly in place. She doubted Beatrice knew the names of her servants either and would never think of thanking a footman or maid for their assistance. Beatrice kept her true nature hidden beneath a veneer of modesty and ladylike decorum. She didn't stride about trading insults with Granby. Beatrice would welcome Granby's incredibly rigid existence in ways Romy could not.

When Granby had spoken of Italy, with more than a bit of longing, the complicated pieces of his life had started to come together for her. By all accounts, Granby's father had been a bitter, controlling man. Granby hadn't so much as traveled to Italy as he'd *escaped*. Romy suspected the man he'd been in Italy was very different from the Duke of Granby. Bits of that man had followed him back to England, but not been allowed to flourish or take root.

A pity, since Granby's current existence was choking him, as evidenced by the way he absently tugged at his collar, unaware of the habit. The gardens. His hair. The coat. Even

Estwood was testament to a different existence. And yet, his duty kept him from embracing the truer version of himself.

Her eyes fluttered shut to keep the gathering tears from falling down her cheeks. How attuned she'd become to him in such a short time. The discomfort Romy caused Granby was real. The man he'd been in Italy wanted Romy, but the Duke of Granby did not. It was actually very simple once she accepted the truth.

Simple, indeed. But it brought her no peace.

❦

"My lady, you look smashing." Daisy's pretty features smiled back at Romy in the oval of the mirror before bending to fluff out the bottom of the gown.

"I do, don't I?" Romy touched a finger to one of the clips strategically placed in her coiffure.

"I am amazed by the things you create." Daisy studied her hair. "If I didn't know better, I'd think them alive and caught between your curls. Each butterfly is different."

"I can't take all the credit for the clips completely. I designed them, but Theo did the painting for me." She turned sideways in the mirror, admiring the way the indigo-shot silk with butterflies embroidered along the hem, floated about her ankles. The skirts parted smoothly to reveal an underskirt also patterned with their beautiful wings. Every time Romy took a step, the gown gave the impression that butterflies were floating out from beneath her skirts.

There was a sharp knock at the door before Theo came through, stunning in a gown of palest pink. Romy designed the gown so that the color faded from a light cream tinged with just a hint of color to a deep pink as it wrapped around Theo's waist and bodice. The silk hugged her shoulders, showing a modest swath of skin. At each shoulder, the silk had been gathered to form a facsimile of a rose with a tiny bit of embroidery in green to represent a stem. Fresh roses dotted Theo's hair.

"Lady Theo," Daisy exclaimed. "You look like the bud of a rose about to open."

"Don't I?" Theo spun, letting her skirts flutter about her ankles. "Wait until Blythe sees my display of bosom." She frowned a bit in Romy's direction. "I thought we discussed cutting the bodice a bit deeper."

"It wasn't necessary." Her sister was generously endowed, and a lower neckline would have been problematic. "I didn't wish you to fall out at an inopportune moment." Romy gazed down at her own less than generous bosom. There was little chance of such a thing happening to her.

"You're a very talented artist, Theo. Daisy is amazed at how lifelike the butterflies appear. Perhaps you should showcase your artistic talent to Blythe rather than trying to entice him with only your bosom."

Theo's mouth parted, a calculating look crossing her face. "That's brilliant. Oh, Romy. You are a genius."

"I am?"

"You've just given me an idea of how I might entice Blythe into eventually offering for me. Thank you."

Romy waited for an explanation, but Theo only smiled to herself and deftly changed the subject.

"Beatrice is going to hate it when the Barrington sisters outshine her, as we are certain to do," Theo said. "Having made the acquaintance of Lord and Lady Foxwood, it is not hard to see where Beatrice's manner stems from. I am grateful Mama is not thrusting *us* toward every eligible title."

"We're very fortunate." Romy didn't want to think about Beatrice tossing herself at Granby like a dinner roll, though she expected it wouldn't be for much longer.

"Yes, we are. We both have the talents of the best modiste

in London at our disposal." She winked at Romy before looking over at Daisy, who had resumed packing.

"Don't worry. Daisy knows. I've few secrets from her." Romy thought about Beatrice's comments at the picnic. "Rosalind has guessed. Do you think she'd tell anyone?"

Her sister shook her head. "At least not purposefully. And I know it isn't a perfect situation, but I am glad you have reached an arrangement with Madame Dupree. At least you can practice your craft even if everyone thinks Madame Dupree has designed their wardrobe."

Strangely enough, Romy had been so preoccupied with Granby, she'd barely spared a thought for Madame Dupree, their partnership, or the shop. The creativity which was such a part of her daily life had deserted her while at The Barrow.

"It is difficult, at times, knowing Madame Dupree will receive the credit, but there isn't any other option. And it is a far more beneficial partnership than I could have hoped for, even if it must remain secret. I'll have to tell Mama eventually. And Maggie. Leo won't mind, though I will refuse to design any of his waistcoats. His color choices are atrocious. Tony may be the only one who will object."

Theo gave her a hug. "He won't. Our brother will think you clever for having found a solution to your problem. I've yet to make the same determination." Her sister fluffed her skirts needlessly. "We should go down. I've promised my first dance to Blythe."

"Theo." Romy took her hand. "Has Blythe given any indication he means to call on you once we return to London? Or given you any indication of his further interest?"

"Don't concern yourself." Theo breezed out the door. "I've everything figured out. You'll see."

❧ 19 ❧

Andromeda was, in a word, stunning.

A masculine sound of appreciation left David as her slender figure entered the ballroom looking as if a cloud of butterflies hovered about her ankles. The indigo silk hugged her shoulders, exposing the lovely peach color of her skin. Butterflies glittered in her hair, peeking out from behind a host of curls streaked with copper.

The lower half of his body rippled with the need to have her. Longing for her settled in his chest. He took a healthy swallow of the scotch he held, hoping to blunt the worst of his hunger.

Lady Theodosia, also spectacularly clothed, followed behind Andromeda, draped in silk of pale pink and cream.

Blythe went immediately to Theodosia's side, taking her hand in greeting before circling her like the rake he was.

She blushed at his attention. Theodosia had made no secret of her regard for Blythe, but she would face some stiff competition tonight in the form of Lady Meredith, who had yet to enter the ballroom.

"Blythe is particularly lecherous this evening, don't you

think?" Haven strolled to David's side, dressed in another coat borrowed from Blythe. His eyes followed the movements of Theodosia.

"Undoubtedly."

"Your aunt has really turned the place out." Haven's eyes roamed around the little-used ballroom with its chorus of chandeliers dangling from the gilt-edged ceiling. Mirrors lined one wall, making the room appear much larger than it was. A request of David's mother, long ago. One of the last things she'd asked of Horace before fleeing The Barrow.

The usual rage he held for his mother on behalf of Horace failed to materialize. He blamed the scotch and took another sip.

Plucking a glass of wine from a servant, Haven regarded him with a frown. "You're drinking."

"How observant you are, Haven. And *I've* observed the lady whom you seem so taken with doesn't seem to mind Blythe's attentions. Why should you?"

A derisive snort came from Haven. "Blythe is like a dog, constantly sniffing around to see where else he can—"

The soft murmur of dozens of voices filled the ballroom, interrupting what was sure to be Haven's vulgar assessment of Blythe. Beatrice entered, as regal as any queen, trailed by her parents. Tiny suns twinkled from the golden strands of her elaborate coiffure, and small diamonds dangled from her ears and throat. David rarely paid much attention to the aspects of a ballgown, but this gown was *magnificent*. Beatrice resembled not a young lady but a celestial being, wandering about mere mortals, far too beautiful to be gracing the ballroom of The Barrow.

"Jesus," David said beneath his breath, eyes riveted on Beatrice's gown, then his gaze immediately shot to the butterflies swirling about Andromeda.

"Magnificent," Haven agreed. "Though I've never cared

overmuch for blondes. I suppose you're determined to marry her. Can't say I agree."

David barely heard him. He glanced between Beatrice and Andromeda. He'd seen both their gowns before as a sketch.

Miss Waterstone entered on her father's arm. He'd seen her gown before, too.

Sketches, strewn over the ground in front of Andromeda, when he'd found her by the stream. He struggled to recall everything he'd seen. Dresses. Gowns. A riding habit. Careful notes written in the margins.

The idea that the daughter of a duke was leading a double life as a modiste was absurd. He had to be mistaken. How in the world would Andromeda accomplish such a thing without anyone knowing? The most sewing the daughter of a duke might be required to do would be tacking a loose ribbon on her slipper.

The bloody butterflies.

His eyes took in Andromeda's hair, spiked with the insects, and then to Beatrice's locks, gleaming with tiny suns. If you looked closely, as he was doing now, one could see the designs of the clips were similar, if not identical. He'd convinced himself she was only passing the time by drawing a gown she'd seen in London. Or sketching a butterfly alighting on a flower. But Andromeda was creating entire ensembles—

Clever, brilliant, unsuitable little shrub.

David took another sip of his scotch, tugging gently at his collar. What an incredibly scandalous hobby for a young lady of Andromeda's station.

Breeding always shows in the end.

He pushed aside his father's comment. Tonight, he wasn't inclined to heed Horace's advice.

Andromeda kept herself to the other side of the room, hovering about the edges, as far from him as possible. She didn't look David's way or even acknowledge his presence.

He couldn't blame her. Not after yesterday.

David's heart seized up inside his chest, constricting until he winced from the sensation. Draining the rest of his glass, he waved to a servant for another, ignoring Haven's raised brow.

"Lady Andromeda is exceptional," Haven drawled. "She's bound to have a rich dowry. I could not give a fig if her mother started life as a lady's companion or her brother is a bastard, not when she looks like that." He nodded in Andromeda's direction. "Despite having been unwise enough to spend time with you."

Haven had no idea what the nature of David's time with Andromeda had comprised, else he would stop talking immediately.

"I think Andromeda and I might get on together. I'd have to fight Estwood for her, though."

"If you go near her, Haven," David replied in his most conversational tone, eyes never once leaving Andromeda's graceful form, "I will take great pleasure in breaking the fingers of both your hands before doing the same to your wrists. You would never hold a gun or a sword with any ability again. A shame, as you've so many enemies."

Haven, to his credit, didn't flinch. "You'll be married to Beatrice"—his words dripped with sarcasm—"and unable to stop me. *Your* behavior toward Andromeda will become fodder for the gossips. Just think of the scandal."

If David took a hold of Haven's chin and smashed his head into the wall, his body would slide down into a rumbled heap. Everyone would assume Haven was already foxed, and footmen would be summoned to carry him up to his rooms.

"Andromeda"—he accepted the glass of scotch a servant had fetched for him—"isn't for you, Haven. I'll kill you if you touch her."

Haven choked on his wine. "Christ, you're serious."

David didn't bother to look at his friend again; all his attention remained on Andromeda as Estwood stopped to speak to her. He pushed away from the wall and Haven, welcoming the way he could feel himself unraveling. The scotch helped.

He never even looked in Beatrice's direction.

"Dance with me?"

Romy turned to see Granby, dark and unfathomable, gazing down at her. He'd watched her almost continuously since she and Theo had entered the ballroom, his eyes following her every step.

Romy had ignored him, of course, resolved to merely get through this evening without her heart being damaged further. The sight of Beatrice, glowing like a golden star in one of Romy's finest creations, unsettled her to no end. If not for Theo, Romy would already have fled to London, uncaring of how cowardly it would be.

"No, thank you, Your Grace." Besides the usual aroma of pine and shaving soap, there was also a whiff of scotch hovering about Granby's shoulders. Glancing down, she saw the glass of amber liquid clasped in one large hand. She'd never seen him imbibe outside of the occasional sip of wine at dinner.

"Don't be difficult, *Romy*." The sound of her nickname on his lips sent a delicious tingle down her arms. A thick wave of hair fell over one eye as he leaned closer. "I dance well."

"I have my doubts."

Granby's gaze lingered over her mouth before it lifted upward. "Butterflies are a particular favorite of mine. I used to catch them as a boy."

"To pull their wings off, Your Grace?"

His lips curled upward as he drained his glass and set it down before taking her hand. She was pulled behind him, like a tiny rowboat dragged by a much larger ship.

"You should be dancing with Beatrice," she bit out. "She has tiny suns in her hair. Much more dramatic than butterflies."

"But I don't want to dance with Beatrice." He pulled her to him, lips nearly brushing her ear. "I know what you've done." The low rumble of his voice traveled up her neck. "You continue to make things so much more difficult. Why? When there are enough obstacles?" His dark gaze settled on the tops of her breasts. "Pink. Or perhaps the color of chokeberries."

Romy shook her head in confusion. He didn't appear to be foxed exactly, only incredibly relaxed. The lovely half-smile on his lips enticed her. "What is it I've done?" Warmth settled at the base of her spine, the pads of his fingers sinking into her skin.

"I've found you out, naughty little shrub." His breath ruffled through her hair, his nose almost nuzzling the side of her neck. "Christ, you smell delicious. I don't care for lavender on principle, but against your skin"—he inhaled again—"I find I like it."

Romy tried to pull back from him, but his hold on her only tightened. "Are you foxed?"

Fingers moved to trace the line of one rib. "Why do you ask?"

"You don't seem yourself."

Granby seemed *very* much unlike himself.

They danced past Lady Foxwood who curled her lips in displeasure as she caught Romy's eye. Beatrice flounced, glaring at them from the wall, looking like a crestfallen angel.

The gown did look smashing on her.

"Only slightly. Foxed, that is. And shouldn't it please you

to know I'm not myself? As I recall, you dislike that other Granby." A thick wave of ebony hair fell across one eye again but this time he neglected to push it back. A smile softened his lips. "You have the most amazing eyes, Romy," he whispered. "Like the sky at night, twinkling with stars. I dream of them."

"The stars?" It was intoxicating, having him speak to her in such a way. The heat of him was seeping slowly through the layers of her skirts. When he spun her, one muscular thigh notched briefly between her legs before retreating, leaving behind a pleasurable curling sensation.

"Or a seascape," he murmured, eyes brushing over her mouth.

Granby argued. He insulted. He did not *flirt*. Not seductively or in full view of the guests filling the ballroom of The Barrow. Not when he was planning to offer for Beatrice.

"I can't imagine the amount of scotch it must take to intoxicate you," Romy said up at him, wanting to touch the length of dark stubble stretching across his jaw and chin. Granby was the sort of man who would always require another shave no matter how efficient his valet. "You're very large."

"I assure you. I am not foxed." There was a sensual half-smile dragging at his lips.

Her stomach gave a delicious squeeze.

"And it does indeed require an enormous amount. Much more than I've already had."

He was utterly charming like this. Playful. And far too appealing. All things he typically kept under a tight lid of control. She'd sensed this other side of him but had only caught brief glimpses until now.

"Too much scotch and you might lose control, Granby." Her breasts teased against his coat as the hand at her waist dipped lower to the swell of her hips.

"There are things, *Romy*," he said, his voice lowering a delicious octave, "which are far more intoxicating than scotch and much more likely to cause me to lose control." The dark rasp of his voice lifted the hairs at the base of her neck. "You, for instance."

"Me?" How seductive she sounded. Flirtatious. "You don't even like me."

"Silly shrub." Granby spun her once more; he tugged her closer and discreetly nipped her earlobe. "I think we both know that is not the case."

"I was a tree nymph, Your Grace." She managed to keep her voice steady, shocked he'd nibbled on her skin. Lady Foxwood eyed them like a hawk.

"You told me," her voice trembled as he led her off the dance floor, "this must cease, Your Grace."

"*David*," he whispered, not bothering to look at her again as he deposited her between Rosalind and Cousin Winnie.

"What?"

"This must cease, *David*," he murmured, releasing her hand before politely thanking her for the dance. "Ladies." Granby inclined his head to Cousin Winnie and Rosalind before strolling off in the direction of Lady Foxwood and Beatrice.

Romy stared at the expanse of his broad shoulders, wondering what the bloody hell had just happened besides the dance. It was the only part of their discussion she understood.

When Carstairs asked her for a dance, Romy readily agreed. Next was Blythe. Then Estwood. Several of Granby's neighbors claimed her next, gentlemen whose names she forgot as soon as they were introduced. Finally, Haven requested a dance.

Once they were gliding across the ballroom floor, she said, "Thank you for your assistance yesterday."

Haven was an excellent dancer, moving with athletic grace across the ballroom floor. Romy thought him quite handsome, in a rumpled, slightly disreputable way. He had the same appeal as a highwayman might. Or a pirate.

"Did I offer you assistance yesterday? Yes, I must have helped you into the carriage or perhaps fetched you an apple."

A smile crossed her lips. "It must have been the apple." How very gentlemanly of Haven to pretend he hadn't noticed his friend taking liberties with her in the grass while the rest of the guests wandered about a grouping of stones. It spoke well of his character.

"You are most welcome," he replied, eyes fixed on someone over Romy's shoulder.

When Haven turned her, Romy saw Theo. Her sister was in the process of apologizing to a servant who was gingerly picking up a broken glass. She must have tripped over the poor man.

"I suppose we are lucky the duke hasn't had us thrown out," she joked. "My sister is single-handedly destroying his estate."

"He is an ass," Haven said quietly. "But he comes by it honestly. Don't give up, Andromeda. I haven't seen him drink this much since we lived in Rome. He rarely allows himself to be—"

"Foxed?" Romy finished for him.

"No. I was going to say *free*." The dance came to an end, and Haven bowed, shaggy hair covering his face.

"Wait." Romy placed her fingers on his arm. "You knew him in Italy?"

Haven was already walking away from her when he said, "Of course. That's how we met."

Romy fanned herself, pondering over Haven's comments only to see Granby moving smoothly across the dance floor,

Beatrice clasped in his arms. They were such a perfectly matched couple. Everyone watched.

Lady Foxwood beamed, avarice gleaming in her eyes, no doubt fueled by the thought that her daughter would soon be a duchess. She gave a satisfied nod to Lady Molsin.

Romy quietly turned away as the reality of the present situation returned to her. It didn't matter how much Granby flirted, drank scotch, and made odd comments to her. Nor did Haven's opinion hold an ounce of weight.

Except the part where he'd called Granby an ass. *That* was certainly true.

I need some air.

After which Romy meant to go up to her room. There was no need to hover in the ballroom like some sort of dejected suitor who'd been refused a thousand times, awaiting an announcement sure to break her heart.

"Cousin Winnie." She took the older woman's hand. "I've a terrible headache. I need to lie down for a moment."

"Oh, dear, no." Cousin Winnie's mouth puckered in distress. "This is what comes of too much sun. I've never known you to be so absent-minded. You forgot your parasol several times."

Romy placed a hand to her temple. "I'm sure you're right. I promise to listen to your advice in the future." She wouldn't. Cousin Winnie also thought she could determine your fortune by reading the leaves of her morning tea.

"I'll make your excuses, dear. You need to be well rested for your journey back to London tomorrow."

Romy nodded and walked out of the ballroom, forcing herself not to look in Granby's direction, though she caught the reflection of him and Beatrice in the mirrors lining one wall. Nothing had changed between them.

She was still unsuitable, at least in Granby's mind.

David *detested* balls. He always had. This one, in particular, was troublesome.

Every guest floating about beneath the muted lights in his ballroom was here for one reason only; to watch him secure a match with Lady Beatrice Howard. Foxwood, far more animated than usual, spoke to Waterstone while enjoying some expensive wine David's aunt had ordered for the occasion. He was practically salivating over having secured a duke for his daughter. Giddy, even.

Only a weak man allows his cock to dictate his decisions.

David took a large swig of his scotch, swirling the liquid around in his mouth before swallowing. He was either slightly foxed or going mad, for he could hear his father's caustic pronouncements quite clearly in his mind, demanding David follow in Horace's rigid footsteps only to be rewarded with scraps of approval.

Every rebellion punished more severely than the last.

His gaze wandered to where Andromeda danced with Haven, and he studied the placement of his friend's hands to ensure they didn't stray over her body. The control he took such pride in was no match for the scotch or the possessiveness he had for the gorgeous girl with butterflies in her hair.

Foxwood was looking in David's direction, waiting for some sign an announcement was about to be made. Even Aunt Pen watched him in expectation.

Beatrice stood at her mother's side, beautiful and perfect, waiting for the cue to join him.

The musicians struck up a merry tune, and several couples took to the dance floor, swirling in front of David until the colors of the lady's gowns made him dizzy. Or it could have been the scotch. He held up his glass. Empty. But he had an excellent bottle in his study.

Rebelling against Horace was difficult. But not impossible.

🦋 21 🦋

After wandering about the gardens for the better part of an hour, her only company the frogs chirping in Granby's pond, Romy made her way silently through the same side door she'd used earlier in the week. She didn't want to run into any of the other guests.

The lights had been dimmed and the hallways mostly deserted as the staff busied themselves at the ball. The small army of servants, headed by Owens, would want to make an impression on their future duchess.

Her heart constricted painfully.

All she'd done was tell a gentleman the length of his coat was incorrect. A good deed, of sorts. And look where it had gotten her. She couldn't wait to return to London and pick up the threads of her life. Designing dozens of new wardrobes would certainly push Granby from her thoughts. She turned the corner to take the stairs and stopped.

There were no stairs.

"Bollocks." She didn't recognize this part of The Barrow and would have to find her way back, delaying her return to her room where she meant to eat a large tray of the tiny frosted cakes she'd been served at tea today. The ones with pink icing were her favorite.

The Barrow was a huge estate, much larger than Cherry Hill, and riddled with dozens of rooms and a warren of hallways. It was surprising she hadn't gotten lost before now.

Light shone down one hall, and she moved toward it, thinking if the servants had lit the lamps, the corridor probably led to a main part of the house. Quickening her steps, Romy caught sight of dozens of portraits lining the walls. She was in the family's portrait gallery, a section of The Barrow she'd passed on her way to dinner.

Sconces threw shadowy light against the walls as she made her way forward, pausing every few steps to peer at Granby's ancestors.

He didn't resemble any of them.

The severe looking gentleman with an earring dangling from one ear and a starched ruff around his neck had a full head of red hair. Next was an elderly woman sitting in a chair, an embroidery hoop dangling from her fingers, looking miserable. Two more paces and Romy stood before a large portrait of an ebony-haired woman in a field of wildflowers. The artist had been very good. Romy could even see a small bee sitting on a forget-me-not in the foreground of the painting. A pebble-strewn beach fell away to a bubbling stream.

Standing before her with a daisy held in one hand was a dark-haired toddler.

Granby.

Romy recognized the area immediately, though there was no footbridge behind the woman. It was the stream where Granby had first kissed her.

"My mother, Emelia."

The deep rasp came from further down the corridor.

Startled, Romy stumbled backward, nearly falling on one of the benches lining the opposite wall.

A massive shadow caused the sconces to flicker before the darkness morphed into a tall, muscular form. Her heart fluttered softly in response to his appearance. Why wasn't he in the ballroom, spinning Beatrice around or announcing her as his future duchess?

Instead, he was here. With her.

"Your Grace."

"I didn't mean to startle you." Granby's voice was low and husky, curling around her waist like a wisp of smoke.

"My apologies, Your Grace, for disturbing you. I took some air in the garden and then—"

"Stay, lovely Andromeda." The words shivered against her skin, holding Romy firmly in place. Granby had discarded bits of his formal wear. The cravat was gone from his neck, the buttons at the top of his shirt undone, exposing the hollow of his throat.

Romy found it difficult to look away from the small triangle of skin. Dark hair sprouted from the spot, which made her consider what the rest of Granby looked like without his shirt.

Warmth shivered across her stomach, pausing to caress her thighs.

The errant bit of ebony hair, the piece that was far too long, fell into its usual place over his left eye, but he made no move to push it away. Light bathed his savagely cut features, creating delicious hollows around his cheeks and jaw. The dark eyes shone with sadness, all signs of his earlier playfulness gone as he brought the glass of amber liquid he carried to his lips.

He resembled nothing so much as a dark, wounded angel, drinking scotch and haunting the dim corners of The Barrow.

"She ran away with her lover." A wealth of pain tinged the words as he looked at the painting. "Leaving me to be raised by him." Granby waved his glass at the portrait of a man with a head of honey-colored curls and blue eyes. He would be considered handsome if not for the cruel sneer decorating his lips. "This *prick* is my father. Horace Warburton, Duke of Granby."

The vulgarity didn't shock Romy; she'd heard far worse from her brothers. It was the vehemence coloring Granby's words. She'd been under the assumption Granby esteemed his late father. She hesitated. "I thought you bore your father a great deal of affection."

Granby snorted in disbelief. "He wouldn't have liked you at all. Much too forthright for his taste."

"Yes. I'm inappropriate. I believe you've told me at least a half-dozen times."

He took a sip of his drink, pointing to the portrait of Emelia. "She ran off. Caused a terrible scandal. She couldn't even find an officer to run off with, just a soldier. Kinkaid is his name. Or was. I believe he died." His massive shoulders rolled. "I never saw her again. Nor have I wished to."

There was a great deal of sadness in the painting of Emelia and Granby. The artist had perfectly captured his subject's melancholy. "I'm sure it wasn't easy to leave, Your Grace."

"How the bloody hell would you know? Shrub."

Romy ignored the immediate flare of her temper at his dismissive tone because he wasn't really angry at her. He was angry at Emelia. She knew the law as well as anyone. Granby was his father's heir. His mother would never have been able to leave the estate with him to be raised by her and her lover. Surely, Granby realized that.

"Is your mother still alive?"

His mouth thinned into a tight line. "Yes."

She studied the portrait of Horace, noting the maliciousness hovering about his patrician features. There was little of Horace in Granby, at least physically. Granby more closely resembled his mother. But Horace had the same air of cold detachment about his shoulders, the ice lurking in his gaze identical to Granby's. Now, seeing the previous Duke of Granby, Romy couldn't imagine that being raised by such a man had been remotely pleasant.

One only has to look at Granby's face to see the truth.

"You find *me* exacting? Intolerant? Arrogant? Superior? Rigid in my beliefs? You, Andromeda, are fortunate not to have made the acquaintance of Horace. Poor Estwood did. Took him years to forgive me." There was a glint of amusement in Granby's words.

"You brought Estwood here to anger your father."

"A brief rebellion." He took a swallow of the scotch. "I had many."

Granby's free hand was very near hers, the long fingers pressed against his thigh. She closed her eyes for a moment and then gently laid her hand atop his.

His big body grew taut, likely enraged she would dare show him any hint of sympathy. Romy expected him to shake her off and dismiss her, demanding she leave him in peace.

Instead, he turned his hand so her fingers could slide between his.

"Did you know I have a brother?" A thick, horrible sound came from his chest as if admitting such a thing caused him great pain.

A brother had never been mentioned. Not by anyone. Not even Cousin Winnie. She guessed at Granby's secret, the irony not lost on her. "I wonder he's not attending the house party."

"He's not welcome." He glared at the portrait of his mother.

Ah. Granby's brother was a bastard, as her brother Leo was. He had to be.

"Do not ask me." His voice had gone icy and clipped. "Or

make judgements about that which you don't understand. Shrub."

"Don't call me that in such a disdainful way." She tried to pull her hand from his, and Granby's fingers tightened.

"I've tried my best to frighten you away." His tone softened, almost pleading. "You've no idea what you've done, Andromeda."

"To you?"

"To both of us. If you had any *inkling* of the liberties I wished to take with you, *Romy*, you might never have wandered down this particular hall tonight. But now it is far too late. And I'm done speaking of my horrible father. And her." He shot another glance at his mother's portrait before looking down at Romy.

The light glanced off his cheekbones, giving Granby a slightly predatory look, his eyes such a deep brown she couldn't make out the pupils. He raised her hand to his mouth, brushing his lips over her knuckles before placing a kiss on her palm. Releasing her hand, Granby raised one long forefinger to trace her bottom lip.

The pleasure of his touch nearly stole the breath from her lungs.

"I plan to take a variety of liberties with you, Lady Andromeda Barrington." The finger moved to trail along her jawline then down her neck, his hand large and warm. Cupping one breast, Granby gently rubbed her nipple through the fabric of her gown until it peaked.

"And if I object?" She wouldn't resist his advances, even knowing how incredibly unwise it would be. He'd made her no promises. Still found her unsuitable. But her entire body burned as if a fire were licking at her skin.

"I bought a fucking painting because it reminded me of your eyes," he said. "I never told you. It hangs in my study. I look at it every day and think of you." His finger drew a lazy pattern over the exposed skin of her shoulder, running over the edge of her bodice before dipping below the neck of her gown. "Every damned day."

"You are to marry Beatrice," she whispered, biting her lip as the tip of his finger slid across her bare skin.

"Does that matter to you, Romy?" His head dipped to nuzzle her neck, his breath fanning across her skin.

"Marginally."

Granby made a sound of amusement before nipping at the delicate skin of her neck. "What do you know of intimacies, Romy?"

Her nickname sounded like an endearment when it fell from his lips. She sensed Granby's restraint was cracking. Peeling away to reveal the man he truly was beneath the ice he'd blanketed himself in for protection, probably from the very man who'd reared him in such strict fashion.

What would it be like if Granby let go? If all his restraint fled?

Wonderfully terrifying.

She wanted all of it. All of *him*. It might very well end in her ruination this evening.

"I know enough of intimacies."

"Because you've experienced them?" His finger paused against her skin before he placed a kiss just below her ear. There was a possessive note in his question, even a hint of jealously.

"No, but my brother does own a gambling hell."

His teeth nipped her skin. "Ah, yes." He licked the spot he'd bitten, scorching her with the heat of his tongue. "But you know what happens there? At Elysium? The intimacies which take place?" The rough sound of his words threaded her body with pleasure.

"Yes. I mean, no. I've not been to Elysium when patrons are present."

A half-truth. She and Theo had snuck in once, telling Peckam at the door they had a matter of urgency to discuss with Tony. He'd left them in Leo's office to await her brother, but she and Theo had explored much of the second floor before Tony caught them.

A low growl came from Granby as he placed a large palm possessively on her stomach, gently nudging her until Romy's back hit the wall. She was trapped, encapsulated in heated muscle and sinew. His fingers stretched across her stomach, sending flutters down between her thighs.

"You're thinking of yesterday aren't you? In the grass?" The big hand flexed.

"Yes." Her voice trembled.

"Were I to find you at Elysium, I would take you into one of the private rooms." He breathed against her neck. "You know what happens there, don't you?"

"I do." Romy knew the basics of lovemaking. Her mother had seen to that. But after touching the decadent fabrics covering the beds in the private rooms of Elysium and seeing the various items in the room, Romy knew her mother had only divulged some of what the act entailed.

"Mmm." His tongue traced the outline of one ear.

Romy tried to take a deep breath and found she couldn't. And it wasn't because Daisy had laced her corset too tight. After visiting Elysium, her natural creativity had taken hold, and Romy had found herself picturing all sorts of things. Things she now envisioned Granby doing to her.

Granby's hand, still holding the glass of scotch stretched above her head while the other wrapped around her waist, captured her against a firm wall of muscle. "A host of depravities are to be found at Elysium." His gaze scorched her. "You should slap me for touching you as I am at the moment."

"Would you find it easier if I did?" She placed a hand on

his chest, right over his heart, positive that he must possess one. Even if he wasn't aware of it.

"Will you kiss me, Andromeda?" There was a flash of vulnerability on his face as he asked.

Romy didn't answer; instead, she slid her hands up the sculpted lines of his torso, feeling his muscles twitch beneath her fingertips and the heavy beating of his heart. She took her time, traveling over his chest before coming to his open collar; she stood on tiptoe and pressed her lips to the hollow of his throat.

A satisfied rumble came from him. "More."

The dark hair lining his jaw chafed her palms as Romy cupped his face, her thumbs smoothing over the slash of his cheekbones.

Granby's eyes fluttered shut, lashes falling across his cheeks like soot.

"You have a beautiful mouth," she said in a bold whisper. "David."

"Christ, you've no idea what you're saying. What you'll do to me."

"I'm not the one who has been drinking scotch," she gently reminded him.

"Do you think it is the scotch which asks for a kiss?" His lashes moved, but he didn't open his eyes. "Rational thoughts desert me when you are near. I forget everything I am because I only wish to be that which Andromeda desires." A shaky breath pulled from him. "Am I what you desire? Do *you* wish me to marry Beatrice?"

Romy's fingers slid into the silk of his hair, knowing his question had little to do with Beatrice. She brushed her lips gently against his, marveling at how soft his mouth felt beneath hers. There was no reason to lie to him about the truth of her heart.

"No, I don't," she whispered against his mouth.

❧ 2 2 ❧

When David first saw Andromeda wandering about the gallery, butterflies floating about her ankles and in her hair, David had thought she was a hallucination, brought on by a combination of scotch and a healthy amount of lust.

He had come to a decision. The scotch helped put his emotions on equal footing with his mind for once. Or it at least blotted out the voice of Horace, screaming his outrage at David's choice. But David finally acknowledged there was more to life than duty.

There was Andromeda.

He grabbed one plump buttock in his hand as Andromeda pressed her lips to his, lifting her up so that she was notched firmly between his thighs. His cock throbbed painfully between his legs, urging David to lift her skirts and take her against the wall, right next to the portrait of Horace.

He knew she was unsuitable, for a multitude of reasons beginning with her bastard brother and ending with a low-born mother. But Andromeda was the only thing which filled the huge, gaping maw within him. She was the promise of happiness. He would never embrace her family or completely put aside his views, but David was willing to *overlook* a great deal to have her. It was the best compromise he was capable of.

She wrapped her arms around his neck, pulling his mouth more firmly against hers, making the most delicious sounds, like a kitten being stroked.

He dropped his scotch, uncaring when the glass fell to the floor. Pulling Andromeda more fully between his legs, he took control of her mouth, his lips sweeping over hers.

She pressed against the hard length of his cock, heavy and tight between his legs, moving her hips in a sinuous fashion.

"*Jesus,* Andromeda," he said, pausing only to clasp her more firmly to him.

"I wish to see the painting," she whispered. "The one that reminds you of me."

He pressed his forehead against hers, their breath mingling. "Are you certain?" David lowered her to the ground, trying not to groan as her body slid over his cock.

"I am." She shot him a defiant look, one he'd grown to recognize. "I want to see the painting. With you. Alone. I'm very sure."

Nodding, David took her hand and led her down the hallway, turning sharply before coming to the door of his study. His fingers paused on the knob of the door. "I wish to be perfectly and absolutely clear. I have *no* intention of marrying Beatrice." It was the closest he could come to some sort of declaration.

"Do you not?" she challenged, a tiny smirk fixed to her lips. "But she is so perfect for you."

"*You* are perfect for me." He flung open the door, gratified to see the fire still burning in the hearth, before throwing the lock.

Pulling her into his arms, David's mouth fell on hers, releasing a lifetime of restraint.

❧

GRANBY'S HANDS RAN UP AND DOWN, LINGERING OVER THE hollows of her body, savagely kissing her, demanding she yield to him. Which was a wasted effort on his part. She would surrender all of herself to him.

A fire crackled in the hearth, throwing patches of light over them both as he drew her to a chair. "Sit." He pressed her down.

She did so with reluctance, her fingers plucking at his shirt. "I don't wish to discuss things further."

One side of his mouth lifted. "Look at the wall. You've a clear view of the painting."

Romy lifted her gaze. The painting was a seascape, drawn from a window the artist was looking through. The sun was sinking below the waves, casting twilight upon the water which the artist depicted in swirls of blues. "It's beautiful."

"The Mediterranean. Your eyes are the same color." He kneeled before her and began to slowly drag her skirts up over her legs.

Romy's petticoats rasped deliciously over her silk-clad legs, sensuously teasing the ache between her thighs. She suspected she knew what Granby meant to do to her. He'd said as much yesterday. Anticipation and arousal rolled over her in waves; she had to press her knees together to stop the throbbing between them.

"What did you see at Elysium?" His teeth tugged at one stocking, while he pushed her legs apart.

"A great deal of feathers."

The vibration of his amusement filtered up beneath her skirts. "There are uses for such things. I vow to show you the ones I know of." He pushed her skirts all the way up, the layers of petticoats puffing out around her.

Romy tried to hold still, but her mind filled with images of feathers and plush material. And Granby.

"Hold your skirts."

Her fingers fumbled against the volume of her skirts, grasping at the silk and petticoats as he pushed her knees further apart. The cooler air of the room brushed between her thighs and across her crease.

Granby's fingers tangled in the dark curls at the apex of her thighs before he blew gently across her already moist flesh. "Beautiful." He grabbed her hips and jerked her forward to the edge of the chair.

Beautiful? She felt exposed. Self-conscious. And horribly aroused.

"I'm going to kiss you." Two tapered fingers slid across her slit, drawing back and forth, the light pressure causing Romy to jolt in the chair.

Granby pressed a kiss to the inside of her thigh. "You should watch me." His thumb drew across her flesh in a teasing fashion, caressing the tiny bit of flesh hidden within her folds.

"I—" She inhaled sharply at the low burn of pleasure.

"Watch me." He leaned over and slid his tongue over her, while pushing her knees further apart. His mouth covered her, teasing and coaxing at her flesh until a low whimper came from Romy's mouth. When he sunk a finger inside her, the whimper turned into a deep, sensual moan, and her hips writhed against the chair.

Granby's fingers thrust gently in and out of her, matching the motion of his tongue.

Oh, sweet Jesus.

Desire pooled between her thighs as she tilted her hips up, frustrated when the action caused him to retreat. He pulled away, nipping at the inside of her thigh, sending a jolt of sensation sweeping up over her breasts. Another finger joined the first two.

"I plan to stay in bed with you for days at a time, pleasuring every exquisite inch of you, Andromeda." He blew another stream of air across her swollen flesh. "The servants will be instructed to leave food at the door. I'll teach you the most interesting things. With my cock. My hands." He looked into her eyes as his tongue ran the length of her slit. "And my tongue, of course."

The most erotic images filled her mind. Of being naked with this man's mouth on her. The entire lower half of her body clenched at the exquisite feeling coiling tightly inside her. She chased her release, panting with frustration every time he paused.

"Do you know when we played bowls—"

Romy didn't care about the bloody game of bowls. "Yes, you cheated."

"Each time you bent to toss the bowl, I imagined lifting your skirts and just taking you on the green. Without a thought to anyone seeing us." He dragged his tongue along her folds.

A low, pained sound left her.

"You watched Lord and Lady Carstairs at the pond that day, didn't you?"

"No. I—"

"Liar." His thumb brushed softly against her engorged flesh. "Did you think of me, Romy? Taking you atop a boulder, out in the open?"

She nodded.

"It arouses you, doesn't it? When I speak to you that way? Tell you what I'd like to do?"

"Yes," she said, ashamed to admit such a thing. "I know it isn't normal. I know that—"

"Shush. Your pleasure is your own."

Her muscles fluttered, clutching as his fingers nestled inside her while his tongue bent to her swollen flesh once more. He drew out her pleasure slowly, deliberately. She would rush forward, nearly embracing the peak of something marvelous, then he would pause, whispering the most outlandish things to her using the foulest language Romy had ever heard.

Every word only increased the sensations ripping through her body.

Finally, he sucked the small, tortured bit of flesh completely into his mouth, his big hands grabbing beneath her so she couldn't move.

Romy came undone. The precipice she'd tried so desperately to attain shattered beneath her feet as she reached it. The skirts of her gown fell from her fingers, her hips jerking upward.

"David."

Her body arched off the seat of the chair as he licked and sucked, drawing out every ounce of pleasure from her body. His fingers thrust harder, as the bones of her body sharpened, the waves of her release cresting to spread across her skin.

When it was over, Romy's head fell back, soft and aching from his ministrations. She could feel the blood pumping through her veins as her heart struggled to regain its normal rhythm.

"That was bloody marvelous," she breathed.

He pressed his cheek against her leg, the hair on his chin chafing the inside of her thigh. *"Sei tutto per me."* The whisper glided across her skin.

Romy looked down at the dark head nestled between her legs and smiled, running her fingers through his hair. "I should have guessed you speak Italian. What does that mean?"

He lifted his head, pressing kisses through the silk of her gown across her stomach, her breasts, until he reached her mouth. "It isn't important."

Then he kissed her, hard.

Romy could taste herself on his lips, mixing with the scotch he'd had earlier. His fingers were still under her skirts, inside her, thrusting gently while his mouth urgently took hers before he withdrew.

They slid to the floor together, the warmth of the fire lingering against Romy's back as they lay side by side together. His tongue explored the inside of her mouth with feverish intensity. Devouring her. With no sign of his previous gentleness. His fingers glided over her shoulders and arms while his mouth made love to hers. The embers of her release flamed back to life again with the merest touch.

He pulled her to her feet, the brush of his eyes against her skin like the finest velvet. Without a word, Romy gave her back to him, agreeing silently to what was to come next, secure in the knowledge of Granby. He might never say the words she wished to hear, but she felt the force of them with every caress of his fingers.

Granby would not be here otherwise.

He undressed her slowly, carefully, his large fingers handling the hooks at the back of her gown with ease. When she tried to help, he only kissed her fingers and pushed them aside as each bit of her clothing fell away to be carefully placed on the sofa. Once she lay naked before him on the rug in front of the fire, he leaned over her, the thick ebony of his hair falling about his cheek and obscuring everything but his mouth.

"You're so beautiful. A painting by Botticelli." A taut nipple found its way into his mouth, to be sucked and stroked by the tip of his tongue. His mouth moved lower, the muscles of her stomach jumping.

Pausing to nip at her hipbone, he said, "You taste delicious, Andromeda." His tongue ran over her folds, still sensitive from his previous ministrations. "But I've other plans for you, little shrub." His breath ruffled the soft hair covering her mound before his fingers pressed into her again, stretching her gently.

Granby's fingers weren't small. She expected other parts of his anatomy were equally large. Biting back a twinge of fear she said, "I was a bloody tree nymph, Your Grace. Had you been more observant, you would have noticed."

"Am I paying enough attention now?"

Romy's breath hitched as his thumb brushed against her already engorged flesh.

Granby laughed softly.

She gave a blissful sigh. There was something so decadent about lying naked before the fire with a large, fully dressed male determined to pleasure her.

He pressed a kiss to her breast. "Wait." His fingers retreated, leaving her frustrated and trembling with her own desire.

When he came to his knees, so did she, though Romy still had to tilt her head to look up at him. Twisting about, he discarded his shoes, which frankly were the size of small boats, and faced Romy again. He hadn't had his coat on when she'd found him in the portrait gallery. Nor his cravat.

She tugged at the buttons of his waistcoat, easing the item of clothing off his shoulders, stretching up as she did so.

Granby kissed the line of her neck, purring softly into her skin. One of his hands palmed her breast.

Romy shivered, feeling the tautness of his larger body, the result of the restraint he held onto for her sake.

"I won't break, you know." Her hands started on the line of buttons on his shirt.

His response was a low growl. Abruptly, he pushed her

hands aside and stood, stripping off the remainder of his clothing in seconds.

Romy closed her eyes.

"It is a little late for modesty, don't you think?" He was kneeling once more before her, hair covering one eye. "Don't be frightened."

"I'm not." Her lashes fluttered open, taking in the naked man before her. Granby was a mass of corded sinew and carved muscle. The firelight played along his torso, giving shadow and depth to his masculine beauty. And he was beautiful, so much so, he took her breath away. Dark hair spread across his chest leading lower to his trim waist and—

So that's what they look like.

His manhood jutted proudly out from a thatch of dark hair between his thighs, pointing directly at Romy.

"Can I touch it?"

A vulgar curse fell from his lips. "Yes. *It* is a cock." He waited to see if she'd be shocked at his coarseness.

She wasn't. Romy had heard the word before. She really was terribly ill-bred for a duke's daughter.

He took her hand, wrapping her fingers around the thickness with a deep groan. The feel was like satin or velvet, smooth and warm. She squeezed, watching in fascination as his *cock* twitched. A tiny drop of moisture appeared at the tip. She bent down, meaning to taste it with her tongue, as he had done to her.

"Romy, what are you—"

She flicked her tongue against the tip, loving the sounds he made as she did so.

"Stop, Andromeda." Gently, he lifted her chin with his fingers. "While I appreciate the sentiment, we'll have plenty of time for such things later." His lips brushed hers before pressing her back.

"Because someone might discover us?" It must have been

divine intervention which had caused her to tell Cousin Winnie she was going to bed. The same could not be true of Granby. His absence would be noticed.

"The door is locked, and the servants' stairs are just down the hall. But even so, I'd prefer not to have a scandalous end to the house party."

They lay side by side again, the length of him positioned against her flesh, which was already aching for his. He cradled her head on one arm, pulling her closer, kissing her with infinite tenderness. Lifting her leg, he settled it over his thigh, positioning himself at her entrance. His thumb moved against her even as he eased his heavy thickness into her.

"Kiss me, Romy."

She did, his mouth swallowing her tiny mewls of pain as her body struggled to accommodate his, mixing with the pleasure of what his thumb was doing to her. With every stroke, she came closer to her release while he filled her, inch by inch. Opening her eyes, she could see the concentration on his face, the endless patience. She was very close to another climax, the exquisite tremors beginning to course down her limbs even as the pressure inside her increased. He rolled her on her back, grabbed one hip roughly and thrust deep inside her.

She cried out, trying to catch her breath, all pleasure forgotten. The pain was far worse than she'd expected. Her mother had likened it to nothing more than a pinch.

Romy thought it more like being ripped in half. Her entire body trembled, twisting involuntarily against Granby's invasion. She hadn't been prepared for it to hurt so much.

He stayed perfectly still, murmuring against her temple. "I'm sorry. Forgive me." Pulling back, he thrust forward again. "It will get better."

A tear trickled down her cheek and he kissed it away. "Wrap your legs around me." The tendons in his neck stood out, the tension in his body evident as he tried not to hurt her further. Another kiss was pressed to her lips.

"It's all right." She pressed her nose into his neck, loving the feel of the crisp hair of his chest dragging against her breasts. "I was only surprised."

He pulled back and thrust again until Romy was sure he would split her in two. He started to move, rocking into her, while his palms stayed on either side of her head.

Romy's body struggled to accommodate him, but with each stroke, the discomfort faded bit by bit into a dull ache. The fullness wasn't unpleasant, but nothing like the bliss she'd experienced before from Granby's mouth and fingers.

He sensed the way her body softened and relaxed beneath his. He started thrusting firmly inside of her, taking up a steady rhythm.

Romy tried to match his movements, clumsy at first, pushing up with her hips until a certain part of her body caught against his—

"Oh, yes," she whispered, her hands running over the muscles of his thighs and buttocks, pausing only when her fingers trailed along the side of an old scar. He drove into her harder, each time pushing her toward the peak they both sought.

Granby took her hands and pinned them above her head.

"Next time," he whispered, "I'll tie you to the bed using the cravat you dislike so much."

The words propelled Romy over the edge. She sobbed, writhing beneath his larger body as another climax shook her body. His mouth covered hers, swallowing the rest of her cries before his own body stiffened.

Warmth rushed up inside her. His face fell into the curve of her neck with a low, shaky groan. He lay still, his breathing ragged against her throat. Pressing a kiss to her ear, Granby withdrew carefully and rolled to the side, pulling her close to his chest.

Romy nestled to him, laying her cheek on the crisp hair of his chest, trying to hear his heart over the mad beating of her own.

23

"Are you well, Andromeda?"

"Yes." Romy snuggled against his warmth, fingers trailing over his chest. *Well* was such a banal word to describe how incredibly wonderful she felt just now. The current state of her mind and body defied description.

"Good." Lips brushed against her temple. "I wish," his voice grew thick, "I could take you to my rooms."

"Why? Do you get cold at night, Your Grace?" she said in a cheeky tone. Granby could do with a bit more teasing in his life. It might become her new focus rather than designing dresses.

He pulled her close, speaking so quietly she had to strain to hear him. "I would be forever cold without you, Andromeda. Denied the warmth of the sun for the remainder of my days."

It was a lovely sentiment. She decided not to tease him further.

Pressing a kiss to her temple, he said louder, "I will speak to your brother upon my return to London. I must first get these"—his frown deepened—"unwelcome visitors out of The Barrow."

Back to being cold and grumpy. Romy's fingernail traced the outline of his lower lip. "Should you not ask me first? If I wish to wed? Perhaps things were not performed to my satisfaction."

A smile hovered about his lips.

He was doing that more often. Smiling. Romy would like to think it was because of her.

"You were satisfied twice by my count," he said. "Besides, even if I hadn't satisfied you," he said, nuzzling the side of her neck, "which we both know is not the case, I've compromised you. Intentionally. I want to wed you. Despite the obvious drawbacks."

Her own happy grin froze on her lips, thinking she'd heard him incorrectly. "Drawbacks?" Romy pulled away though he tried to hold on to her. "You still find me unsuitable?"

Granby stayed silent, reaching for her again.

He did.

What was it about her? Would he prefer she behave more like Beatrice? Or was it because she possessed a bastard brother? "What drawbacks, David?"

His fingers circled her wrist to hold her still. "It isn't important. I am willing to overlook such things. I want *you,* and you want me."

"Not at the moment, I don't." She pushed away from him and came to her feet, grabbing her chemise and tossing it over her head. "How dare you throw Leo at me when you have your own spare branch on the tree."

Granby's face paled. He stood, angry now as well, jerking on his trousers. "Don't ever speak to me of that again. *Ever.* My family doesn't acknowledge such transgressions."

"What a horrible way to refer to a human being. And I

don't plan on speaking to you again after tonight, so speaking of your *bastard brother* shouldn't be a problem."

"Christ, you are so naïve."

"You bloody, pompous ass." She shivered, feeling cold all over. "I am the daughter of the Duke of Averell. Don't you dare pretend to be better than me."

Granby snorted, an arrogant sound of derision she wished to slap him for. "Yes, a duke *and* a lady's companion of dubious origin."

Romy took a step back. "A lady's companion is an honorable profession," she whispered, pained at his obvious scorn for her mother.

"How many dukes in London run a pleasure palace, Andromeda? Or have bastard brothers they welcome into their home? Your father's own exploits are legendary." He pinched the bridge of his nose and took a deep breath. "You cannot possibly be so obtuse."

She opened her mouth and shut it. Apparently, she was.

He tried to take her hand, and she stepped back, out of reach, and tried to put on the remainder of her clothes. A near impossible task without help. A sob lodged itself in her throat.

Granby spun her around like a porcelain doll, helping her dress with surprising efficiency. Taking a deep breath, he said in that calm, chilly tone she detested, "You are overwrought and not thinking clearly."

"You assume I am thrilled"—she turned back to him —"that you are willing to *lower* yourself to wed me? As if you are doing me a favor? What were you going to do, Your Grace? Not allow me to see my brother? Or perhaps ban me from seeing my mother? Was I to pretend they don't exist?"

A tremor passed through his fingers as he hooked up the back of her gown.

A small cry left her. Dear God. That was *exactly* what he'd meant to do. Her family was well respected. Highly thought of. Granby was wrong. He had to be. "Perhaps the portrait of Horace is, in fact, not a painting, but a mirror," she spat.

He tugged the fabric of her gown so hard, the fragile material nearly tore. "You don't know what you're saying," he snapped back. "You've no idea what you—"

"I am not overwrought. You are a miserable prig, and *this* was a mistake." She balled up her hose and placed them in the hidden pocket of her gown. Her hands shook as she grabbed her slippers. "Take your hands from me this instant, lest I taint you more than I already have."

"I am not the only one who shares such views. I am trying to protect you." His words glinted with ice. "And we *will* marry. You might even now be carrying my heir."

Romy slapped his hands away and strode to the door, her fingers stilling on the knob. Tears spilled from her eyes though she tried to stop them. *How could he?* Did he have any idea of how much he'd hurt her?

"My brother is not a drawback, Your Grace. Nor my mother. And I *adored* my father. And no matter how big a rake he was, Marcus Barrington was still twice the man you are."

The very tops of Granby's cheeks reddened. "You will listen to me—"

"No, actually. I won't. Take your stupid, outlandish tenets that you live by, and go marry Beatrice. Float about the *ton* with the rest of discerning society. I bid you good evening, Your Grace. I believe the ball is still going on. Enjoy yourself."

❦

ROMY FLED THE STUDY, HER HANDS SHAKING, AND MADE her way up the servant's stairs as quickly as she could, careful to keep to the shadows, terrified someone might see her in her state of disarray. While her gown was properly laced, her lips were swollen, and Granby's scent was all over her skin.

What have I done?

Ruined herself for a man she loved.

She stopped on the top stair as a painful sob tore through her; she pressed a hand to her chest, willing the agony to subside until she could reach the safety of her rooms. Romy *did* love Granby, despite him being an absolute ass in the worst way possible.

She strode down the hall in the direction of her room.

Granby meant to *acquire* her like one of his bloody frescoes, merely *overlooking* her imperfections because he desired her. But he would never accept her completely.

That wasn't love. She wasn't sure what to call it.

Romy had *almost* shared her deepest secret, the dress designs. Madame Dupree. What a foolish thing that would have been. Granby would never allow his duchess to be involved in trade, even discreetly.

Throwing open the door to her room, she slammed the heavy wood behind her. She was shaking so badly, her legs threatened to buckle.

He's ruined the most beautiful night of my life. And my heart.

"My lady?" Daisy came forward, a book in her hand. "It's so early. I didn't expect you until close to dawn." Her eyes grew wide as she took in Romy's appearance. "My lady," she said, eyes growing concerned. "Are you hurt?"

"I'm perfectly fine, Daisy. The ball was tedious. Boring. I'm weary of this house party and its guests. Will you have a bath drawn for me? I wish to wash the stench of the ball from me."

Daisy jerked her head. "Immediately, my lady." She came forward and took Romy's hand, giving it a tight squeeze.

"Please, get me out of this gown." At Daisy's widened eyes, she said, "Now. Immediately."

A few minutes later, Daisy left her standing with a robe draped around her shoulders, pretending not to notice the spot of blood staining the linen of her chemise, and went to order her bath.

Romy slumped into a chair. Viciously, she tore at the butterfly clips in her hair, tossing them about the room like pebbles. She stared at her beautiful gown, knowing she would never, under any circumstances, wear it again.

I thought he loved me.

Love? The late Duke of Granby had made absolutely sure his son was raised without such a pedestrian emotion, if the conversation in the portrait gallery was any indication. Instead, all Granby could think about was how unsuitable Romy was because her mother had once been a paid companion. Insinuating he wasn't the only one who looked down on her family. Or her father. A man who acknowledged his faults and strove to become a better man. Something Granby obviously didn't have a clue about.

Angrily, she wiped the tears from her cheeks.

Granby assumed ruining her would guarantee marriage.

He was wrong.

❧ 24 ❧

David woke with a start, his arm stretching across the bed, disappointed to realize it had only been a dream. Andromeda had been naked before him, her hair fanning out across the coverlet of his bed with butterflies floating around her head. The butterflies increased in number, swirling about their naked bodies as his mouth fell between her thighs.

As the remnants of the dream faded, a hollowness took hold, spreading out across his chest.

I have not lost her. She is only angry.

David dropped his head back on the pillow, ignoring the slight ache in his temples. The decision to wed Andromeda had flourished well before David had taken her virtue in his study, before he'd so much as poured a glass of scotch, else he would never have touched her.

But he had touched her. Claimed her. *To ensure she would marry me even after realizing how I would separate her from her family.*

There was far too much scandal and speculation in Andromeda's family for him to ever embrace the Barringtons.

Not to mention the bastard. He had assumed she knew how many in London viewed her family. Or at least *suspected*. Did she expect him to welcome Murphy to his dinner table? Before David realized it, Andromeda would be welcoming *his* bastard brother to visit.

He threw back the covers, placing his feet on the floor, oddly reluctant to call for his valet and make his way downstairs. Fear twisted in his gut, the worst he'd ever known.

She was only overwrought.

He told himself Andromeda's anger at him might well be for the best. A certain amount of detachment would be beneficial going forward. She would expect displays of affection. Tender words. Tokens. He'd no idea how to do any of those things. But he would ensure she was happy. Cared for. Content.

He thought of the words which had fallen from his lips last night.

Sei tutto per me.

You mean everything to me.

The ache in David's chest increased, lingering even as he rang for his valet. David caught a glimpse of himself in the mirror.

Perhaps the portrait of Horace is, in fact, not a painting, but a mirror.

David stared at his reflection. He felt slightly ill, and he didn't think it was due to the scotch he'd had the night before.

His valet rushed into the room, apologizing for taking an entire minute to answer David's summons. David searched for the man's name and couldn't recall it.

"I overslept." David raised a brow and gave the man a meaningful look.

"Palmer," the valet supplied, not daring to meet his eyes.

"I should like to make my way down, immediately.

Palmer." He would find Andromeda at breakfast and take her into the gardens. Kiss her until her mood cooled. Apologize for the clumsiness of his words. Once she was calm, she would see he was right.

The best laid plans often go awry.

"That was one of the least pleasant conversations I've ever been part of in recent memory." Aunt Pen stood at the window, not turning as she addressed David. "Carstairs and his wife are leaving."

"I wished them well on their journey as I came down for breakfast. Carstairs maintained a vacant look on his face while I addressed him. Possibly I should have reminded him who I was."

"That is unkind." A small chuckle left her. "Carstairs is lovely. It's his gossiping wife I don't care for. At least you won't be forced further into their company now that you don't mean to marry Beatrice."

"I do not," David stated with conviction. Beatrice as his duchess, sharing his bed, held not the slightest appeal now.

"Ah." Aunt Pen leaned closer to the window. "There go the Foxwoods. Finally. I thought you'd have to pry Lady Foxwood's fingers from the doorframe or force her into their coach, as reluctant as she was to release her hold on her hopes of Beatrice becoming a duchess. Foxwood was furious, Granby. He will not take this insult lightly."

"It was not intended as an insult. I never formally offered for Beatrice. Foxwood's expectations exceeded the reality of the situation."

Aunt Pen left her perch at the window to sit down on the sofa. "I realize it is still early, but I could do with a sherry."

"Of course." David stood and went to the sideboard.

"How much truth is there in Foxwood's accusation? That your affections had been stolen by the brazen Andromeda Barrington?" She accepted the sherry from him.

David poured himself a scotch, looking down at the butterfly clip grasped in his free hand. It must have fallen from her hair last night as they'd made love. He'd nearly destroyed it with one of his boots.

Like I have Andromeda.

David put the clip in his pocket, ignoring the flood of unease filling him. She hadn't been at breakfast. A note had been sent to her room inquiring after her health, but David had received no reply. He'd been about to leap up the stairs to her room and demand entrance when Aunt Pen had summoned him to the study, where David had been greeted by the furious glares of the Foxwoods.

"Some," he offered.

"I'm surprised. Beatrice was such a logical choice." Aunt Pen sipped at her sherry, a speculative look gleaming in her eyes. "Though I never cared for her. Your decision to marry Beatrice was motivated only by the knowledge that Horace would have approved."

David didn't want to speak of Horace. "I suppose Foxwood won't be selling me the land I want now. I'll spend a fortune in rail going the long way around."

"Don't change the subject, Nephew." She wiggled her glass. "A bit more, if you please."

He went to the sideboard, grabbed the entire decanter of sherry, and placed it on the table before her. "Don't become a sot, Aunt Pen."

She shot him a look of confusion before a laugh bubbled out. "Granby, are you making a jest?" Her eyes twinkled at him, and David was struck by an unexpected rush of affection for her.

"I suppose I am." He sat in the chair across from her, the

same chair in which he'd pleasured Andromeda the evening before. The seascape hung before him, exerting its calming influence over David.

"There will be gossip, Granby. Are you prepared for that?"

David didn't answer. He wasn't sure of very much right now except his desire to have Andromeda. "I've compromised her," he said bluntly.

The glass of sherry hovered just before his aunt's lips. "Good Lord."

"Not Beatrice," he assured her. "Andromeda."

"I knew who you meant. Beatrice garnered little of your attention, but Andromeda . . ." She paused. "You rarely took your eyes from her the entire house party."

"Even if I had not compromised her, I would still wed her."

"How interesting," Aunt Pen said. "Have you discarded your narrow view of the world so quickly? What about good breeding? Bastards? Pleasure palaces?" A tiny smile lifted her lips. "Horace would be so displeased."

"Horace is dead."

"You've finally noticed."

David's hand gripped the glass. This conversation was taking far longer than necessary. He'd only wanted to inform Aunt Pen of his decision as a courtesy. "Once we are married, I'll ensure her family is kept at a distance. I've no intention of welcoming her bastard brother into my home."

"Or your own brother, for that matter," Aunt Pen added sharply.

"I don't have a brother." The bastard his mother bore her lover didn't count.

"How convenient, Your Grace," Aunt Pen continued, "to just hide all the things which make you uncomfortable instead of accepting them. I'm hoping you'll prove more tolerant with Andromeda."

There was a hint of mockery in his aunt's tone. "There are certain aspects of Andromeda I am willing to overlook, as difficult as it is."

"Indeed? How thrilled she must be to know that despite such flaws, you still wish to marry her. Do you suppose Andromeda will just toss her family away like spoiled pudding? I will be curious if she accepts you, Your Grace."

"As I said, I've compromised her. It is no longer her decision."

"Ah. You took the decision from her. *Intentionally*. Perhaps Horace isn't dead after all."

David stood. He needed to find Andromeda, and he wasn't in the mood for another cryptic conversation with his aunt. "I'm sure you have things to do, Aunt Pen." His voice was cool. "Seeing the remainder of our guests off." Dismissing her as politely as possible, David headed in the direction of the door.

"You are very arrogant, Nephew." Aunt Pen's words stopped him. "And you overestimate your own allure."

He'd no idea why Aunt Pen was intent on insulting him this morning. He'd thought she'd be happy at the prospect of Andromeda. Who he suspected was probably out walking before her trip back to London, waiting for him to find her. "How so?"

His aunt pursed her lips. "Andromeda and her sister left The Barrow at first light."

25

Romy looked across the coach at Theo. A book lay open on her lap, though she hadn't turned the page in at least a half hour. Her sister hadn't made any protest at being awakened so early and being shoved, with little ceremony, into the coach to return to London. Not even a mild complaint had left her at not being able to tell Blythe goodbye.

All of which was very odd.

"I apologize for taking our leave so early this morning."

"I'm sure you had your reasons for forcing me up at dawn and dragging me into the coach without so much as a biscuit or cup of tea. Sneaking out as if we were thieves. I hope, at the very least, you left a note for Cousin Winnie and one for Lady Molsin."

"I did." She'd written them each an apology for departing so early before crawling into her bed last night and collapsing into a puddle of tears.

"You left the ball last night." Theo stated the obvious.

"I was tired. A headache." More heartache, but she declined to say so.

"Another one? You seem plagued by them as of late. Perhaps you should see a physician when we return."

"Did Blythe like your dress?" A flush crawled up her sister's cheeks. "Goodness, Theo, don't tell me he stole a kiss?"

"I definitely did not kiss Blythe," she assured Romy. "Granby left the ballroom shortly after you did. He neglected to return as well."

"Did he?" Romy looked out the window. "He was drinking a great deal of scotch. Perhaps he was foxed."

"What happened, Romy? Between you and Granby?" She put her hand up when Romy opened her mouth. "Don't bother to deny it. I'm not stupid, and I am your sister. Besides, he's been making cow eyes at you since we arrived. I didn't need my spectacles to witness it."

Romy snorted. "Really, Theo? Cow eyes? Can you think of any gentleman less likely to moon over a lady than Granby?" It hurt to even say his name.

"Did he finally steal a kiss?" Theo peered at her. "Isn't that what he requested from you after he beat you in bowls? Blythe assumed so."

She bit her lip. "Blythe is mistaken." Granby hadn't stolen anything. She'd given him her kisses as well as her virtue. Even now, she didn't regret allowing him to make love to her. It was what had come after that pained her so.

Romy shifted in her seat, trying not to wince at the soreness between her legs. Daisy, loyal to the very roots of her hair, had put a mix of herbs into Romy's bath last night to ease the sting, promising the ache would fade in a day or two. Unless the gentleman was well endowed.

Bollocks.

Theo slapped the top of her book. "Are you in love with him?"

Romy remembered standing before the portrait of Emelia

and taking Granby's hand. The anger choking the low rumble of his voice when speaking of his parents. That was the moment. It was then Romy had realized she was truly in love with Granby. Not in the grass when they'd been discovered by Haven. Or when he'd stripped her bare and made love to her.

When she'd taken his hand and felt his fingers slide around hers, locking them together, Romy's love for him had opened her heart, expanding to hold his.

A tear rolled down her cheek. "We cannot be together. It is impossible."

"Why not?" Theo leaned across and placed a hand on Romy's knee.

"Because regardless of what Mama thinks, love does not overcome every obstacle." Romy's voice raised. "I have so much love for him, Theo." She pressed a hand against her chest. "But my love will *never* be enough." Romy raised her hand to wipe at the dampness on her face. She had to stop weeping over David Warburton, Duke of Granby. He didn't deserve her tears or anything else. "Sometimes your affections are for the wrong person."

"But the way he looks at you . . . I just thought—"

"Desire, Theo. Nothing more. Certainly not affection. Granby likes to bed beautiful women." Too late Romy realized what she'd said. "What I mean is—"

"Say no more." Theo moved from her seat, settling next to Romy. "We will not speak of him if you don't wish to." She made clucking sounds, her arm going around Romy to pull her close. "I never knew what you saw in him anyway. Great block of ice."

Romy leaned her head on her sister's shoulder, feeling Granby's hand laced with hers. Then, despite her best intentions, she burst into tears.

❦ 2 6 ❧

Romy's mother pointedly looked across the table at her, putting aside the letter she had been reading.

Romy drizzled a bit more honey on her toast and smiled back at her mother who was much improved of late. Since she and Theo had returned from the house party at The Barrow, Romy had spent a great deal of time reliving bits and pieces of her relationship with Granby. The more she examined their final discussion, the more Romy was sure she'd done the right thing in deciding not to see or speak to him again.

The first few nights, in her own bed, staring at the canopy above, she'd wept. He'd broken her heart. But Romy had been raised to be a woman who did *not* sob over a gentleman's disregard, though she was certain when her mother had conveyed such sage advice, she had likely been under the assumption the man in question had merely stolen a kiss.

Romy waited for regret over their night together, but it never came. She loved Granby and probably always would, but she hoped it would fade in time, allowing her to find happiness with someone else. She planned to confess everything except Granby's name to her adoring future husband. Any man she married would love her for who she was. Flaws and all.

"Is something wrong?" Olivia said quietly, her eyes on the letter Mama held.

Poor Olivia had been anxious of late, owing to the fact her maternal grandfather, Lord Daring, had suddenly taken an interest in her after ignoring her existence for most of her life.

"Don't worry, dear; the letter is not from Lord Daring." Her mother's eyes fixed on Romy. "He is not the source of my concern. Nor should he be yours."

Olivia took a deep sigh of relief.

"Is it from Leo?" Romy asked. "Does he say when he'll return home?"

"No. He is still wandering about New York. The letter is from Cousin Winnie. She and Rosalind have both caught a cold, which is why she has written."

"What a shame," Theo said. "Rosalind has a weak constitution. Has Torrington called on her?" Theo asked, mentioning the earl who Cousin Winnie hoped would marry Rosalind.

"She doesn't say. She had more important matters to relate." Her mother was still staring at Romy. "Is there something you wish to confess to me, Andromeda?"

Romy put down her toast, the honey sticking in her throat. "I can't imagine what you mean, Mama." There were several things she needed to speak to her mother about, Madame Dupree being foremost. Unless it had something to do with Granby and that bloody house party.

Her heart started to thump loudly in her ears.

"Apparently, the Duke of Granby did not offer for Lady Beatrice Howard as was expected at the house party you attended. Winnie was terribly surprised. As was everyone else. Including Lady Beatrice herself."

It wasn't a shock Cousin Winnie would write and tell her mother such a thing, especially if she couldn't visit in person. "I'm sure Theo and I mentioned that to you when we returned, Mama."

"Don't bring me into this," Theo whispered as she bent to pick up her napkin.

"Oh, you did mention it." Her mother pushed the paper she'd been reading earlier across the table toward Romy. "I just find it appalling you didn't tell me everything. Cousin Winnie's letter now makes everything abundantly clear. I went to her, you see, after overhearing a comment at the small soiree I attended given by Lady Cambourne."

Romy's fingers reached for the paper and just as quickly retreated.

"Very well. I shall read it to you," her mother intoned.

"Poor Lady B. Mistakenly assuming she'd be made a duchess. Note to all those impeccably bred young ladies of London. Be careful who arrives uninvited to a house party."

Olivia looked out the window, Theo down at her plate.

"I'm not sure, Mama, what this has to do with me," Romy said stubbornly.

"I'm not finished, Andromeda." Her mother picked up another paper to her right. "This item is quite well written."

"A certain young lady is following in the footsteps of her brother and engaging in trade," her mother recited. *"Her education must have been very fine indeed to have included dressmaking along with dancing and French."*

This was very bad.

"How curious." Romy pretended disinterest and drizzled more honey on her toast, uncaring when it began to pool on the plate.

"And finally, my favorite."

"Lady A. possesses talents unheard of for a young lady of her station. Dressmaking and ensnaring the affections of a duke are top among them."

Romy's toast fell to the plate, plopping into the middle of the honey.

"I am not sure which I should be more concerned about at the moment, Andromeda. The fact that you are in *trade* of some sort and failed to inform me or the scandal that you are the cause of Granby not offering for Lady Beatrice. Please help me, for I can't choose which is worse."

"Mama, I—"

Her mother held up a hand. "I'd heard things, most especially at Lady Cambourne's. I am not completely insulated here. I wrote to Cousin Winnie immediately, wondering why she hadn't called on me to tell me herself that my daughter was to become the latest scandal in London. She has told me everything."

"Cousin Winnie tends to exaggerate," Romy said.

"Cousin Winnie, bless her, noticed nothing out of the ordinary, not until you danced," she raised the letter up, "far too closely to the duke." She slapped the vellum down. "Granby was expected to announce to everyone he and Beatrice were to be engaged. Then you both disappeared from the ball."

Romy looked down at her plate, watching the honey drip over the edge onto the tablecloth. Pith, their butler, would be most upset.

"It was not until the following morning, after you and your sister fled the house party, which, by the way, did nothing but make you look guilty, that Winnie heard from Lady Foxwood that Beatrice and Granby would not wed as his affections had fallen elsewhere. She then proceeded to chastise your cousin for being a poor chaperone and me for allowing you to be in trade."

Romy wracked her brain, trying to figure out how Beatrice could possibly have found out. The only way would be if she saw Romy's sketches which, except for the day in the woods, had been in her room. A cold trickle of dread trailed down her spine.

Beatrice had been in her room at The Barrow.

"Why would Lady Foxwood say such a thing, Andromeda?" Her mother's voice raised an octave. "You told me upon your return home that you disliked the duke in every way."

"He is most unpleasant," Romy offered. Dear God. She hadn't been out of the house except to see Madame Dupree or to walk in the park; she'd been too afraid of bumping into Granby. This was far worse.

Her mother's eyes narrowed as a grim smile tightened her lips. "My dears," she glanced at Theo and Olivia, "I need to speak to Andromeda in private."

"Of course." Theo stood, shooting an apologetic look at Romy. "Let us take a turn about the gardens, Olivia."

"And pray catch Phaedra as I am certain she will burst through the doors at any moment. I don't wish us to be interrupted." Her mother looked at the two footmen. "Leave us. Shut the door behind you. Should you see His Grace wandering about, please ask him to come to the breakfast room."

Both men bowed, closing the doors quietly behind them.

"You are in trade." Her mother calmly stirred a lump of sugar into her tea. "I'm to assume your hobby has become more?"

"Not exactly." She wet her lips and proceeded to tell Mama how it had begun innocently enough. She'd gone to the modiste's as a way to pass the time and keep from dwelling too much on her father's illness. Assisting young ladies with their wardrobe choices had naturally happened. Madame Dupree noticed and asked to see Romy's designs. "Now we are partners in her shop. She plans to expand. Carry ready-made clothing for the working class." Romy looked down at her hands. "I'm very good at it."

"You are. But you are also the daughter of a duke."

"Yes. I'm expected to marry well and preside over tea." She looked up at her mother.

"Which brings us to the next point." Her mother's gaze pierced her. "Granby. I've raised all you girls with the firm belief a gentleman doesn't define you. Neither I nor Tony would force any of you to marry against your will if you didn't wish it, or to marry at all."

"I know." A lump formed in Romy's throat.

"But I also cannot allow your reputation to become so tattered that other young ladies are crossing the street to avoid you. Think what such a thing would do to your partnership with Madame Dupree, which isn't even legal, by the way. Tony will have to see to that."

"Mama—"

"I've never told you, but I was not a maiden when your father and I met. He was not my first lover."

Romy blushed at her mother's frankness. It was one thing for her mother to speak to her of what to expect from the marriage bed, quite another to imagine her mother doing such things, especially with a man other than Romy's father.

Or even *with* her father.

"I was fortunate that I never found myself with child. My already dire circumstances would have become much worse." She stood and came around the table to sit next to Romy. "And I didn't love him, that first man. Are you in love with Granby?"

A sob came from Romy's lips. "Yes. But we cannot be together."

"Clearly he doesn't want to marry Beatrice Howard. Lady Foxwood is busy shredding your reputation over the fact."

"No. He wants to marry me, but—"

The breakfast room doors burst open to reveal her brother Tony looking splendid in an indigo coat and fawn-colored riding breeches, splattered with bits of dirt. He'd been out riding, which usually put him in a wonderful mood.

"He ruined her," Tony snapped, jerking the gloves from his hands. "Bloody fu—"

"Anthony," her mother cautioned him. "No vulgarities. You've been spending too much time at Elysium, apparently, to have such things slip into your speech."

He turned to Romy, blue eyes so like her own, blazing with fury. "It is all over London. You're a scandal, Andromeda. *You.* I expected Theo to do something like this. She's always so self-contained. It's bound to unravel at some point."

Thinking of Blythe and her sister's behavior, she said, "Give her a bit more time."

"Definitely Phaedra," he spat, ignoring her. "But you? I'd have never thought you so reckless. To brashly meet him during the ball where he was to offer for Lady Beatrice Howard."

Romy angrily wiped at her cheek. "There is no need to yell at me, Tony. After all, you set the bar for scandal rather high when you ruined Maggie at a ball in this very house. Perhaps it is just another example of our *eccentric* behavior."

"Eccentric?" Her mother looked at her.

"Yes, Mama. That's what it's called in polite society. They think us eccentric, though I'm sure that is the kindest word that is used. I have a bastard half-brother of whom none of us are ashamed, and he runs a pleasure palace."

"Gambling hell," Tony groused.

"It doesn't matter what you call it, Tony. You are in trade, with your bastard brother, running a notorious establishment. But we all pretend it's perfectly normal, and it isn't. And your own reputation isn't exactly above reproach."

"We aren't speaking of me, but you."

"Scores of your former lovers populate every event we attend in London. Poor Maggie."

Her brother's handsome features pinked. "That is my past. She understands."

"No, she *accepts* you for your past. But is it any wonder Mama prefers Cherry Hill and hates society? Or maybe it is because she was a lady's companion before marrying Papa." She drew a deep breath. "It isn't normal. You are my family and I love you, but we aren't at all like other titled families. We pretend we are, but we aren't. Now that I'm out, and so is Theo—it has recently come to my attention that even a duke's daughter can be considered unsuitable."

Tony flopped down in a chair. "Bloody hell. I'd no idea."

"You wouldn't." Romy bit her lip, relieved he'd forgotten about her own shame for the moment. "You live in a bubble of your own magnificence. Beatrice detests me, as does her friend Rebecca, now Lady Carstairs. I may have threatened them both once when they were gossiping about you and Maggie, and neither has forgotten it. Lord and Lady Foxwood treated both Theo and me as if we were beneath them." She turned to her mother. "Is this why you kept us at Cherry Hill and we rarely came to London?"

All the color had leached from her mother's face. "Before we married, your father's reputation was worse than your brother's, as you are aware." Her mother looked as if she'd say more, but instead, she rose and picked up her teacup. "Andromeda, I'd like to speak to your brother. Why don't you go upstairs and rest? Maybe sketch me a new day dress?" A weak smile creased her lips. "We'll speak of this later once I've had time to digest the situation."

Romy nodded and moved to the doors. "I won't marry the Duke of Granby. I'm not a tainted bit of stew he must be forced to eat," she said with conviction.

"Of course not, dear." Her mother waved her off.

Amanda Barrington, Dowager Duchess of Averell watched her eldest daughter escape the breakfast room. It was terrible to see her child in such pain and not know the best way to help her. She suspected that if Andromeda had gone so far as to compromise herself, it was because she'd fallen in love. Andromeda wasn't rash, however. And from what Amanda knew of Granby, he was many things, but not dishonorable.

"Shall we retire to your study, Tony? I find myself in need of something stronger than tea." He stood and escorted her down the hall; en route, she waved away Pith, who came to ask about the evening's dinner menu. Amanda had to constantly remind him she was no longer the mistress of Averell House but her daughter-in-law, Maggie.

Once Tony shut the doors and poured them both a glass of brandy, though it wasn't even mid-morning, her stepson sat next to her on the sofa, taking her hand.

"What would you have me do?"

Amanda had to look away from him, for Tony looked so much like his father, her beloved Marcus, there were days it was difficult to face him. She missed her husband every second of every day. But she supposed that was what the rest of her life would be like until they were together again.

'Don't you dare grieve me, Amanda. Well, possibly a little bit.'

She shook away the memory of her husband and turned to the task at hand.

"Don't have him killed." She shot Tony a look. "And for God's sake, don't tell Leo. Though I miss him dreadfully, I'm grateful he isn't in London."

"He took advantage of her."

"I don't believe that is what happened. Andromeda has been raised to be strong, forthright, and not shy about sharing her opinions. There is no one less likely to be taken advantage of by a gentleman. When two people fall in love, such things happen, which is why I'm puzzled she has refused him."

Though her daughter's impassioned speech about the Barringtons had certainly given Amanda much to consider.

"Granby came to Elysium asking for me and left a note, requesting to meet with me in the park."

Amanda surveyed her stepson's muddy boots. "And you did. *He* told you he'd ruined her, didn't he?"

"Yes. There is speculation, of course, about her stealing his affections, but no one has come out and said he ruined her. Except for that bloody big block of ice."

Amanda's brows raised. "Block of ice?"

"He has all the warmth of a frozen pond and told me in no uncertain terms he means to marry her. Demanded he do so with all haste. But I'm not inclined to allow him to have her, especially since my sister just referred to herself as a tainted bit of stew."

"I see." Granby wanted Andromeda. What had occurred between them to cause such a rift? Knowing her daughter as she did, Amanda knew Andromeda would never have given away her virtue lightly. She loved him. It was painfully clear. "What do you know of Granby?"

"He's a cold bastard. Just like his father. Terrible scandal when his mother ran away with her lover. Known for his exacting nature and lack of humor. His only redeeming quality, from what I can tell, is his business acumen. He is often in the company of Mr. Estwood, a businessman of some reputation."

Her thoughts ran back again to Andromeda's impassioned speech earlier. How the Barringtons existed in a bubble of their own making, oblivious to those who might not esteem them, dukes or not. It made them sound incredibly arrogant. But there was more than a bit of truth to Romy's words. She and Marcus had known there would be challenges when they married, which is why they'd raised the girls at Cherry Hill, rarely visiting London. It had been a very long time, but she supposed some of the older members of society, those who knew she'd been a lady's companion, like Lady Dobson or Lord Daring, still lifted their noses at her.

Of course, Lady Dobson was now living in genteel poverty, having had to sell her house in town and leave society. Greedy old bitch. Amanda felt not an ounce of pity for her.

"Did Granby give you the impression he finds us . . . somehow *beneath* him?"

Tony's face hardened.

"Don't get angry, Tony. Winnie has told me the previous Duke of Granby was strident in his views of a person's origins. It would be nearly impossible for his son to not share such attitudes. And Leo *is* a bastard." She squeezed his fingers, thinking how much worse things would become if the knowledge that Amanda herself was the illegitimate daughter of the Earl of Wight leaked out. Being a former lady's companion was the least of her sins. But everyone who knew the truth was dead.

Except Lord Daring.

Amanda blinked, refusing to give any of her time or thought to her former employer and Olivia's grandfather. "Granby wants your sister but not the rest of us. I expect your sister objected. She is in love with him—"

"Rotten bastard. I'm not giving Andromeda to him."

"Tony," she said gently. "It is not your choice. Not really."

"I don't know if I can stomach having him as her husband. Leo will detest him. I won't force Romy to marry him unless . . ." His voice trailed off. "Unless she is with child. Even then, I would be more inclined to send her off to the country than marry him. I don't like Granby. Not a bit. Reminds me of a giant vulture. Whatever could she possibly see in him?"

"Love is rather unexpected, as you well know. But you could try to be kinder to Granby, given the forces that shaped him. After all, the two of you have much in common besides Andromeda."

Tony snorted. "Hardly. I can't see that we are anything alike."

"You both have bastard brothers," she said as Tony's eyes widened. "Though I think you like yours a bit more."

27

"Your Grace, the Duke of Granby is calling for Lady Andromeda."

Romy looked up from the game of chess she was playing with Tony, her shoulders instantly stiffening. The week since confessing to her mother and brother had been terrible. She'd been whispered about no matter where she went, even Madame Dupree's. When she and Theo had run into Beatrice and Lady Carstairs in the park the other day, both women had given them a cut direct. In full view of every carriage passing by.

Romy had wanted to scream to everyone on the path that Beatrice was welcome to Granby. She didn't want him.

"Ah. I wondered when he would darken my doorstep."

"You invited him?" Romy nearly tossed the rook she held in her hand at Tony's head. "Why would you do such a thing when I've told you how I feel? The talk will go away. It is already fading," she lied.

"I merely said he was welcome to have the opportunity to convince you of his suit. Nothing more. And the talk hasn't even begun to fade."

Pith cleared his throat. "What shall I do with him, Your Grace?"

Romy pursed her lips. She had a great many options for Pith as to how to dispose of the Duke of Granby. "You should tell him, Pith—"

"To await Lady Andromeda in the drawing room. Thank you, Pith." Once the butler left, he turned back to her. "You must, at the very least, receive him, Romy."

"Must I?"

Her brother stared at her intently. "I do not think you are as averse to Granby as you pretend to be, or you would not have allowed him to ruin you."

Romy sucked in her breath. It wasn't something she wished to discuss with Tony.

"At the very least, you can pretend to court for a time and then jilt him. I'm sure Foxwood would enjoy that. But in the meantime, *your* reputation suffers."

"It is all idle speculation. It wasn't as if anyone actually saw us together." She thought of the day at the stream, when she and Granby had run into Lord and Lady Carstairs. There wasn't a doubt in Romy's mind who was feeding the gossip mill.

"That is all it takes sometimes. I admit, Granby would not be my choice for you. I find him humorless with little to recommend him."

"Cold. The warmth of frost on a pond," Romy snipped back.

"I thought it a stream. But that was before the ball." He moved his bishop. "I ran into Carstairs the other day."

Bollocks. "Did Carstairs tell you what *he* was doing? He and Lady Carstairs were fishing. Naked, Tony." Her eyes widened as she tried to keep from blushing at the memory.

"Sounds delightful. Good for Carstairs. I'm glad to hear he's other hobbies besides hunting."

Romy glared at her brother and moved her queen into place. "Checkmate."

DAVID STALKED BACK AND FORTH ACROSS THE FINE RUG OF the Duke of Averell's drawing room. He'd been cooling his heels for the better part of an hour while he waited for Andromeda to appear. Averell had called on him earlier, making his position clear. If Granby wished to court Andromeda, she must agree. He would not force his sister to accept Granby. No matter what had occurred between them.

"And what of a child?" David had snapped at Averell.

"My position will remain the same," Andromeda's brother answered.

David should have guessed. The Barringtons liked producing bastards.

He continued to pace, growing more annoyed by the second. It had been an entire month since he'd seen her. When he'd found out she'd left The Barrow, David's first thought had been to have his coach readied immediately and go after her, but he was so bloody angry at her for not allowing him to explain. The hot rush of anger, so unlike his usual cool detachment, had unnerved him even further, so he'd decided he'd wait a day or two and allow Andromeda to come to her senses.

Later that evening, after enjoying the quiet of The Barrow now that his guests were gone, he'd gone to his study, taken one look at the painting, and told himself he was a bloody idiot. He would leave for London first thing in the morning and demand Andromeda listen to him.

But the next day, a series of torrential thunderstorms had drenched the countryside for the better part of a week, ruining the roads to London and trapping him at The Barrow.

By the time David had finally made it to London, the city was already rife with gossip about the house party. Aunt Pen, who'd traveled back with him, apprised him of the situation after calling on several of her friends.

David kept his temper in check, but just barely. The usual control he was known for deserted him when faced with the prospect of losing Andromeda. Aunt Pen, in a move to block the gossip stirred up by the Foxwoods, slyly admitted to several of her friends that her nephew had indeed found Lady Andromeda fetching. What man would not? But that was a far cry from anything else. Lord Foxwood, she implied, wanted his daughter to be a duchess far more than Beatrice herself wanted it.

Lady Carstairs, however, refused to be silenced. David would need to pay a visit to Lord Carstairs and impress upon him the importance of shutting up his bloody wife.

The click of the door disturbed his thoughts, forcing him to turn.

About time.

The sight of Andromeda standing before him struck David dumb. His gaze ran over every remembered curve of her body, searching for some sign of welcome in the gorgeous blue of her eyes. He was disappointed to find none.

Christ, I've missed her so much.

She dropped into an elegant, exaggerated curtsy, her skirts fanning out around her. "Your Grace."

David moved toward her, inhaling the soft scent of lavender, remembering the way she'd felt in his arms. The sense of completion he'd found only with her. He had sown his share of wild oats. Kept a mistress when he'd felt like it. But bedding a woman had always been no more than the release of physical need. Not so with this one woman whose virtue he'd taken on the floor of his study. Desire for Andromeda rushed through his veins, forcing his heart to thump painfully beneath his ribs.

He reached out to tuck a stray bit of hair behind her ear, a reflex borne of his overwhelming need to touch her.

Andromeda flinched, stepping away from his fingers.

Still angry.

"Why have you come, Your Grace?"

Frustration bloomed inside him. She was *compromised* and could be with child. Everyone was whispering about them, thanks to Foxwood and Lady Carstairs. Her reputation was in danger. And his aunt had drawn his attention to an item in one of the gossip columns implying Andromeda was in trade. As a modiste.

Even Andromeda would need to admit she couldn't go about designing dresses for the other ladies in the *ton*. He'd have to put a stop to her hobby immediately, though he applauded her ingenuity. She could design and create to her heart's content. But she couldn't actually *be* a modiste.

"You know why I am here, Andromeda. We must marry." Greedily, his eyes strayed to the gentle swell of her breasts and delicate line of her neck. He thought of tasting her again. Burying himself inside her. Lacing his fingers with hers and just speaking to her.

The last desire was the fiercest.

Andromeda raised a delicate brow at his declaration. "Must we?"

Did she not understand what it cost him to come to her? By the look on her face, the answer was no. And she didn't seem to care. Taking a deep breath, David measured his words carefully, not wishing to make the situation worse. "We parted on bad terms, Andromeda, and that was not my intent. I wish to apologize."

"Apologize? Do you even know what for, Your Grace? Or

are you only throwing words out at me in an effort to placate me? I'm fairly certain it's the latter."

Damn her. "I used an unfortunate choice of words in the study. I only meant to convey—"

"How grateful I should be that despite so many flaws in my lineage, you are willing to overlook my imperfections and marry me? Tell me, how many of my deficits did you overlook when you took my virtue on the floor of your study? I suppose I should be pleased my meager charms blocked such from your mind long enough for you to bed me."

The rejection shouldn't have stung so badly; he'd been subjected to years of disapproval from Horace. But having Andromeda tell him she didn't want him was far worse. Did she have any idea how he'd struggled with this? With her? He'd apologized. Why couldn't that be enough?

"We *will* marry."

She shook her head. "No. We will not."

"Excuse me?"

"I refuse your most generous offer, Your Grace. Pith will show you out."

"A poor choice of words was used," he hissed. "I misspoke." His jaw tightened, feeling Andromeda slip through his fingers like grains of sand.

"Did you know, Your Grace, I liken myself to one of the paintings or frescoes you are so proud of; beautiful and aesthetically pleasing until you notice a flaw in the canvas. Or a crack in the tile. Perhaps the colors aren't as glorious as they once were. You ignore it for as long as you can, but every time you view the painting, the imperfection begins to gnaw at you more. You have it reframed. Restored. But it doesn't matter because *all* you can see is the *flaw.*"

"Andromeda—"

"Someday," her voice grew thick with emotion, "you will grow tired of pretending you don't see the imperfections you find in me. Will you then ask the servants to take me down, cover me with a cloth, and relegate me to the attic?"

"You are not a fucking painting," he roared, his control finally snapping.

There wasn't so much as a pinking of her cheeks at his vulgarity. She stood her ground, glaring right back at him.

"Your language doesn't bother me, Your Grace. After all, my mother began life as a lady's companion. My bastard brother owns a pleasure palace. Clearly, I am low-bred since I didn't so much as protest when you took my virtue."

"Stop it." David tugged at his collar, unable to take a deep breath. "The words I spoke . . ." He reached inside his pocket where he'd carried the butterfly clip, smoothing his finger over one delicate wing. "They were not—"

"I think you should leave. There is nothing more to say." She turned, and he caught her arm.

"You love me," he stated with absolute conviction, watching as her lashes fluttered down to hide the anguish David had glimpsed in their depths. "Don't bother to deny it."

"I won't. But I fear, Your Grace," her voice trembled, "that I cannot and *will not* spend my life with a man to whom I am nothing more than a possession. A possession he owns despite his dislike of its *provenance*. In time, you will be inclined to discard me for being without blemish."

"Never." The very idea of bedding another woman repulsed him. "I want you." He reached for her so quickly, she had no time to move away. His mouth captured hers, all his anger, frustration, and longing for her pouring from his lips.

Andromeda flailed her arms at him, before a choked sob shook her body. She sagged against him, a small whimper sounding from her lips. He could feel every delicious curve of her body as he pulled her closer, running his hands up and down her spine. Their need for each other suffused the air of the drawing room.

Why couldn't this be enough for her?

Andromeda suddenly wrenched away from David, shaking her head in denial as her gaze on him grew sad. *Wounded.* "If you cannot accept *all* of me, Your Grace, my family, my bastard brother." She paused and drew a shaky breath. "My partnership with Madame Dupree—"

David struggled to regain his breathing, hearing the dismissal in her tone, and snarled, "A duchess *cannot* be a modiste. Or be in trade. Even if I should overlook everything else." Ice coated his words though he tried to stop it.

"Then you accept *none* of me." A tear escaped one eye and slid down her cheek. "I will not be your duchess. Marry Beatrice. She is in London. The Foxwoods will welcome your attentions. Her lineage is unblemished."

"Perhaps I should seek her out." He regretted the words the instant they left his mouth, knowing they were untrue.

Andromeda wobbled as if he'd slapped her, pain creasing her lovely features before she lifted her chin. Defiant to the last. Nodding sharply, she walked toward the door, proud as any queen.

"Good day, Your Grace."

❧ 28 ❧

"I thought I might find you here."

David looked up to see Aunt Pen waltzing into the drawing room. He wanted to study the seascape and drink scotch, not listen to her riddles. He'd had the seascape brought to London, discarding the painting which had formerly graced the wall. "I'd prefer to be alone."

"A pity." She came around and took in the chair across from him. "You look in dire need of companionship."

He picked up the decanter from the table and poured another glass of scotch. He'd been doing quite a bit of that since leaving The Barrow. Drinking scotch. Rambling about this house instead of meeting Blythe at their club. Haven had come to dine once or twice, but other than that, David had kept to himself. He hadn't even gone riding in the park.

Only Aunt Pen intruded on his self-induced solitude.

His aunt, upon their return to London, had declined to open her own London home, stating she would prefer to take up residence with David. He hadn't cared enough to tell her to leave.

"Out paying calls, Aunt Pen?"

"I had tea with the Duchess of Averell today. Lady Andromeda's sister-in-law. Lovely young woman. She's a pianist. Did you know the duke plays as well?"

David turned back to his study of the painting. "I believe that was part of the scandal, the fact that he compromised her *on* a piano. There's even a nasty rumor he had her in his rooms at Elysium before they wed. She's the product of a tin miner, if I'm not mistaken, and the duke is a notorious libertine." He shrugged. "At least before their marriage."

"He fell in love. Just as you have."

Is that what this horrible emptiness was? The sensation he was bleeding from wounds no one else could see? David's fingers curled around the glass he held. "I don't think I'm capable of that emotion, Aunt Pen." If this was love, he wanted no part of it.

"You think you aren't worthy of it, which is quite different."

"Are we having one of our mysterious conversations in which you speak but actually say little because I am supposed to come to my own conclusions?" He waved her away. "I'm not in the mood for this exercise. I'd rather look at my painting."

"She does love you."

"Not to belabor the point, Aunt Pen, but Andromeda would rather be compromised, unwed, her reputation in tatters, than marry me." He lifted his glass, staring at his aunt through a haze of scotch. What a tragedy he hadn't indulged sooner in the benefits of a glass or two on a regular basis. "Even though I was willing to overlook certain *aspects* which came with Andromeda—all the unwanted *baggage*."

"Is that why she left? Because you were stupid enough to voice those opinions to her?"

David clamped his lips firmly shut.

"You did." Aunt Pen's mouth popped open, aghast. "No

wonder she fled The Barrow before the sun had even risen. There is nothing quite like having been compromised by the man you love only to be told you don't meet his expectations. No one likes to be told they are flawed and disappointing," she said sharply.

The very last thing David wanted to do was sit in his own home and be chastised by Aunt Pen as if he were a lad. "I'm well aware I did not assess the situation correctly." His finger tugged at his collar. "You may leave."

Aunt Pen snorted, watching the movement of his fingers. "I'll do nothing of the kind. It is time we have a very frank discussion."

"Must we? As you can see, I'm busy." He held up his glass.

Aunt Pen untied the ribbons of her bonnet and tossed it on the sofa behind her. "I'm curious. What did your father tell you to explain my absence after your mother left? That I found the scandal so horrifying, I could not even look at my own nephew? That your mother abandoned you in a second, running off with her lover without care or regard for you?"

Horace had indeed said all those things and a great deal more. "I don't wish to discuss ancient history." Nor did he want to debate the motivations of his father. David was certain, with further examination, he would not like what he saw.

"Leave," he snapped at his aunt.

I've no idea who I am anymore.

"What a cruel, cold man Horace was. You know I *begged* my brother to allow you to come to me, or for me to stay at The Barrow after Emelia left? I *begged*, David. And I was refused. Repeatedly. When you went away to school, away from his influence, I wrote you. Sent you gifts."

David tried to swallow. "I wasn't aware." He'd never received even a note.

"When Horace became ill," she continued, "I took the opportunity to become part of your life again."

Aunt Pen had been at The Barrow when David had returned from Italy and had never really left, becoming a fixture in his life. What had it cost her, to help nurse the brother she despised?

Pain pressed against his heart. Aunt Pen had come because of him. Not Horace. And he'd treated her with the same cold contempt her brother had.

"Horace was in love with his own superiority. Lording over everyone the fact that he was a bloody duke. Treating his servants as if they were trained dogs, put on earth to cater to his whims; except, he knew the names of his dogs."

"What of it?" David croaked. He remembered clearly helping a maid carry a bucket of water to mop the floor shortly after his mother had fled The Barrow. The maid had been struggling, the bucket far too heavy for her. Horace had beaten David with a horsewhip, intentionally leaving scars which would serve as a reminder not to transgress in such a way again. "I don't know the names of every one of my servants." In fact, David had stopped looking at the people who served him all together.

"Horace liked to rebuke Emelia for the slightest infractions, mocking her low birth, deriding her manners, always when he had an audience. I'm sure it was worse in private. When she finally had the courage to leave him, no one was surprised. The scandal was enormous, even so. Made worse by the stories your father spread of her."

A weight settled over his chest. "Go away, Aunt Pen, or I will have"—he struggled to remember the name of his butler—"*someone* remove you."

"You don't even know the poor man's name." Her chin shook as if she struggled with something horrible. "You've become just like him. I thought when you went abroad—I'd hoped . . ." Her voice trailed off into another sniff.

The choking sensation increased around his neck.

"My mother broke his heart," David insisted stubbornly, knowing the words Horace had spoken to explain away his excessive drinking, always done in private, were false.

"My brother didn't have a heart. Let us talk about the elephant in the room, David."

Jesus. Could they just stop talking altogether? Every inch of his body was bruised and aching, emotions, so long buried, having broken free.

"Horace meant to remarry. When you escaped to Italy, free from him for the first time in your life, my brother planned to marry a girl barely out of the schoolroom. He meant to sire *another* heir. Surely you knew."

David tugged hard at his cravat, finally tearing at the silk and tossing it aside. He struggled for air, thinking of his father's shriveled body lying against the coverlet of his bed in The Barrow, his face twisted into dislike at the sight of David. Screaming for his physician.

Once he'd grown tired of ranting, Horace had reached for David's hand. It pained him, he'd told David, to know Emelia's blood flowed in David's veins. He'd been intentionally hard on David, cruel, some might say, but all out of affection.

"I suspected."

She tentatively laid her hand over his. "Can you not see what a monster he was?"

David forced his eyes back to the painting, struggling to contain the absolute horror of what he'd become. He'd seen the hatred in his father's eyes. Overheard him sending for his London solicitor. He had not been deaf to his father's last words.

No, I've only chosen to not listen.

Aunt Pen leaned forward and bravely placed a hand on his arm. "If you continue down your current path, David, you will lose Andromeda *forever*."

Forever. A lifetime without her.

His hand slid into his pocket, touching the butterfly clip.

"I don't think that is what you wish."

"No." The word stumbled out of his mouth, thick and heavy.

"Do not let Horace define who you are. You can choose to be different."

David took in a lungful of air. "What if I cannot?"

"It is not too late." Aunt Pen pulled a letter from her pocket and placed it on the table between them. "Start here. You must purge the bitterness from your heart, but it will not be easy. It would be much less complicated to simply retreat to The Barrow."

The handwriting was unfamiliar. The simple wax seal told David it was from no one of great import. He broke the wax and unfolded the paper.

My beloved son.

David slammed the vellum onto the table. "You cannot expect this of me." Bitterness soured his stomach.

"If you would be the man Andromeda would have, you must start here. Read it." She stood and walked to the door. "I'll be in the back parlor working on my correspondence, should you need me."

David stared at the letter, feeling betrayed by his aunt for forcing him to accept something he could not. The clarity with which he now viewed Horace was bad enough.

Ill breeding always shows in the end. You must stamp it out lest the stain spread.

As Horace had meant to stamp him out for being Emelia's son. Aunt Pen would never lie about such a thing. David had absolutely no doubt that had his father succeeded in marrying again and producing another heir, David would have awoken one night with a knife at his throat.

Hands shaking, David poured more scotch into his glass. Bits of conversations with his father, punishments meted out, rules repeated, all raced through his mind.

Carefully, he picked up his mother's letter.

I will begin this letter as I do all the others I've sent, by telling you I love you.

Hours later, David cast a bleary eye at the clock, wondering if Aunt Pen would demand he have dinner with her. He'd read the letter from his mother a half-dozen times while sipping scotch. It was obvious his aunt had been in touch with his mother because Emelia knew all about the house party and his intent to marry Beatrice.

It was a hard thing for him to accept his mother's love, having gone so long without it. David had been jealous of the unknown, faceless bastard son his mother had borne her lover, Kinkaid, from the moment Horace had informed him, somewhat *gleefully,* he now realized, of his brother's existence, when David was eleven. His brother had Emelia.

And David was left with Horace.

He reached into his pocket for the butterfly clip, the tips of his fingers caressing the wings, thinking how clever Andromeda was. He wanted her now, at this moment, with an ache that threatened to bring him to his knees. Not because he wished to bed her, although that would certainly improve his mood, but David only wanted her near.

Had he not been insulted by an annoying creature at a garden party, David might never have acknowledged the truth of his existence.

"I miss you, little shrub." He pulled the clip out. "So much."

Romy smoothed down the skirts of her ice-blue gown, smiling when her fingers stuck against the small pocket hidden within the folds of silk. The gown had been delivered by one of Madame Dupree's assistants only this morning. The waist, with its series of tiny pleats, required Daisy to lace Romy's corset a bit tighter than usual, but the look was worth it.

Lady Compton walked past, crimson skirts sweeping out around her.

A lovely design. Lady Compton had been assured the gown had been created completely by Madame Dupree. The modiste had gone to great lengths to ensure every one of her clients knew the whispered rumors of Lady Andromeda Barrington designing gowns were patently ridiculous. Yes, she admitted, Lady Andromeda had a flair for color and fashion, a talent which she was only too happy to share with those who frequented Madame Dupree's establishment. But to suggest a pampered duke's daughter was a modiste *and* Madame Dupree's partner? Ludicrous.

Thankfully, the talk had begun to die down, though Romy

was infuriated Lady Beatrice Howard had found out her secret. She was forced to avoid Madame Dupree's, a concession she'd made at the request of the modiste herself, though Romy still sent designs with fabric suggestions and other notes.

Yet another reason to dislike Lady Beatrice Howard. Romy didn't bother to acknowledge the other.

Carefully, Romy picked her way through the crowd. The skirts of her gown were much fuller than usual, belling out around her and giving Romy cause to avoid some of the younger gentlemen who didn't watch where they stepped. Lady Ralston's ball was a complete crush, as usual. Pomade, perfume, and shaving soap along with the acrid scent of too many bodies pressed together singed her nostrils as she struggled to make her way to her mother's side.

"She's no coward, I give her that much."

The words floated on the air just to the left of Romy.

"Walking about with her head held high. The Beautiful Barringtons." A snort. "One should call them the *Brazen* Barringtons. I wonder if she made the gown herself?"

Romy glanced out of the corner of her eye. She wasn't acquainted with either of the women, though she recognized one as a client of Madame Dupree's.

"I can hardly merit such talk. I doubt she can sew a hem." A sharp giggle. "Though perhaps her mother taught her. I'm sure the dowager duchess learned to thread a needle as a lady's companion."

Romy's fingers curled inside her gloves, but she pointedly ignored both women. Now that she was no longer encased in her bubble of ignorance, it was illuminating to hear how society viewed the Barringtons. No one would *dare* offend the Duke of Averell or her family outright, but now Romy heard the snideness beneath their courteous words and the thinly veiled insults hidden inside genteel conversation.

She blamed Granby for destroying her blissful ignorance.

While the talk about the Duke of Averell's sister secretly masquerading as a modiste was scoffed at, the gossip about Romy enticing Granby enough so he tossed aside Lady Beatrice Howard had not. Beatrice was painted with angelic and saintly brushstrokes while Romy was forced into the role of scheming enchantress. She was now the owner of a battered reputation.

"Ignore them. I do." Her sister-in-law, the Duchess of Averell, sidled up next to her, taking Romy's arm in hers. "They're merely jealous. All will be well, Sister."

The current situation became more intolerable to Romy each day. It wasn't just the gossip, though that was certainly unfortunate. Nor the damage done to her reputation. It wasn't even being banned from visiting Madame Dupree's.

It was Granby.

His massive shoulders and giant booted feet had not visited the Averell mansion again, which Romy told herself pleased her, even though it didn't. Nor had she seen him stomping about at the events she'd attended. The only reason she knew the Duke of Granby to still be in London was an item appearing in the gossip columns claiming that Granby had been seen calling on Beatrice.

A group of ladies clustered at the far wall, her mother and Cousin Winnie among them, waving their fans. Cousin Winnie refused to leave her mother's side, feeling it her duty to protect her cousin's widow from any who would cause her distress.

Romy's mother looked beautiful in her off-shoulder gown of gunmetal silk. And very angry.

Lord Torrington danced into her field of vision, a bored Rosalind held in his grasp, her skirts swirling about her ankles.

Rosalind caught sight of Romy and lowered her eyes,

likely still feeling guilty over directing Beatrice to Romy's room at The Barrow. She'd forgiven Rosalind, of course, because how could her cousin know Beatrice would simply waltz in without knocking? Or that Romy had left her sketches out?

"He's here, by the way."

"Who?" Romy said, knowing full well who Maggie referred to.

"Granby."

Romy scanned the ballroom, but for a man so large, Granby was surprisingly impossible to spot in the crush. She smoothed a non-existent wrinkle in her skirts, determined to stop the twist of excitement at seeing him. Though she'd refused him, the love in her heart had not quieted.

"Is my mother faring well this evening?" This was not the first outing Romy and her mother had attended as of late, simply the largest. Together, with Tony and Maggie at their sides as well as the indomitable Cousin Winnie, they'd tolerated the whispers at the theater and at a small soiree given by Lady Hatterfield.

But this was Lady Ralston's ball. *Everyone* was here.

"Amanda is fine, Romy. Your scandal has given her incentive to be out amongst society. Frankly, I'm more concerned for Cousin Winnie. I've never seen her so upset. And stop changing the subject. Granby is *here*."

"I heard you." Her stomach clenched again. "You needn't worry. I don't think he'll speak to me or any of us. I've heard he's courting Beatrice again, so I doubt Granby has any interest in me." There was a wistful sound to her voice which unsettled her.

"No, I mean he is *here*. Now. Bearing on us from the rear. Goodness, he's large."

Romy spun about, flustered, looking for a way to disappear. Turning to her brother, she took a step, thinking to find sanctuary behind his back.

Tony shook his head, stopping her. "Stand your ground," he mouthed.

"Lady Andromeda."

The low rumble vibrated down her shoulders, stirring up her desire for him. The longing for him was always present, just beneath her skin, flaring up at the most unlikely times. She'd spent weeks trying to force it from her system.

No, not weeks. Much longer than that. Since their first heated encounter at Lady Masterson's garden party. Romy had been drawn to Granby then, only she hadn't known the extent of their attraction for each other. Or the effect it would have on her heart.

He found her *lacking*. Imperfect.

But in Granby's defense, taking note of the dozens of eyes drifting in the direction of the small group of Barringtons, he wasn't the only one who felt that way.

We should be called the Blind Barringtons.

Granby loomed over her, darkly handsome in his impeccably tailored formal wear. Her eyes immediately went to the length of his coat before glancing up at him. The ebony waves of his hair had been brushed back, but a handful of impudent locks were inching ever closer to his left eye.

"Your Grace." Romy swept down into a perfect curtsy. At least she could do that much correctly. "My sister-in-law, the Duchess of Averell."

"Your Grace." Granby greeted Maggie politely, his eyes never leaving Romy's face.

The ballroom seemed to hold its collective breath, waiting to see what would occur. Fans fluttered in the sudden quiet as heads turned in their direction. Romy had the oddest sensation of being a goldfish swimming about in a tiny bowl with a mob of children pressing against the glass.

"I believe you promised me this dance, Lady Andromeda." He took her hand with a sharp, barely polite nod in the direction of her brother. Granby wouldn't deign to ask permission, it seemed.

Romy glared right up into his beautiful, arrogant face. "I fear you are mistaken, Your Grace."

Granby shot her a warning look before whisking her onto the dance floor, ignoring the twist of her hands as she sought to release her fingers from his grip.

"Don't cause a scene, little shrub." The corner of his mouth twitched.

"Are you smiling, Your Grace?" Her heart was struggling within the confines of her ribcage, her entire body tingling at his nearness. "Your mouth is making the most unusual contortions. Perhaps you are only having a fit of apoplexy. Pity. We'll have to leave the dance floor."

She tried to pull him in the other direction. A useless effort. It was like trying to move a mountain.

He swung her into his arms as the musicians began to play. "You look beautiful, Andromeda." The shock of hair fell further over his eye, making him look younger and more approachable. Unbearably attractive.

Romy cocked her head, studying him. He seemed different tonight. The coating of ice was missing, for one thing, besides the smile flitting about his lips.

Granby's mouth. The remembered feel of his lips and tongue against her flesh sent shivers across her skin. "How kind of you to say, Your Grace."

"Did you make the dress?"

The question caught her off guard, as did the way her nipples puckered inside her gown as he breathed against her ear.

"Don't trip, Andromeda. You'll tear that lovely gown. I'd prefer to do that. Tear the gown from you, that is."

Heat spiraled around her core, though she desperately tried to stop it. The attraction between them sparkled beneath Lady Ralston's multiple chandeliers, intoxicating and sensual, drawing her closer to him. She was certain everyone at Lady Ralston's ball noticed.

"What would you say, Your Grace, if I told you I stayed up until the wee hours, stitching away like a common seamstress? How horrified you'd be. Your senses might well not recover."

His gaze on her hardened into obsidian. "Lower your voice." He swung her about so forcefully, her slippers lifted off the floor. "Do you wish to draw more attention in our direction?"

"I'm used to being observed as a member of the tattered Barrington family. I'd no idea we were considered so outside the confines of society until you forced me into awareness. Now I see condemnation at every turn, no longer blind to it. You have my thanks."

"Stop," he whispered softly, pain and regret leaching into his words. "I did not come to argue."

She was so surprised at the unexpected emotion in his voice, Romy couldn't reply for a moment. "Then what did you come for, Your Grace?"

"You, of course."

A delicious tremor ran up her spine impelled by the feel of one large hand splayed across her lower back. His fingers sank into the silk of her gown, hiding them from view as he squeezed the top of her buttocks.

"I am wholly unsuitable, Your Grace, as you've pointed out to me numerous times," she sputtered, wishing with all her heart he'd not come here to torture her tonight. She had worked so hard to put her feelings for him aside.

"Are you certain of that, Andromeda?" His voice was low

and quiet, whispering against the curve of her cheek. His scent, warm male skin and pine, teased her nostrils.

No. Quite frankly, she wasn't sure of anything.

Granby said nothing more, and Romy stayed silent as well, not wanting to interrupt the sensation of being in his arms with more heated words. She closed her eyes, pretending everything was different between them, if only for the length of a dance.

The song ended much too soon. Romy's eyes fluttered open as Granby led her off the dance floor, his hand, large and warm, curled around hers protectively. He stopped just short of her brother, bowing solemnly to her. When he straightened, the barest brush of his fingers caressed her stomach.

The slight touch unnerved her, knowing what it was he asked. "There is nothing that need concern you, Your Grace." Her courses had come and gone, heralding that she was not with child. She'd been grateful, of course. And slightly bereft.

The intensity with which he observed her had Romy looking away.

"First, you are forever my concern, whether you feel it merited or not." He gently tugged on the silk of her gown. "I came to tell you I must leave London for a time, Andromeda. No more than a fortnight at most. There is a personal matter requiring my attention." His words faltered. "When I return, we need to talk."

"I've nothing more to say."

"Yes, but I *do*." Annoyance, the kind she was used to from him, flickered from the depths of his eyes. "And you will listen." He looked away for a moment as if struggling to remain calm. "Please."

Romy stared at him. He was *very* different tonight.

Granby nodded politely to her brother and Maggie once more before taking his leave of her, heading in the direction of the rooms set aside for cards. Romy had a difficult time looking away from the broad expanse of his back, remembering the feel of all that muscle beneath her palms as she had lain beneath him.

Turning away, she lifted her chin, daring anyone at this bloody ball to so much as shoot her a speculative glance.

But the only person in Lady Ralston's ballroom who watched her was Lady Beatrice Howard.

DAVID MADE HIS WAY TO THE ROOM SET ASIDE FOR CARDS, finding a spot next to Haven who sat alone. Not surprising. Haven, in addition to his propensity for dueling, was also an excellent card player, so much so he was occasionally accused of cheating by players with less skill. If his friend lived to a ripe old age, it would be a miracle.

There were a few murmurs and side glances as he sat down, none of which would be silenced once talk circulated that he'd danced with Andromeda.

Haven nodded in greeting.

Blythe, always offering advice no one asked for, had impressed on David two things necessary to make sure the gossip about him and Andromeda died down. If the fire had no fuel, it could not burn. First, silence Lady Carstairs. Immediately. She detested Andromeda and was responsible for keeping much of the speculation alive.

David had gone to see Carstairs the very same day, impressing on him the importance of a holiday in the country for him and his wife. Lord and Lady Carstairs had left the city yesterday.

The second was Lady Beatrice Howard. Her status as the most sought-after jewel in London had been damaged, causing Lord and Lady Foxwood embarrassment. David must put out the story that Beatrice had refused *him* during the house party, which she would embrace, and force her parents to do so as well. Even now, the gossip that David had been refused by Beatrice was making the rounds at Lady Ralston's ball, which accounted for the pitying looks he received.

"How was your discussion with the lovely Lady Andromeda Barrington?"

"Stubborn. Hostile. Dismissive. Exactly as I anticipated. She's terribly consistent and possesses a formidable temper."

"That doesn't bode well for your future." Haven shuffled the cards he held, though no one sat at the table save him and David.

David waved down a passing servant. "Scotch. A big bloody glass of it."

The servant looked in Haven's direction. "My lord?"

"Scotch as well." He turned back to David. "I see you're back to enjoying spirits again."

David merely grunted in response.

"I admire that about Andromeda. Her absolute lack of fear where you are concerned is her best feature. She's not impressed with you at all." Haven snorted. "Christ, Gran. I can't believe you meant to marry her and then cut her off from her family."

"You gave me the bloody idea."

"Fair enough. But I didn't think you'd take me seriously. Or be stupid enough to mention your intentions to her."

Haven could benefit from a sharp jab to his nose. It had already been broken once. Breaking it again wouldn't matter. "I *didn't* tell her. She guessed." He peered over Haven's shoulder, painfully aware of the looks and whispers being sent his way. "Take great care, Haven, that you do not admire what belongs to me *too* much in my absence."

"She's not a cloak or a horse you've purchased, Gran. I'm not sure Andromeda would appreciate your implied ownership of her person."

"I'm well aware. But my advice to you still stands." David might be gradually throwing off Horace, but there were some aspects of his personality that would never change. Possessiveness being one of them.

If he must accept *all* of Andromeda, and David meant to, then she must accept all of him.

"I will ensure neither Estwood nor any other gentleman oversteps his bounds," Haven said. "How long will you be gone? Is it estate business?"

David's fingers drummed on the glass in his hand. He'd been deliberately vague about his reasons and his destination with both Blythe and Haven. Only Estwood knew.

"A personal matter," he said to Haven.

He could have sent Andromeda a note that he was leaving town. Or dared to call on her. But he had an inkling she would have refused to receive him. And David had wanted to see her, with a need that bordered on desperation.

She was the only reason he'd come to Lady Ralston's. Over the last few weeks, without Andromeda, David had realized how much her presence in his life had altered him. He hungered for only a moment of her. To smell the lavender on her skin. To have her insult him, which David quickly realized was more flirtation than actual offense. He wanted to talk to her about his mother.

And Horace.

Even now, as Haven droned on about the poor playing of Lord Benedict who had approached their table for a game, David heard nothing but the sound of her skirts wrapping about his ankles as they danced. The weeks since she'd practically had him thrown out of her home had been nothing short of agonizing.

He wouldn't survive a lifetime without her.

❧ 30 ❧

David's coach, a sleek black conveyance that was exceedingly well-sprung, rolled to a stop before a small, tidy cottage two days' ride from London. The cottage sat isolated at the edge of a glen outside a tiny village David wasn't even sure merited a spot on a map. It was as good a place as any to hide from a vindictive duke, especially one known for his cruelty, who might very well kill you if you were found.

David pushed aside the thought of Horace.

But he was unable to push away the distaste rising up inside him. He couldn't help it. Most of Horace was gone, but not all of him.

He sucked in his breath. The letter Aunt Pen had given him to read from Emelia Warburton, now Kinkaid, had been one of many. Knowing Horace wouldn't have allowed her to correspond with David and not wishing to give away her location, Emelia had sent the letters to Aunt Pen instead. Dozens of them, even after Aunt Pen had been banned from visiting The Barrow.

Even after reading his mother's words, knowing what

she'd suffered during her marriage to his father, the resentment refused to abate. A hardened bitterness lay bundled up inside him so deep, David wondered if it could ever be dug out.

Aunt Pen had wanted to come, but David had refused. Her need to coddle him had become annoying.

The only person he wanted as he sat, waiting to face his past, was Andromeda.

His hand immediately went to his coat pocket where the butterfly clip rested, a talisman he carried everywhere. He would tell her everything when they were on speaking terms. Then he meant to keep Andromeda naked in his bed for several days. And marry her, of course. Though David wasn't sure which he'd do first.

Two chickens came from around the side of the cottage followed by a tall, lanky boy of about sixteen. Large feet kicked up the dust in a pair of boots that had seen much better days. The lad was whistling. It sounded like the same improper tune that had spilled from Andromeda's lips when he'd found her by the stream.

David took it as a sign.

The lad stopped abruptly, finally looking up and taking notice of the coach, mouth popping open before he dashed into the cottage.

A low hiss escaped him. The boy was obviously the *bastard*.

A familiar flash of disgust unraveled inside, but David successfully pushed it away. It was difficult to ignore the attitudes he'd been raised with, but it was not impossible. He *was* trying. Still, the jealousy David felt at the sight of his brother was not as easily dismissed. Renwick, that was the mongrel's name—

David inhaled sharply, the control he maintained on his emotions once more firmly in place.

An older woman appeared at the door of the cottage, dressed plainly, with an apron around her waist. She stared dumbly at the coach, waving away the comforting hand Renwick placed on her shoulder, though he continued to hover protectively behind her.

Ren. She refers to him in her letters as Ren.

His mother wiped her hands on the apron around her waist, hands visibly trembling, as she nervously regarded the vehicle sitting in her yard. There was no mistaking the crest on his coach. And Aunt Pen had told her Horace had died nearly five years ago.

David hadn't written her. His thoughts couldn't translate into coherent written words.

The footman flung open the coach door, bowing as David stepped out.

"Thank you, Miller."

If the footman, dressed in the finest Granby livery, was surprised David knew his name, he was too well-trained to show it.

"Jones," he said, addressing the driver, "we passed a tavern on the way. Why don't you, Miller, and—" He struggled for the other footman's name, a lad not much older than the by-blow—

Stop. This was why he'd come here first. He couldn't run the risk of insulting Andromeda's bastard brother over dinner one night. She would hate David for it.

"Beets," the young footman supplied.

"Yes." David nodded with a sigh. He had a footman named for a vegetable. This was why he'd never bothered to learn their names before. "It's been a dusty ride up from London. Why don't you take my trunks to the inn and have an ale?" He'd taken rooms at the village's only inn, not knowing how long his stay would be. Or if he'd be welcome.

Christ, he wasn't sure he wanted to be here. It felt as if his skin was being peeled off with a blunt paring knife.

"Yes, Your Grace."

The coach rolled away as David and his mother stared at each other across the dust and chickens, neither of them speaking.

The dark hair David had inherited from her was gone, replaced with a mass of silver curls pulled back at the base of her neck. Emelia was still a striking woman. Beautiful, even, despite the hard life she'd led since leaving The Barrow. She and Kinkaid had this small farm and little else. In her letters to him, Emelia had expressed no regret over the life she'd chosen.

Except for leaving me.

Estwood had looked into Kinkaid's background for David, as well as the ownership of the cottage. Kinkaid was the son of a moderately prosperous farmer who'd fallen on hard times. He'd become a soldier when his father's farm was sold, but Estwood had been unable to find out how Kinkaid had met Emelia in the first place. They had struggled financially, especially when Emelia's family had disowned her over the scandal of leaving the Duke of Granby, but the pair had been otherwise happy. After fleeing to this charming backwater to hide, they had presented themselves as married, though they didn't wed officially until Horace died. Kinkaid followed Horace, barely two months later, so Emelia was a widow twice over, though he doubted she had cried over his father.

"Your Grace. I wasn't expecting you," she said from the doorway.

"My apologies for not informing you of my visit," he replied politely, though his fingers clenched tightly against his thighs to stop the rage. Disgust. Scorn. *Anguish.* The pain of the boy he'd once been screamed out in pain as the only person whom David had truly loved, had abandoned him.

Moisture gathered behind his eyes, and he looked away, ashamed. *Christ.* Andromeda had done this to him. She and Aunt Pen. They'd conspired together to unman him.

Weak. I always knew you were your mother's son. I'll have to make a proper duke of you.

He turned back to Emelia, watching as she dabbed her eyes with the corner of the apron tied around her waist. She looked about to burst into tears at the sight of him.

"Will you come in for tea, Your Grace?" She pushed at Ren who stood behind her. "I've a spice cake. Your favorite." Her hands fluttered to her throat. "I mean, you used—"

"A slice of cake would be most welcome." An ache started inside him, looking at the woman he hadn't seen since he was a child. She had remembered spice cake was his favorite.

Ren glared at him with warning as David followed Emelia into the cottage, stooping low beneath the doorway.

"If you so much as bring a tear to her eye, duke or not, I'll make you regret you ever came here."

David paused and took in his bastard brother, no more than a lad, whom he'd spent the vast majority of his life detesting. Scornful words about his brother's parentage begged to spew from behind his lips. He leaned over, gratified when Ren stepped back a pace, and answered.

"I already do."

31

Romy pulled a pin from the tiny cushion attached to her wrist, tacking it on the hem of the gown she worked on. The storeroom had once been used for fittings before Madame Dupree had enlarged her establishment, but Romy now used the area as her workspace. It was good to be back at the modiste's shop, surrounded by so many of the things she loved. Her sketches were strewn across a table in the middle of the room, while the remainder were tacked on the wall along with corresponding swatches of fabric.

The muted sounds of Madame and her assistants filtered through the walls, but Romy kept well out of sight. The talk about her plying a needle as modiste had ceased to circulate, and she'd returned to Madame Dupree's, albeit discreetly. She no longer roamed the front of the shop, offering her advice to young ladies. It was deemed too risky by both the modiste and Romy's brother.

After the Ralston ball, the gossip about her and Granby had slowed to a trickle. According to Theo, who heard it from Rosalind, Beatrice had finally confessed *she* had refused

Granby during the house party but had been too fearful to tell Lord and Lady Foxwood of her decision. She dismissed Romy as nothing more than an attempt on Granby's part to make her jealous.

Now, instead of gossip, Romy was the subject of sympathetic looks and unwanted pity.

While it wasn't flattering to be thought of as a consolation prize in Granby's pursuit of Beatrice, Romy dared not contradict any of the talk. Her reputation was battered enough for now. The entire affair left her with an oily feeling in her stomach, as if she'd eaten too much cream sauce. Granby had been adamant he would not marry Beatrice, but maybe not for the reasons Romy had originally assumed. She meant to ask Granby if he ever returned to London.

He'd told her he wished to talk to her. He'd be gone at most a fortnight, he'd said.

Not an entire month.

No one, not even Haven, who called on her with strange regularity, though she suspected he was really looking for Theo, or Estwood, who had taken her to view a collection of Egyptian mummies, had spoken to Granby.

It doesn't matter. He finds me too flawed for him. Unsuitable. He is an icy giant incapable of love.

Unfortunately, repeating those lines every time she thought of Granby, which was far too often, didn't make the *lack* of him any easier to bear. He'd broken her heart and stomped upon it, yet still, she longed for him, even knowing he couldn't return her feelings. Not really. Physical desire was certainly wonderful, as she'd recently found out, but it could not replace love.

I want him to love me for me. Drawbacks and all.

She breathed out, rubbing the patch of skin over her heart. Before Granby, Romy would have scoffed at the notion that she, a duke's daughter, was considered remotely unsuitable. But the Barrington Bubble, as she liked to refer to the protection her parents had encased her and her sisters in for so many years, had popped.

It was amazing the things one learned about the Barringtons if you only listened.

Ruffling the lace on the bodice of the gown she worked on, Romy took a bit of ribbon, trying it against the shoulder. She hadn't quite forgiven Granby for his view of her. It chafed against her heart. Was it worse to be unloved because she was unsuitable? Or preferable to be unloved because Granby wasn't capable of the emotion?

She leaned back against the table, indescribably sad, thoughts of him taking all the wind from her sails. The dress before her no longer held any interest. Nor did her sketches. What she really wanted to do was go home, sit on a chair before the fire in her room, and wallow in self-pity. Maybe cry. She'd done so last night, but it hadn't helped.

"I thought I might find you here, though I didn't expect you to be so distressed, especially when surrounded by mounds of fabric and fripperies. Did someone steal your pins? Destroy a bolt of tulle? I know, someone unraveled your ribbons." The words rumbled from directly behind her.

Romy turned, hiding her surprise and happiness at his appearance. He'd been gone for a *month*. Not that he owed her a note or any bloody sign he was still alive but—

"I'm out of feathers. The peacocks have been most uncooperative. I'm quite despondent."

Granby stooped a bit as he made his way through the doorway, his hat dangling from one hand. "I was hoping your melancholy was brought on by missing me."

Romy's skin prickled in the most delicious manner, warming as he drew near. "Perish the thought, Your Grace." Didn't Granby know she carried a piece of him in her soul? Stolen from him that night in the study?

His ebony hair looked a bit longer, curling around his ears and collar in a wild manner. The savage slash of cheekbone and nose were pinked as if he'd been out in the sun for hours without a proper hat. All that sun must have melted the icecaps he usually wore on his massive shoulders, for there was only a hint of chill when he spoke.

Most unusual.

Romy had to grab the edge of the table with her fingers to keep from throwing her arms around him. She'd missed him that much.

Granby came forward, cocking his head at the dressmaker's dummy along with the sketches strewn about the room. "You've been busy."

"You've been gone," she finally croaked.

"You noticed. But I did mention I'd be gone when last we spoke."

"For a week, possibly two," she said, cringing at the needy sound of her words. "How did you know I was here?"

"You *did* miss me." Warmth lay banked in the darkness of his eyes. "I've missed you too. And Madame Dupree let me know of your whereabouts."

She sniffed the air, catching leather and horses. "You're rather dusty," she said, noting the state of his coat and boots.

"I returned home only today and came straight here."

Romy gave him her back and stacked the remaining sketches strewn across the table. "Well, you can return home. There is no need for you be here unless it is to watch me do unsuitable things."

"What if I chose to do those unsuitable things with you?"

She squeaked at the touch of his tongue against the curve of her ear. "There are things I must say, Romy."

"My position has not changed, Your Grace. If you cannot accept all of me—" She took a shaky breath as the warmth of his chest pressed into her back.

281

"I can have none of you. Yes, I remember quite well."

"Then you must also recall I come with a variety of draw-backs, as you call them. Things which may offend your tender sensibilities. You've deemed me unacceptable."

Two big hands landed on either side of her, trapping Romy against the table. Blood pumped through her body, her heart beating wildly. A coil of arousal twisted low inside her with an insistent ache, begging for attention, a common occurrence with Granby in the vicinity. If so much as one wicked thing came from his beautiful mouth, Romy would be lost.

"Terribly unsuitable." Granby pressed against her, the hard length of him rubbing sinuously against her backside. "I've stayed away from you as long as I could. Time enough to allow your anger toward me to mellow." One of his hands disappeared as he nibbled at the back of her neck. "I was working on my own imperfections, as it happens."

"I see." She gasped at the feel of his hand running up the back of her legs, even as the other settled on her waist before sliding up the front of her dress. The dress she wore was one of her oldest. She'd been in a rush to get to Madame Dupree's this morning and had chosen the dress because it required no corset and only a petticoat or two.

"What are you doing?" Her voice raised an octave as Granby's finger slid between the crack of her buttocks before cupping her with his hand. His fingers tugged lightly at the soft hair of her mound, sliding back and forth.

"Examining *your* imperfections." A finger pressed into her heat, circling and teasing at her flesh. "All this wetness is for me. I knew I was missed."

Romy's hands trembled against the table. "You should leave. You may call on me later."

"And run the risk you will not receive me?"

Her forehead pressed against the table as she struggled to

retain some dignity, but all Romy could do was shamefully push her hips back against him. His fingers moved purposefully over her flesh as a small moan left her.

"I would." She gasped as his forefinger flicked gently against a sensitive spot. "Receive you."

"Can't take the chance. You seem averse to talking, or at the least, allowing *me* to speak." He pressed a kiss to the back of her neck. "I'm hopeful I can persuade you to listen." His teeth grazed her upper back, nipping at her skin through the worn calico she wore. "I think perhaps I will take all of you." He pulled Romy's hips up, exposing her more fully. "Every tiny"—his finger teased against the small, painfully engorged bit of flesh hiding within her folds—"bit of you, Romy."

Gasping for breath, she whimpered at the torture he inflicted, dizzy from the way her body molded to his and the pleasure scorching her veins.

"Madame—" She tried to retain some semblance of control. Granby's large body covered hers, his fingers caressing her flesh, pausing only to thrust one digit inside her before retreating again.

This was not how she'd expected her morning to proceed.

"Madame Dupree has been paid an enormous sum to ensure we are not disturbed. And by the way, she is no more French than I am." The cooler air of the room slid across her buttocks and the back of her legs as Granby lifted her skirts up to her waist. There was a rustle of clothing and then the hot thickness of him pressed into the back of her thigh.

One hand gently reached to the back of her scalp, turning her head so Granby could press a tender kiss on her lips before carefully forcing her head down, so she lay against the table.

"What I've figured out, Andromeda, while I was gone working on my *own* imperfections, is that I am not good at expressing myself with words." His fingers stroked and teased, sending a bolt of sensation down the lower half of her body.

"Please," she whispered against the table, nearly mindless with pleasure. Every caress of his fingers sent her closer to her release. She could feel it tightening inside of her.

"Are you listening, Romy?"

"Yes." She slapped at the table with an open palm. "Your Grace."

"I finally have your attention. Good. Now, we can blame Horace for forcing me to be the cold bastard I am, but the fact remains . . ." His fingers continued to press and retreat until she wanted to weep.

"I will take *all* of you, Andromeda Barrington."

"All of me?" She was panting, her flesh swollen and painful, her nipples so peaked they might scratch the old wood of the table beneath her.

"Yes. Haven't you been listening? Every luscious bit I find —" His voice grew raspy. "I cannot be without you, Andromeda." He thrust into her, pushing Romy across the table with a low groan. His hands took hold of her hips, lifting her so that her feet didn't touch the floor.

Romy clawed at the table as her body stretched to accommodate him. He withdrew, then surged forward again, eliciting a cry from her.

"Andromeda," he whispered into her hair before his lips trailed down her shoulder. He gently lifted her chin. "Look, naughty little tree nymph."

She had forgotten about the old, chipped mirror in the corner of the room. Madame Dupree had spoken of tossing it into the alley but never had. The mirror faced them, reflecting perfectly the act that was taking place on a table used previously only to cut fabric.

Granby loomed over her, a dark god bending over the nymph he'd captured. The mirror did not reveal his face, obscured as it was by the thick strands of ebony hair. One massive hand moved up and down her back before settling at the base of her neck, holding her in place while he continued to ravish her with each savage thrust of his body into hers.

Her eyes stayed on their reflection, feeling Granby claim her. *Seeing* him do it. The sight increased her pleasure, as he had known it would.

"I didn't mean to hurt you." Granby's voice was rough. "Doing so nearly tore the heart from my chest. Do you understand?"

"Yes," she panted, watching her reflection writhe against the table. Romy's body sharpened. Tightened. Her toes pointed inside her shoes.

Granby's fingers stopped. He stayed inside her but didn't move.

Damn him. Romy slapped her hands against the table again. "David," she begged.

"Do you accept my apology?" A low moan left him as he thrust gently. "Please, forgive me."

"Yes." She whimpered, twisting her hips about. "I forgive you."

"Good," he purred against her back before his fingers pinched gently, slamming into her, his free hand coming around to cover her mouth.

Romy screamed her release into the palm of his hand as Granby's cheek fell against her back, moaning out his own release. The table creaked beneath them, protesting violently over the way it was being used. Waves of sensation rolled over her, rippling across her skin until Romy lay limp across the scarred oak, gasping for breath.

With a soft groan, Granby withdrew from her. She watched his reflection as he took a handkerchief from his pocket, gently cleaning her and then himself before tugging down her skirts.

He nuzzled into her neck, turning her over to face him, kissing her with great tenderness. "I like the gown, by the way," he said nodding at the dressmaker's dummy.

"I won't give it up," she said, waiting to see frost gather about his lips at her statement. "All of this. Madame Dupree. I won't." But Granby only nodded and kissed the end of her nose. He stood, peering down at her from his great height, eyes roving over her still-trembling body and swollen lips.

"You are a magnificent little shrub. I'm keeping you. *All* of you." He leaned forward, drawing his fingers across her breasts and over her stomach before he straightened and strolled out the door. "Come for tea tomorrow. There's something I want to show you. You can pretend you are calling on my aunt."

She nodded, brain still fuzzy from the intensity of their reunion and the turn her morning had taken. "Yes."

32

"Please wait here, my lady. Lady Molsin will be down in a moment."

Granby's aunt had sent her a note only that morning asking Romy to call on her. At least the messenger said it was from Lady Molsin, but the very masculine, barely legible scrawl at the bottom, beneath his aunt's polite invitation, told her it was not.

You are not a painting.

Romy deliberately didn't tell anyone, not even Theo, where she was going. Her mother had assumed she'd gone to Madame Dupree's, as she so often did. She really shouldn't have arrived at Granby's home unescorted, but Lady Molsin was in residence, and the invitation *was* from her if anyone should inquire.

Romy admitted to herself she was nervous. Granby's mood yesterday had been tender and gentle, despite the roughness with which he had taken her against the table. A bloody marvelous experience she hoped would be repeated. Last night, sitting in her bath, she'd relived every moment, her hand straying between her legs, stroking gently, as Granby had done.

Daisy had interrupted with a stack of towels at a most inopportune moment.

As striking as the knowledge that Granby was more fiery passion than ice was knowing Romy's own nature was just as passionate. One word from him and her mind summoned up a host of erotic thoughts and images. He seemed pleased by that part of her. It was the other bits of her life she was concerned about.

Granby claimed to want all of her. Romy was here today to ascertain exactly what that meant to him.

She looked up as the door opened, and Granby strode into the room.

"Thank you, Helmsworth."

Romy didn't do a good job of hiding her shock. Granby knew the butler by name. *And* he had thanked him. She took in his appearance as he came closer. Deliciously rumpled as if he'd only tumbled out of bed.

The very thought of Granby, naked, between silken sheets, caused her thighs to squeeze together.

And he was smiling. *At her*.

"Good day, Lady Andromeda," he greeted her politely, his gaze landing on her mouth then brushing across her bodice.

"Your Grace, are you well?" she said, mostly to hide her own reaction to his presence. Her entire body hummed as he drew near. The cravat was tied properly. The length of his coat perfect. His waistcoat even possessed a splash of red. Warmth crept up her cheeks.

The knowing glance Granby gave her told Andromeda he knew full well the power he wielded over her.

"Of course," he groused back. "Why would you think me unwell?"

"I worry that you've hit your head," she said tartly, pleased when his lips tilted into a scowl. "The Granby I know doesn't smile so much as you."

"I am only happy." He leaned down and pressed a chaste kiss on her forehead. "Stop acting as if I'm addled or gone mad. Although, I find you to be a particular type of madness."

Hope flared up inside her. She knew Granby desired her physically, that had never been in doubt. The spark between them burned brighter than ever. But had he truly put aside his previous attitudes in regard to her family? It would break her heart to have Granby not accept Leo. Or be unkind to her mother.

Or not return the love she had for him.

But first, Romy meant to be honest. "I've come to realize, Your Grace, some of the deficits you see in the Barringtons may not be without merit. I see them now, our eccentricities." She held up her hand when he opened his mouth to speak. "I'm not certain you will ever be comfortable sitting across a table from Leo, for instance."

"I'm uncertain of that as well."

A horrible drop of her stomach met his words. "I am not sure what your intentions are in regard to me, but—"

"You know very well what my intentions are, Andromeda. Honorable, in all ways except when you are naked. Then I make absolutely no promises." He shrugged. "Though you were not naked yesterday when I fucked you on the table at Madame Dupree's, I thought I made myself clear all the same."

She drew in a shaky breath, the vulgarity and the images sending a wave of heat down her body. Which Granby knew full well it would.

"You're blushing. Shall I explain, in great detail, what I would like to do to you right now?"

"No. Please don't." Her gaze shot to his mouth. *Bollocks.* "That isn't necessary."

"Later then. And I will welcome Leo to *our*"—he emphasized the word—"home to dine. I'm bound to be uncomfortable at first, but I will conduct myself appropriately. I'll even be pleasant to Averell, though I don't like him at all. Is that blunt enough for you?"

Romy wasn't certain how to reply. She'd never met anyone who didn't think Tony to be smashing. "My mother—"

"Is a lovely woman. I applaud your father's choice. Elysium will be your next point, and I have grown more accustomed to the association with the provision I remain a member in good standing. *And* as long as I am given leave to take you into the private rooms when the mood suits us."

Another flush stole up her cheeks. She could never allow her brothers to know such a thing.

"You are fine with Elysium?"

He waved a massive hand before her. "Not completely. Nor Leo. But I will get there. The point is, I am not *averse* to growing accustomed. Acceptance takes time, does it not?"

"Yes." She would have been more concerned if Granby had told her he was completely at peace with all the Barringtons' imperfections. But it was reasonable to allow him time because he was open to the idea. He may not be so agreeable in terms of Madame Dupree once he knew the extent of Romy's relationship with the modiste.

"Still, you must know, I am not only designing gowns for Madame Dupree when the mood hits me. I am a partner in her establishment. I am in trade, Your Grace. Discreetly, of course. My name will never be above the door nor is my part ownership ever discussed but . . ." She paused. "If we were to marry—"

"We *are* going to marry. As soon as it can be arranged. Christ, I should just throw you in my coach and take you to Gretna Green this instant," he shot back, the rumble of his voice full of ice chips.

Now *that* sounded like Granby.

"If we married—"

"When we marry," he corrected.

"You will have control over what I own. You could take it from me in a second. I can't let you." She shook her head, her mind at odds with her heart. "No matter how I—"

He came over to the sofa and kneeled before her. "I will *not*, Andromeda. I have art. Gardening. Building things. You should see the planned renovation I have for the west wing of The Barrow," he said. "I will not take away from you that which you *need* to be yourself. Not Madame Dupree. Your silks. Your bastard brother. Or your family."

A tear slipped down her cheek. It was a beautiful speech.

"You must trust me in this, Andromeda. I admit, there are attitudes so ingrained in me from my upbringing which will take time for me to put aside. Like a thorn which must work its way out of your skin. Others I may never completely vanquish. But I will make every effort to accept all of you, as you must do for me. I'll show you something which may help to give me the benefit of the doubt."

"What about love?"

"Love?" The gravelly sound of the word on his tongue slid up under her skirts.

She really could not express herself clearly when he was bent on seduction. Granby would have her on the sofa before the tea cart arrived, and she couldn't allow it. Not until things were settled between them.

He went completely still, his hands no longer caressing her thighs. "You think I don't love you."

She bit her lip, vowing not to start weeping.

"Andromeda." He took her hands and pressed them to his lips. "Did you ever seek to translate the words I spoke to you that night in the study? *Sei tutto per me.* You are everything to me."

Another tear slipped down her cheek. *What a lovely senti-ment.* "I am?"

"Yes." He pressed a kiss to her thigh. "I am not good with words, Andromeda. I will never be the sort of man who writes you poems or compliments your eyebrows. You'll be fortunate if I bring you flowers, though I may try to grow you a bougainvillea."

She had no idea what that was, but it sounded lovely.

"I am rife with imperfections, including my inability to tell you that which you need to hear." A deep sigh escaped him as he reached into his pocket to place one of her butterfly clips in her lap.

"I could not bear to be parted from you, so I carried this with me." He paused, a forlorn look flitting across the harsh features of his face. "I will be difficult. Cold, at times. I'll scowl. Demand. Expect obedience, though I know you'll never give it. We will argue, a lot, I imagine. But you must never doubt how much I love you." He placed her hand over his heart. "It beats for nothing and no one else but you, Andromeda Barrington."

"David," she sobbed. "You love me."

"Of course I do. Haven't you been listening?" He leaned up, kissing her until Romy grew breathless and his hands strayed over her bosom. With a groan, he pulled his lips from hers as a knock sounded on the door.

"Damn it. I asked them to wait a full half an hour; it hasn't been that long. Tea has arrived."

"I don't want tea," she said against his mouth.

"I'm well aware of what you want, little shrub. But I've done *something,* and I wish to show you. I think you'll be pleased."

"More renovations?" She took full measure of the very sparse, masculine décor of the drawing room.

"I suppose you could say that. But not the furnishings.

You know much more about what sort of damask my bottom should be on than I." He stood and pulled her up to stand beside him. "Come."

The door opened to reveal Lady Molsin, another woman, and a lad of no more than sixteen or seventeen. Romy smiled at the trio, her eyes running over Granby's guests, waiting to be properly introduced.

The woman was about Lady Molsin's age. The silver of her hair was bundled in a graceful chignon at the base of her neck, her dark eyes warm as she took in Romy with a shy smile on her lips.

Romy felt as if she knew her. Possibly she'd come into Madame Dupree's.

The young man at her side shifted, drawing attention to his feet. They were enormous.

"How lovely to see you again, Lady Andromeda." Granby's aunt came toward her, even as she locked eyes with Granby and waved at the pair behind her.

"Andromeda." The rumble of his voice grew hesitant as if the words were hard for him. "I wish to introduce you to my mother, Emelia Kinkaid."

Romy's mouth popped open.

"I've finally managed to render you speechless," he said curtly. "A momentous occasion."

She recovered quickly. "Mrs. Kinkaid, a pleasure."

"You must call me Emelia. This is my son, Renwick."

"Ren, my lady," Renwick greeted her. He made the mistake of gazing at her a bit too intently, and a soft growl left Granby.

Ren stepped back immediately, though he didn't look the least ashamed to have been caught admiring her. And not at all impressed with being threatened by the Duke of Granby.

This was Granby's brother. His *bastard* brother. Looking between them, Romy could see the similarities in their build.

They both possessed their mother's eyes, though Ren's hair was a shade lighter than Granby's.

I've been working on my own imperfections.

Romy slipped her hand into Granby's, feeling his big fingers close over hers.

A sigh of contentment left him.

He'd left to forgive his mother and give his acceptance to the brother he hadn't wanted to acknowledge. That was why he'd been gone so long. What must it cost him to have done so? Her heart swelled with love for him.

"Is this what you wanted to show me?" she whispered.

"Yes." He looked down at her, a trace of ice shadowing his eyes. "I didn't only do it for you."

"I know." This was hard for him. Excruciating, even. But so important. She squeezed his hand and brought it closer to her, nearly into the folds of her skirts.

"But I approve all the same, Your Grace. With all my heart."

EPILOGUE

The wedding of a duke was a spectacular affair even if it was the wedding of the Duke of Granby. The bride, one of the Beautiful Barringtons, lived up to the moniker, for there had never been a more stunning young lady. Her dress alone was nothing short of spectacular, created by the most exclusive modiste in London, Madame Dupree.

Though everyone speculated the dress had been designed by the bride herself.

The Barringtons were there in full force, excepting their bastard, Leo Murphy, who was away on business. There were some who wished he'd never return to London, but that would leave Elysium to be run completely by the Duke of Averell.

It would be far better for Murphy to resume his proprietorship of the establishment.

Lady Andromeda seemed a curious choice for a duke known for his aloof manner and dislike of scandal and eccentricity—two things the Barringtons possessed an abundance of. The previous Duke of Granby would never have approved his son's choice. But the duke's large form hovered protectively over his new duchess as they exited the church, pausing only to bring her fingers to his lips, smiling as he did so.

A love match, the gossips speculated. Another Barrington eccentricity.

The duke and his duchess waved as their carriage struggled through the packed streets filled with well-wishers and those wanting to catch a glimpse of the new Duchess of Granby in her wedding finery.

Invited guests spilled from the church. The remainder of the Barringtons and their ward Olivia Nelson, granddaughter of the Earl of Daring. The Marquess of Haven, probably wearing a borrowed coat, for everyone in London knew he was as impoverished as they come. The Earl of Blythe. Mr. Harrison Estwood, a financier. Miss Lucy Waterstone, walking arm in arm with Miss Rosalind Richardson.

Then three women left the church which caused several gasps from the crowd of onlookers.

Lady Molsin and the Dowager Duchess of Averell were both well known to society, but it was the third woman, holding her chin up as she descended the steps, who drew everyone's eyes. It had been years since anyone had caught sight of her, and the former Duchess of Granby's appearance in London was nothing short of shocking. Most had assumed her dead. Whispers hovered in the air as her gaze passed over the crowd with determination, daring anyone to challenge her presence at the duke's wedding.

None did.

THANK YOU FOR READING THE DESIGN OF DUKES. I hope you enjoyed reading Romy and David's love story. If you did please leave a review.

Want more Beautiful Barringtons? Click here for the next in the series THE MARQUESS METHOD.

Lady Theodosia Barrington has long been infatuated with the Earl of Blythe. Desperate for Blythe to declare his intentions and offer for her, Theo paints a scandalous, self portrait of herself and sends it to the earl as a gift.

A reckless decision and one she regrets immediately.

She has to retrieve the miniature at all costs before her reputation is destroyed. But when she sneaks into Blythe's home to take back her gift, it isn't her adored earl she finds but the disreputable Marquess of Haven.

CLICK HERE FOR THE MARQUESS METHOD.

SIGN UP FOR KATHLEEN AYERS NEWSLETTER

https://kathleenayers.com/newsletter/

I love hearing from readers. Email your thoughts, comments or suggestions to kayersauthor@gmail.com

AUTHOR NOTES

What if you had the soul of a fashion designer but were born a duke's daughter?

I'd like to think that even though women at the time had to bow to society's norms, the most clever young ladies, (like Andromeda) found a way to follow their dreams, especially if they had mothers like the progressive Dowager Duchess of Averell.

During the 1840's a modiste shop gradually became less a spot to just be fitted for a gown and more a one-stop place for women's fashion. Women were having entire ensembles created for themselves including purses, hats, gloves and other accessories. Andromeda, with her talent for fashion, seemed the perfect Barrington to be on the cutting edge of this trend, secretly designing "looks" for her peers in society.

Some of you may have noticed the sewing machine on my cover – I can hear you shaking your heads that the sewing machine wasn't patented until 1846 by Elias Howe. Very true. It's a few years after Andromeda's story but I'd like to think she'd buy a sewing machine the moment she saw one.

Barrows, as most of my UK readers are familiar, are man

made mounds resembling small hills. They've been excavated since the late 1700's and are thought to be burial or religious sites. I don't pretend to be an expert but in doing research I found the barrows, stone circles and such dotting the English countryside to be incredibly interesting...enough to take a few liberties here and there.

ALSO BY KATHLEEN AYERS

The Beautiful Barringtons
The Study of a Rake
The Theory of Earls
The Design of Dukes
The Marquess Method

The Wickeds
Wicked's Scandal
Devil of a Duke
My Wicked Earl
Wickedly Yours
Tall Dark & Wicked
Still Wicked
Wicked Again

Printed in Great Britain
by Amazon

35108453R00172